Hot Puck

Hot as Puck

Book Four

Rhian Cahill

Hot Puck
Hot as Puck Series Book Four
By Rhian Cahill

For more information visit:
www.rhiancahill.com

Schellie.
For always cheering me on.
Mr. C.
For putting up with my crankiness as I tried to get this book finished
during this big transition in your life.

PROLOGUE - NAT

March

"What do you think?"

"You told Blake he was twenty-one."

"He will be when you join the league."

"Hmm..."

"Ignore his age, Nat. Concentrate on what's important."

"He's good. Young. But good." Good is an understatement. The kid was born to be a goalie. My eyes find Mason's. "Really good. Really young."

"You said that." He laughs. "I think he's your guy, but other teams have to be looking at him."

"Of course they have." My gaze moves back to the screen where the spliced together reel of Chase Hawkins saving goal after goal continues to play. "When the time is right, he'll have his pick of teams."

"Yeah, he will. But he's a family guy."

"What does that mean?" I watch another puck deflected with ease.

"He doesn't party like the rest of his teammates. Doesn't hook up with any girl that offers. From the info I have, he doesn't date at all. His single focus is keeping his grades well above a pass and improving his skills on the ice."

"Who's feeding you the information?" The video plays on and it's like watching a thirty-year-old veteran. The skills this kid has—and at nineteen he is a kid—are on par with any goalie currently playing in the league.

Hell, I'd go as far as saying he's one of the best I've seen.

And I've seen a lot.

The last few years have been filled with watching hockey. Current players, retired players, college players. You name it, if they play hockey and are anywhere near being eligible to play professionally, I've watched them.

But this is the first time I'm seeing Chase Hawkins, and I don't understand why. The kid should be on everyone's radar. And maybe he is. Maybe there are eyes on him, watching and waiting. Waiting for the perfect moment to pounce.

Like I said, he's young, but not so young we can't offer him a deal now. And if we do, he's got time to grow—mature. The Rogues are more than a full season away from taking to the ice in the national league, he can continue to hone his skills in college, tick over a birthday—I glance at his stat sheet in front of me—two birthdays, before he joins the team for our first pre-season game.

"You want to meet with him?"

My gaze snaps to Mason's. "Can you get me in without anyone knowing? The media frenzy hasn't died down from the franchise announcement. Every move we make is being splashed across every media outlet in the country."

"I can try. I know his dad, as well as his old coach. Might be able to get us a chat with one of them first. Off the record."

"Do it. In person or video chat. No calls. I want to see their faces when we talk." Pushing back my chair, I stand and point at the screen. "And send me that so I can show Walker and Blake."

"Blake's seen him play. She might remember him if you mention his name and St. Paul."

"I'll ask her." Shouldering my bag, I head for the door.

"Before you go."

I turn back to face Mason.

"I wasn't sure when the four of you first talked about making a bid for a national franchise. I may have said some things I wish I hadn't."

He holds up a hand to ward off the comment burning my tongue and my lips twitch at his perceptiveness.

"But since then, every move you've made has been solid. Insightful. Strategic. You know what you're doing and you're building a good franchise, one a lot of players are putting their hand up for, and right now there's little information out there about the team other than who owns it. I think—no, I *know*, the Rogues are going to be a Cup-winning team."

"That's the ultimate goal, but we'll take goals scored in every game we play, win or lose. As long as we're competitive in our first season, we can build from there."

"I won't offer to cross my fingers because I don't think you need me to."

"No. We don't. You sure you don't want a job?" I ask with a small smile. It's been a running joke since the idea of KAW owning a hockey team was first floated.

"Can't leave Cash."

"I can understand that." I wouldn't expect him to leave his teenage son despite him no longer being with the boy's mother. "But if that ever changes, give me a call."

PROLOGUE - CHASE

April - 13 months later

I've been preparing for this moment for months.

Months of knowing Mom was going to die and there was nothing I could do about it. Nothing *anyone* could do.

It still doesn't seem real.

But here I am, standing in the same place I did less than two weeks ago with a thirteen-year-old clinging to each hand and a four-week-old strapped to my chest.

Thankfully, Candace is asleep and, if I'm lucky, she'll stay that way for the rest of the service.

Cass and Stell are wide awake though. Well aware of what's happening. Both standing with matching poses of stiff spine, chin up, lips pressed tight in a thin line, and tear-filled eyes that refuse to leak.

I knew we were going to be burying Mom—my gaze darts to the fresh grave beside hers—but I never expected to bury both my parents before I turned twenty-one.

Didn't expect to become guardian to my three younger sisters either.

Especially with Candace only a few weeks old.

I still don't know how I got here. Standing beside Dad's ten-day old grave while they lower Mom into the one next to him.

Two weeks.

That's all it's taken to turn my life upside down, inside out, and sideways.

A few months ago, I was a carefree twenty-year-old, living my best college life, being scouted by top NHL teams.

Now I'm a single parent of three.

Over the last few weeks, a few well-meaning people have suggested I let my sisters go into the system so I can get back to my life.

Fuck, in the days after Dad was killed, even Mom tried to convince me letting Candace be adopted was the best option for all of us.

What kind of option is destroying our whole family in a matter of weeks?

Not. Happening.

We're a family and we'll stay a family. I refuse to give up any of them.

I might be scared right down to my fucking bones, freaking out more times than not every single day, but the only way I'm letting go of any of my sisters is if I'm in the ground next to Mom and Dad.

I'm the only family they have left—the three of them all *I* have left.

We belong together.

Whatever it takes, I'm keeping them with me. Raising them the best I can.

And it's not like I'm some college dropout and we're hurting for money.

Dad had several life insurance policies in place, and the family's successful chain of sporting and outdoor equipment stores is thriving. Bringing in a good profit as well as a wage if I want to manage the store closest to our mortgage-free family home.

I haven't decided what to do there.

If I don't work, I can concentrate on raising the girls. Take my time getting used to this new role in their lives—in mine.

What I can't do is go back to college.

Play professional hockey.

Those dreams may as well be in the ground with my parents.

Cass and Stell squeeze my hands simultaneously, pulling me from my thoughts.

The priest, or whatever he is—I can't even remember the guy's name at this point, never mind his title—moves toward us, a sympathetic, pity-tinged look on his face that tightens every cell in my body.

It takes everything in me to stand still, let him come.

I want to run.

Run fast and far and not look back.

Pretend the reality in front of me—both my parents in the ground—isn't happening.

Except I can't do that.

I've got three little girls relying on me.

I can't let them down.

I *won't* let them down.

Whatever it takes, I'll make sure my sisters have the lives my parents would have given them if they were still alive.

NAT

July - 3 months later

In the minutes since I pulled up outside this two-story house in suburban St. Paul, I've taken the time to study the place. I'm looking for anything that gives me inspiration.

I've been planning this trip for weeks—months—and I still don't know how to approach this meeting.

Not that it's scheduled.

Or a meeting.

I'm ambushing Chase Hawkins.

He disappeared from college and the NHL scout radar without notice. Maybe his departure didn't go unnoticed, but it certainly didn't cause any ripples, no comments or rumors. And with the skills the kid has, I don't understand it.

Especially when the reason behind his withdrawal from school and hockey is a tragic one.

Maybe that's why everyone has stayed quiet—stayed away—kept his departure from the sports scene off the radar.

Then again, perhaps, like me, they're all still in shock over what happened.

Four months ago, Chase was preparing, along with his father and teenage sisters, to welcome a new member of their family while they waited for another one to slip away.

In a cruel twist of fate, only weeks after the newest member of the Hawkins family joined the world, Mitch Hawkins was on his way home from the hospital where his wife lay dying of cancer when he was hit head-on by a drunk driver.

The death of Sienna Hawkins had been expected—anticipated in a macabre way. Not Mitch's.

His untimely death rocked the grieving Hawkins family to the bones.

And left Chase the guardian of his three younger sisters. One only a baby.

I'm not sure how I'm going to convince him to uproot himself and his siblings for a move to Baton Rouge. They've experienced so much change in the last few months. So much devastation.

Is the offer we have really good for them?

I've been over it again and again. Hashed it out seven ways from Sunday on my own, with the girls, as well as a few other trusted advisors, and as much as I don't want to cause any of the people living in this house more change, the consensus of all is to make the offer.

Taking a final fortifying breath of cool air, I switch off the rental car and climb out. It's hot, not as hot as the south, but still warm enough to warrant air conditioning.

My gaze sweeps over the area as I make my way to the sidewalk. The yard is overgrown, the garden beds full of weeds instead of flowers, and there's a few things hanging out of the mailbox.

The urge to pull the mail from that box and take it inside—sort it out and take care of it to lift one small thing from Chase's shoulders—sweeps through me.

I clench my fists and keep walking.

If he's receptive to listening to our offer, if he even considers it, I'll gladly spend a few extra days in St. Paul helping organize anything he needs help with.

Jerked to a stop, I look down to find my heel stuck in a crack in the pavement. I have to give it a good hard yank to pull it free, and to be safe, I slip the shoe off and examine the heel.

Luckily it doesn't appear to have any damage, and I slide my foot back in and take a careful step toward the house.

When my other foot wobbles on another crack, I stop and frown at the path beneath my feet, study the front yard with more care.

Even if Chase shuts the door in my face today, I'll find a local landscaping company—pay them from my own pocket—to come clean things up, mow the lawns, tidy the garden beds, plant some low maintenance flowers.

The backyard too.

The kids need a safe place to play.

Decision made, I head for the house again, but when my foot wobbles on another crack I slow my pace, shake my head, and mutter, "Shouldn't have worn heels."

Although my shoes aren't wedge heels, they're not stilettos either, and shouldn't have this much trouble walking along a path, even a cracked and crumbling one.

I might not know how to approach this meeting with Chase but I'm still the general manager of the Baton Rouge Rogues, newest NHL franchise, here to offer him a lucrative contract with the team and as such, this morning, before I left the hotel, I dressed for business.

Power suit skirt—no need for the jacket in this heat—in a deep, almost black blue, a starched white blouse in a thick fabric that isn't see-through even when wet, and my favorite pair of two-inch Dior heels.

Another glance around the neighborhood has me wondering if jeans and a t-shirt might have been a more appropriate choice. After all, I am meeting with Chase in his home. Without notice.

Too late to second guess my wardrobe choice now, I shake off concerns about my outfit and walk up the steps to the porch.

There's a stroller to the left of the door, a blanket and a few baby toys in the seat. To the right, a two-person glider that looks worn in and comfortable, and farther along the porch a small table sits between a couple of rocking chairs.

The yard and front path might be an unkept mess, but the house itself isn't. The paint isn't peeling, the windows are sparkly clean, and the stairs and porch floor don't creak when I walk on them.

If you ignore the uncut grass, unweeded garden beds, and crumbling walkway, the house is the picture-perfect suburban family home. And I know the Hawkins family has lived within its walls from the day Mitchell Hawkins married Sienna Durum and moved his new wife in.

A niggle of doubt tugs at my belly.

Accepting our offer would pull the Hawkins children from the only home they've ever known.

The conflicting emotions I feel about offering Chase a pivotal spot on the Rogues is something I've never dealt with. Once I make a business decision, I stick to it. Forge ahead until I get what I want, how I want it.

The only decision in my life I floundered over and lived to regret was marrying Johnathon Whitman.

Not that I had any other options at the time.

And I am rectifying that mistake now.

Pressing the bell, I step back and wait for someone to answer the door.

The ding-dong of the bell quickly fades away leaving only silence and I wonder if anyone is home.

Chase should be here. The older girls should be in their summer school program like every other weekday, but Chase is usually home with the baby in the mornings.

I'm poised to press the bell again when the faint sound of a baby crying catches my ear. The sobbing gets louder and louder to the accompaniment of thumping feet and the low rumble of a deep voice.

When the door flies open, through the screen I see a barely clothed man bouncing on his toes, a squirming baby held against his bare chest, her butt and head cradled in his big hands, while she wails her displeasure for all to hear.

And for the first time in years, my insides clench—throb.

I suppose this is what women mean when they say their ovaries explode.

The hunk of male perfection in front of me is all man. Nothing kid-like about him.

He's the hottest thing I've seen—possibly in my life—and from one heartbeat to the next my long dormant-believed-dead libido is resurrected.

I'm so shocked by my body's reactions I can't speak.

Not even when he pushes the storm door open and moves to the side.

"Thank fu"—his gaze darts to the baby on his shoulder— "fudge, you're here. Come in. She woke up hangry. Her butt is clean, and her bottle is in the warmer."

In my flustered state, I don't question him. Don't ask what the hell he's talking about. Just step inside the cool house, and when he hands over the crying baby, I take her, cradle her to me and rock side to side as though I've done it a thousand times before.

"The kitchen is that way." He throws out a muscled arm and my insides do that weird clenchy-swoony thing again. "I'll be in the office in the basement if you need me, but the call should only last thirty minutes. It's just a check-in with the store managers."

The baby on my chest continues to wail, but I can't take my eyes off the man in front of me, his body now in full view.

My stare has him looking down. "Shit!" Wide eyes bounce back to mine. "Shoot. I meant shoot. I need to get dressed and I'm already running late."

He doesn't wait for me to reply, he turns and heads up the

stairs two at a time. When he reaches the top, he looks back with a frown.

"Her bottle should be ready now. I put it in the warmer before I took her upstairs to change her diaper."

"Oh." I jolt out of the lust-daze I'm in, disguise it as a rock of the baby, and offer him a smile. "Right. I'll get her fed and take care of her until your meeting is done. No rush."

Turning away from the sight of him in nothing but his underwear—and holy hell, that ass!—proves more difficult than I expect, but I do it and head in the direction he indicated.

Except for the neglected front yard, the outside of the house is the picture of perfect suburban family life, and inside is no different. It's like a movie set. Even with the clothes and toys and general daily bric-a-brac of family life scattered around the place, it's neat and tidy.

And clean.

When I enter the kitchen, I find a large open space filled with light streaming in through the row of windows facing the backyard. A big island dominates the center of the room.

On one side is the work area—countertop, oven, fridge, sink, dishwasher. On the other, a row of stools is tucked under the counter edge. Behind them the space holds a well-used comfortable looking couch and a plethora of baby equipment and toys on a colorful baby blanket spread out in the middle of the warm colored timber floor.

A glance at the countertop near the fridge finds the bottle warmer easy to locate. When I pull the bottle from the device and turn the baby so she's cradled in my arms instead of over my shoulder and she sees what I have, the crying stops.

Instantly.

Her rosebud mouth remains open as though she's about to let out a yell, but her eyes are glued to the bottle in my hand.

"Is this what you want, baby girl?"

I've had little experience with babies this small, enough to know how to hold them and to check the temperature of formula before sticking a nipple in a little one's mouth. It takes a bit of juggling, but I manage to check the warmth of the milk then offer it to the now quiet baby.

Candace.

The baby's name is Candace.

The older two girls are Cassidy and Crystal.

I need to remember that. Use their names when I think about or speak to them.

And I assume the man upstairs is Chase. In his panic to be ready for a call while getting Candace changed and fed, and finding me on his doorstep, neither of us introduced ourselves.

Moving over to the sofa, I lower myself to the soft-as-it-looks-cushion without jostling Candace.

Although I needn't have worried. Her little mouth is latched onto the nipple and is not letting go. She's already sucked down a good amount in the minute or so she's been drinking, and I hope it fills her belly long enough for Chase to return.

Because I have no idea if this little one is only on formula or if she needs solid food as well. She's not quite five months and my knowledge of babies doesn't stretch to when they start eating solid food. Does she have teeth?

No. Drew is seven months and only just teething.

Looking around, I don't see a highchair and breathe a sigh of relief. If Chase isn't back, I don't want to have to search out anything that might tell me what to do once she finishes her bottle.

With Candace content for the moment, I let my gaze roam the room and take note of all the pictures on the walls. Family photos from years gone by right up to the newest one, a group shot of the whole family, probably taken within hours of Candace being born.

My stomach clenches.

Taking this family from their home is going to be difficult.

Despite the circumstances, I believe Chase deserves a chance to play in the NHL. And if anyone can give him a chance to shine on the ice, it's the Rogues.

We're built for families. It's part of our mission statement. To support every player and employee of the Rogues organization in and out of their job.

We built Rogue sportswear the same way and the two companies are closely entwined, especially now we've constructed our newest sportswear manufacturing plant in Baton Rouge.

The hollow sound of air being sucked from a container snaps me out of my thoughts and focuses my attention back on Candace.

"Wow. No wonder you were screaming your lungs out. You were starving."

Removing the bottle from her mouth, I tuck it between my knees then lift her to my shoulder. I might not have had much to do with babies this small, but I know you're supposed to burp them after they finish a bottle.

I get a good loud, body-jolting burb followed by two smaller ones and I pull her away from my chest, a smile on my face, but I almost drop her when from behind me a booming voice yells, "Fuck!"

CHASE

I have my pants up over my hips and I'm tugging a shirt over my head when it dawns on me what I just did.

"*Fuck.* I left my baby sister downstairs with a fucking stranger."

Yanking the shirt down off my face, I sprint from my room. I have to grip the side of my jeans to keep them from falling off. I don't have time to button and zip. I need to get to Candace.

There's no noise filtering up the stairs. No baby gurgles or whispered words or squeak of baby toys. And every worst-case scenario from Candace being dead on the floor to she's not even in the house flashes through my head as I beeline for the lower floor.

I'm not even sure my feet touch the steps as I take them two and three at a time.

The front door is closed, the foyer empty. The living room shows no sign of life—or death. And my heart is lodged in my throat, the thing beating a million miles a minute as I tear through the house in search of my sister, and the woman I handed her to.

My chest and gut clench painfully.

Who knows who I fucking handed Candace to! It could have been a serial killer for all I know.

I'm panting for breath when I fly into the kitchen. My gaze lands on the empty bottle warmer before it ping-pongs around the rest of the room until it lands on the back of a head of dark brown hair.

"Fuck!" Bending in half, I press my hands to my knees and suck in gulps of air. "Holy fucking shit."

Instead of the shout I started with, the last three words are no more than a whisper. The chaotic emotions bouncing around inside me have zapped every single molecule of air from my lungs and constricted my airways so tightly I'm surprised I can get anything through them.

The last minute—that felt like a fucking hour—has to have taken a decade off my life. Fuck. At the rate my heart is beating I might be having a heart attack.

"Fuck me," I mutter when the constriction of my chest eases enough I manage to pull in a full breath.

It takes everything I have to straighten, to raise my gaze to the sight that delivered so much relief I almost hit the floor.

When I do, the woman I let into the house not ten minutes ago is standing on the other side of the couch looking at me with concern.

And now that I'm looking at her, *really* looking at her, I can't believe I thought—

"You're not the babysitter from the agency are you." It's not a question. It's obvious whoever this woman is, she isn't the twenty-four-year-old nanny I was expecting.

This woman looks older than that and definitely not dressed to take care of a baby with her straight knee-length skirt and white blouse.

"No. I didn't get a chance to introduce myself before."

She cradles Candace against her chest so naturally a pang of regret twinges in my chest. I was never that at ease with my sister the first few times I held her.

Shit. I've been holding her for months and I'm barely at ease with her now.

The woman moves around the couch in my direction, and I'm rooted to the spot as I watch her come. I can't pinpoint the emotions flooding me.

Relief, gratitude...*excitement?*

What that last one is about I can't say. But I can't deny the buzz of elation filling my veins.

When she's closer she holds out her hand. "I'm Natalie Redding."

The name rings a bell, but my heart is still beating like a rock band drummer on speed and I can't pull my thoughts together enough to figure out the reason she's familiar.

I stretch out my hand to meet hers. "Chase Hawkins."

She smiles at me as we let go. "Yes. I know." She pats my sister's back. "And this is Candace."

"I..." I snap my mouth closed. I don't know if I should be worried she knows us or not. "Yes, that's my sister, Candace."

Obviously, she isn't here to hurt either one of us because she's had Candace alone for long enough to have done whatever she fucking pleased. If she's another reporter here to—

My phone beeps, reminding me I'm supposed to be on a call. "Shiii...ooot!"

Fuck. I really need to curtail my swearing. Should probably curb it in my head too.

"You need to get on a call," she says, and I open my mouth to argue, but before I can she adds, "Why don't I keep Candace occupied downstairs where you can see us?"

Candace is already looking sleepy and if I've learned one thing over the last few months it's letting her sleep too much during the day means no sleep at night. For anyone.

"Can you keep her awake until I'm off the call? She's a night owl and we're trying to correct that by keeping her up more during the day."

"Sure. Are there toys to play with down there or should I grab some of these?"

She's already moving toward the pile of toys I haven't packed up from this morning. "Leave those. I have a basket of things downstairs in the office." Too many things, but that's another story.

"Okay. Lead the way."

Turning, my gaze lands on the fridge and the manners Mom and Dad instilled in me snap into place.

Facing her again, I ask, "Do you want a drink? I have cold water and juice in the fridge, or I can make coffee or tea."

"I'm good. And you need to make that call."

"I do, but they're okay if I'm a few minutes late. It's not the first time this one has kept me from being on time or made me miss one altogether." It's why I organized a sitter. *Shit!* My gaze meets Natalie's. "I was expecting a babysitter."

"I figured. If she arrives while you're on the call, I can come up and answer the door." She must see the panic in my eyes because she quickly adds, "I'll leave Candace with you if I do."

A breath of relief rushes out of me, and I'm amazed I'm still standing at this rate. My lungs and heart haven't had a workout this strenuous in months. Not since Dad—

Nope. Not going there right now.

It's hard enough living in this house, taking care of my sisters, taking his place in the business, without thinking about the senseless loss of Dad.

Not that Mom's loss makes any more sense.

"Chase?" My eyes focus on Natalie again. "Are you okay?"

Shaking off my depressing thoughts, I offer up a smile. "Yeah. I'm fine. Just a lot on my mind."

"I can imagine." Her gaze dips to Candace. "Let's get downstairs. She's getting heavier and I think I might need something other than myself to keep her from falling asleep in the next few minutes."

"Right. Of course. Let's go." I turn and lead the way.

"And maybe you could, um, tidy up before you get on screen. If it's a video call."

Her words stop me in my tracks. With a frown, I glance over my shoulder at her. "Huh?"

She's smiling at me. And it's not one of pity either. I've had enough of those sent my way in the last three months.

No doubt she knows our story, at this point it feels like the whole world knows it, although I'm sure it's only those closest to the family, the local community. It's not like I've ventured far from home since everything went ass over tit.

My priority has been keeping the girls in a routine, keeping things as normal as possible, which when I think about it is total bullshit because how the fuck can anything be normal ever again?

"Your pants are still undone, and your shirt is on backwards."

"What?" Looking down at myself, I see my left hand still clenching denim at my waist and a huge print of my parents' company's logo on my chest, not the discreet one I expect to find over my left pec. "Fuc—udge! I mean fudge!"

A light laugh comes from behind me, and it's quickly followed by the gurgle that passes for laughter from Candace. Both sounds send a wave of warmth through me.

With a sheepish grin, I turn to face Natalie and nod to the door that opens onto the basement stairs. "Head on down, you'll see where I've got Candace's things set up. I'll get fixed up and be down in a second."

"Do you need me to give her anything else to eat?"

"No. We aren't at the solid food stage yet." *Thank fuck.*

I know I'm going to have to look into that soon. She's waking more and more hangry between bottles, but I just haven't had the bandwidth to deal with one more thing.

There are a few other things more important right now. And a few things I plan to take off my plate after this meeting.

The thought of the meeting has me spinning around and racing upstairs again. And if I pass the front door and check it's locked and arm the alarm, no one would blame me.

I'm a twenty-year-old solely responsible for three underage girls.

And my gut might be telling me the woman in my house is safe, trustworthy, but it's better to be safe than sorry.

Although in my previous life my gut never let me down. Never steered me in the wrong direction when it came to where the puck would go—

I stamp on those thoughts as pain lances my chest.

That life is over.

Never to be revisited.

And the sooner I accept that and move on the better.

The girls need me to be the best parent figure I can be. I might be clueless most of the time, but I had two really good role models for the first twenty years of my life. I have to believe their guidance has imbedded itself in my subconscious over the years.

If I can draw on even a tenth of what they showed me, I'll be thrilled. The other nine tenths are what books and the internet are for.

Plus, there's Candace's doctor. She's been a world of help since Dad died.

Dammit. Shaking my head, I clear all thoughts of Dad's death from my mind.

Easier said than done when I'm expected to be his replacement in the business. It might have taken me months, but I've come to the conclusion that I'm not cut out to be a parent and work. At least not right now.

Maybe when I get the hang of this parenting thing, I can look at taking a more active role in the company. For now, I'm going to leave the running of the stores to the managers and appoint Kent Quinn manager of the managers.

Kent will be my point person. And I'll leave it to him to hire his replacement, because honestly, I know very little about the business my family owns, and Kent's been with us from the beginning.

Dad never included me in any meetings or store visits. He knew my dream was to play in the NHL and only join him in the business after I retired from the ice.

But that was when he thought he'd live until both of us reached retirement age.

I could sell the business. Invest the money in other things to earn an income to support me and the girls, but the sporting and outdoor equipment stores aren't just mine. And I refuse to sell anything—the house or the business—before the girls are old enough to make a decision.

Candace is too young, and Cass, Stell, and I will make the decision for her, but the twins are old enough to remember our parents, our life before, and I refuse to take any more away from them.

Whether I want to work in one of our stores or not, I'll keep hold of the legacy our parents left us.

I glance around my childhood bedroom. The one I've only lived in part-time for the last few years.

Mom kept everything as I left it. The wall of old hockey sticks. The hockey print bedding. The shelf of pucks—one from every shut-out game I had during my years in college—is the only new addition.

Otherwise, the room looks exactly like it did when I lived here.

Never thought I'd be back in this room permanently.

Not like this.

As much as it hurts to be here, it also comforts.

Being surrounded by their things, walking through the rooms they spent so much time in, brings solace I know we all need right now.

Especially the girls.

I have no idea how I'm going to guide my sisters through their teenage years. Mine were hockey, hockey, hockey. Early days, late nights, game weekends. The girls aren't into any sport or activity beyond what's required of them in school.

My phone beeps again reminding me of the call I should be on and I run my fingers through my hair, try to tame the tangled mass. It needs a cut.

One more thing I don't have time for right now.

That changes in the next hour.

Smoothing a hand down my now righted shirt, I tug the material to remove any wrinkles as I walk toward the stairs.

Time to be the only legal-aged owner of a multi-million-dollar company.

NAT

Listening to Chase on his call tells me two things.

One, he knows little about the business his parents built beyond what it is.

And two, he needs help.

Lots of help.

With the girls, and the business the four of them have inherited.

He's making moves to give himself a break by appointing Kent Quinn overseer of the stores. It's a smart move; the man has worked for Chase's dad since the first store opened its doors.

That knowledge doesn't stop me from shooting a quick message to Eli. I want all the information I can get on Kent and the business Chase appears to have no desire—or energy—to manage.

I can't blame him. He's spent his entire life training to play professional hockey. And now he's been forced to give up that dream to take care of his sisters.

Theirs isn't the first tragic story I've heard, but I have to be honest and admit, it's the one that has affected me the most.

The others were part of the various charity organizations I or KAW has supported over the years. It's one of the reasons Rogue sportswear is now one of the largest supporters of the underprivileged in the country.

Too many children go through life without the basics, and we made a pact the day we formed KAW and started our first sportswear line to help those in need.

Half of the profit the company earns is given to charity. In the beginning we picked a few different ones each year but now we have our own organization that runs numerous charities as well as giving to others all over the world.

The dilemma I have with wanting to help Chase and his sisters is they aren't underprivileged. Yes, they lost both their parents in tragic circumstances and Chase is barely an adult responsible for his younger siblings, but they aren't destitute.

Their parents have left them well taken care of financially.

More than. From my quick research prior to coming here, I know Limitless is a multi-million-dollar business.

I can't work out if my need to help them is because I want Chase to play for the Rogues or something else. I need to factor in my reaction to him when he opened the door.

Is it deeper than a simple attraction to a good-looking man?

I may have met Chase for the first time today, but I know him. I've pored over his stats and watched too much video of him to not know who he is.

But is my need to help just because I want him as the Rogues starting goalie?

I don't know. All I do know is, his lack of interest in running his family's business is a point in my favor.

I think.

It's easy to hear the frustration in his voice. See the concern in his eyes when he glances over at where I am on the floor attempting to keep Candace awake.

Despite my best efforts, I think it's a losing battle.

Her little eyelids keep dropping and staying that way longer and longer. Although it is super cute when they pop back up, her eyes going wide as though her brain suddenly realizes she's missing out on something.

I've tried to keep the noise to a minimum but the longer we lie on the floor, the harder it is to keep her occupied enough to keep those baby-blues open and focused.

Not that her eyes focus that well yet. It's amusing to watch her go cross-eyed trying to see clearly when I wave one of her toys in front of her.

The doorbell echoes through the house above us and my eyes meet Chase's.

"Okay, everyone good for now? We can schedule a call for tomorrow if anyone has any concerns or wants to discuss the changes after having time to think about what I've just laid out," Chase offers the group on his screen.

One by one they say goodbye, leaving Chase and Kent.

"Are you sure this is what you want, Chase?"

"It's what we need right now. I need someone to do the overseeing so I can concentrate on taking care of the girls." His gaze moves over to me where I'm now standing with Candace in my arms. "They need me to sort things out at home before I venture into the business."

"All right but let me know if you have questions or ideas or anything. You know I'm here for you and the girls no matter what it is you need. Your dad took a chance on me, and I wouldn't be where I am without his support and encouragement. I owe him."

"I'm sure he'd say you owe him nothing, but I appreciate the offer, and I'll definitely take you up on it regarding the business."

"Make sure you do. And give the girls our love. Jade hates that she can't help you out right now," Kent adds. "But with her mom living with us and the kids—"

"Kent. Stop beating yourself up about it. Tell Jade to stop too. We're okay. And we'll be better now you're taking things off my shoulders." The doorbell buzzes again. "I gotta go. Someone is at the door."

"Call if you need to."

"I will. Bye." Before Kent can say anything else, Chase disconnects the call. With a harshly blown out breath he lowers his head. "I feel like I'm letting them down."

"Who? The people on the call?" I ask as I walk over to him. Candace is getting heavier by the second and her little head is resting on my shoulder.

"Yeah, them too. But I was talking about my parents. They didn't struggle taking care of everything and I can barely get everyone dressed in the mornings."

"Chase. I'm going to be brutally honest with you. Yes, you are failing at some things. But that's to be expected. You've gone from being a college student whose only concern was grades and improving hockey skills, to a business owner and parent of three young girls. And you did it in the blink of an eye."

"But—"

"No." I hand him Candace when the doorbell goes again. "There are no buts in this. It's a huge shift in your lives and no one, least of all your parents, would expect you to handle it all with ease. I'll get the door."

I don't want him to wallow in self-pity, but I don't have time to talk about this more right now. I'm assuming the nanny he organized has finally shown up.

I'll be dispatching her immediately. There is nothing I hate more than lateness. And maybe it's not my place to dismiss her but Chase needs someone who isn't going to be late helping him right now.

The only thing I've ever been late for was my own birth. It will take some juggling, and I'll need Eli to pick up some slack as well as Trevor. The two of them will have no problem freeing up some time to take some of my load while I dig in here and help Chase find his feet.

By the time I get upstairs I've formulated a plan of action, and as soon as I've seen to the tardy nanny, I'll put it in motion.

Opening the door, I find myself lost for words.

The woman on the porch looks more like a puck bunny than

a nanny and when she opens her frowning mouth my suspicions of her grow.

"Oh. You're not Chase." She tries to see past me into the house. "Wait. Are you his mother? I thought you were dead."

The frown she gives me is more a sneer and for the life of me I don't understand her motives. Is she pissed she thinks his mother is still alive?

I hear Chase behind me but don't open the door wider. I don't want this woman interacting with him yet. The need to protect him from whatever this is grips me tight and there's no way I'm letting this woman near Candace.

"Can I help you?" I ask, moving through the door and pulling it snug against my back.

"Where's Chase?"

"Mr. Hawkins is busy at the moment. Can I help you?"

"Yeah, you can let me in. I'm his nanny."

"Are you?" I arch an eyebrow. "And what time were you supposed to start?"

"Oh, well, I didn't know who I was nannying for, so I had to go home and get changed before I came here, and there was an accident on the—"

I hold up a hand. "I don't need to know anything else. Mr. Hawkins will contact the agency to let them know your services are no longer needed."

"What? Since when?"

"Since you failed to show up at the specified time and when you finally did arrive, you're dressed for a night on the town, not a day at home taking care of a newborn and two teenagers."

"Teenagers?" She takes a step back. "No one mentioned teenagers. Just a baby."

"And Chase."

"Well, yeah."

"How old are you?"

"Why? What's that got to do with anything?"

"Everything when you're expected to care for three children."

"I've been babysitting for a decade and nannying full-time for the last five years while studying online for my degree."

I have to hand it to her, once pushed she shows a backbone and while I don't have proof what she's saying is true, if the agency Chase used is reputable, it should be the truth.

"Good for you. But as I said, Mr. Hawkins no longer needs your services. He'll contact your agency who will contact you. And you'll be compensated for your time today." I move back into the house.

"But—"

"I apologize for any inconvenience caused," I say as I close the door between us.

I wait. I can hear her muttering on the other side of the door, and it brings a smile to my face.

I'm not a malicious person. Hell, look how charitable I've been with my soon to be ex-husband. But I can't deny the little thrill I get from removing that woman from Chase's life.

And it has nothing to do with me wanting him to accept a contract with the Rogues.

"Is she gone?"

Chase's voice makes me jump and I spin around to face him, my back pressed to the door. "Yes."

"Oh, but..." He drops his gaze. "I guess I don't need anyone now."

I study him. I can't tell if he's happy about giving up an active role in his family's business or not. "Do you want to need someone?"

"No. I don't want anyone taking care of the girls but me." He raises his gaze to mine. "But that's not realistic, right? At some point I'll need to get a job. Not for money but for myself. I'll need help then."

"Maybe. Or the twins might be old enough to help."

"I don't want to put that on them. They should get to be kids, teenagers, and not have to look after their baby sister."

"I didn't mean full-time. Is Candace down for her nap?" At

his nod I push off the door and head toward the kitchen. "How about we have that drink, and I explain why I'm here."

"It's not to save me from women dressed to hook themselves a man?" He chuckles. "I thought your outfit was inappropriate for taking care of a baby, but she took the cake with what she was wearing."

"Hmm..." In the kitchen I make my way to the coffee machine. "You know how to use this?"

"No." I glance at him, and he shrugs. "I don't drink coffee."

"Ah, still taking care of yourself even though you're not playing." It's the first time I've mentioned anything to do with hockey.

He eyes me carefully and I can tell his brain is spinning. "Oh! Oh shit! I just worked out who you are!"

I smile. "And who's that?"

"You're Natalie Redding."

"Yep. We established that before your call."

"Yeah, but I didn't connect the dots then. You own Rogue sportswear."

"KAW owns it and I'm one fourth of KAW, so yes, I own Rogue sportswear."

"You're the COO."

"Correct."

"What the hell is the COO of Rogue sportswear doing in my" —he jolts back a step—"Do you want to buy Limitless?"

"No. That's not why I'm here but if you were thinking of selling, I'd be interested in talking."

"Why else would you be here? Did you know Mom and Dad? I don't recall seeing you at their funerals but then I don't remember much of those few weeks. Hell, lately I don't remember what I had for breakfast most days."

"No. I didn't know your parents, although I did know of them. Limitless does stock our products after all." I smile. "I'm here to see you."

"Me? Why?"

"How informed are you about the latest in the league?"

"I haven't watched a game since…" he trails off, but he doesn't need to say the words. I know when he stopped taking note of NHL news.

"Well, the league announced the newest franchise."

"Yeah, that was before. Baton Rouge Rogues. Seems weird to have a team in the south but as it's not the first and the others have been successful, I guess they know what they're doing."

"Yes. The Rogues."

"Aren't they due to enter the league this coming season?"

"They are."

"Have they announced the team?" There's excitement in his voice and I hope it remains when he hears why I'm here.

"No. Well, that's not true. We've announced—"

"We?"

"KAW owns the franchise."

"Ah, right. Makes sense. You own a sportswear business, why not a sports team."

"Yes. But my involvement is more than owning the team. I'm the general manager."

"Female GM?"

I don't think he's against it, but he is surprised by it. "Yes. Our assistant coach is female too."

"I think I remember Blake Watts being mentioned." He shakes his head. "Honestly, most of what I know about the hockey world has been shoved into a back corner of my mind."

"Let's not force you to figure this out. I'm here, as the GM of the Rogues, to offer you a contract as our starting goalie."

His mouth drops open. If his jaw could unhinge it would be on the floor, I'm sure. And before he can argue about all the reasons why he can't even think about accepting the offer, I step in his direction.

"Hear me out. I don't want you to think about the girls or your family's business or anything else. What does Chase Hawkins, hockey goalie, want to answer?"

CHASE

For a minute I freeze in place.

My mind can't comprehend Natalie's question. Her words stick on a loop in my head.

"What does Chase Hawkins, hockey goalie, want to answer?"

Over and over and over.

"What does Chase Hawkins, hockey goalie, want to answer?"

Round and round until things start to come unstuck and I know the answer.

Or at least I did.

In a different life.

Not this one.

In another life I worked and worked and worked for the chance to be offered a position in the NHL. But starting goalie?

Fuck yeah!

Every one of my dreams had me starting in goal for an NHL winning team.

Except all of those dreams and wishes and hard work were a lifetime ago and, in *this* life, the one I find myself living now, I'm a twenty-year-old *parent* of three.

And that's when things really come unstuck.

And I come unglued.

In more ways than one.

My body jolts and out of my mouth bursts laughter so unhinged even I can hear the insanity in it. But I can't control it—can't stop it.

The sound grows louder and louder and more demented and is so far beyond my ability to rein in it makes me laugh harder.

Motherfucker.

I've lost my damn mind.

Or she has.

She can't be serious. The Rogues can't possibly want me to play for them. I'm a kid raising kids.

That thought makes me laugh so hard I have to wrap my arms around my waist to hold my sides because my whole body feels like it's going to explode.

My chest aches. My gut aches. And my heart aches for all that I can no longer do.

I'm not sure when the switch happens. When I go from deranged amusement to heart breaking distress, but one minute I'm laughing my ass off, the next I'm sobbing like a toddler in the arms of the woman who just offered me the world.

I cry harder when the reality of what I have to say sinks in.

I cry harder for everything I've lost.

I cry harder for what my sisters have lost.

But I cry the hardest when the realization of never being able to share this momentous moment with my parents—never seeing either of them again—kicks my heart so hard my ribs ache.

Words are being whispered in my ear, but my fractured mind doesn't understand them. I just know the sound is a constant murmur that draws me closer.

My forehead rests on Natalie's shoulder, my arms wrapped tightly around her like she's the only lifejacket in a thrashing sea. The snug hold of her arms encircling my waist presses our bodies together, and every wall I've held in place since my parents' died crumbles, and I bawl like I've never bawled before.

And she holds me through it.

Lets the storm of emotions inside me fall onto her shoulders while her arms banding my waist keep me grounded, keep me from collapsing to the floor.

I have no idea how long it takes, how long she allows me to use her strength, but when the sobs finally slow, when the tears start to dry up, I stay exactly where I am. Stay in the safe place she's given me.

Despite the tears and anguish, it's the calmest I've felt in months, and I can't bring myself to move.

In the weeks since everything changed, I haven't broken down once. Not like this. Not this bone dissolving grief that has left me weak and her shirt soaked.

"Why don't you go take a shower and lie down? I can keep an ear out for Candace and give her another bottle or whatever it is she needs when she wakes, just tell me what I need to do."

She pulls back to look at me but doesn't let go and I'm grateful, I'm not ready to leave the comfort of her arms. I'm not sure I ever will be.

"Do you need to pick up the twins?"

I shake my head. "They're getting dropped off by their friend's mom, Mrs. Harper." My voice is raw, jagged around the edges and scraping my throat in a way it never has.

"Okay." She looks at the clock on the oven. "Why don't I make you some lunch while you shower and then you can take a nap."

"I..." My throat chokes up and I have to swallow to clear the lump from the back of it. "I'm okay. I can make my own lunch."

"Chase."

Her arms move, slip away from my waist so she can bring her hands up to cradle my face. Her skin is soft and warm against my cheeks, and I want nothing more than to lean into her again. Let her hold me up.

But I can't.

I need to be strong for the girls. I'm all they have.

"Don't." She keeps my head still, her gaze drilling into mine. "Don't take it all on when you don't have to. It's okay to accept a little help. It doesn't mean you're failing, or you don't care."

"Why?" The croak in my voice is still there, my throat still aching with rawness. "Why would you do this?"

"Because I've been where you are without the younger siblings. In my case it was an elderly aunt who needed care, so I know how hard it is, how easy it is to take it all on, to think you're alone. But I was lucky enough to have someone to force help on me. Let me do that for you. Let me help take some of the burden off your shoulders. Just for a little while today."

"I should—"

"You should do what I said. Take a shower, have something to eat, then lie down. It doesn't have to be long. Just rest for a bit without worrying about anything else. I'll take care of anything urgent."

"I"—shaking my head I try to clear the fog my crying jag left me in—"Are you sure?"

"Yes."

Her answer is firm, no room for anything but acceptance, and the relief that flows through me is breath stealing. Even though I want to argue, I know I can't stay upright for much longer.

"All right. I'll shower. See how I feel—"

"Nope. You have three things to do for the next few hours."

She removes her hands from my face and pulls completely free of my hold and I'm struck by how natural holding her felt. So natural it feels weird not having her in my arms now.

Raising a fisted hand, she flicks up her index finger. "Shower." Her middle finger joins the first. "Eat." Then she rounds out the trio with her ring finger. "Rest."

"I can rest down here." I'm not sure why I'm pushing. My mind and body are drained, and I want to lie down and forget about all the things I need to deal with, let someone else handle them even if it is for only a few minutes.

"There's too much distraction down here. Plus, I'm going to search your pantry and see what I can put together for dinner and I'm bound to make noise doing it."

I'm not sure why that surprises me, but I can't keep the shock from my voice when I say, "You're making dinner?"

In answer she plants her hands on my shoulders and spins me around before saying to the back of my head, "Yes. After I make you a sandwich or something for lunch. Now go, I'll be here taking care of anything that needs taking care of."

I step forward when she gives a little push. I could easily have stopped myself but I'm raw and weak from crying and the grief weighing me down, and the thought of not being the one in charge for a even a few minutes, never mind not having to worry about cooking dinner, is too much to resist.

My feet drag as I make my way out of the kitchen and just before I leave the room, I glance over my shoulder. Natalie is where I left her, arms crossed over her chest, a stern do-as-I-say-or-else look on her face.

And maybe it's the bone-weariness I'm feeling after purging my grief, or maybe it's the no-nonsense glint in her gaze, whatever it is, I do as told, and head upstairs to the bathroom.

Once behind the closed door it doesn't take me long to strip and step under the shower because the more I think about soothing my aching body with hot water, the more I want to do it.

The first blast of water is cold, but as it warms, the spray does its job and washes away some of the tension holding my body tight. Closing my eyes, I tip my head back and let the calming sensation soak through my skin to my bones.

Warm and relaxed, I lean against the wall and angle the showerhead my way. I don't bother with soap. I did that when I showered earlier today.

But this isn't about getting clean. Not in the physical sense. It's about clearing my head, washing away the stress of the day.

I didn't think my decision to step back from the business was weighing on my mind, but the longer the call went on the more I realized how much I hated having to step back.

Not because I want to be in charge of my parents' life work, but because I *should* be in charge of it. I'm the only one capable of running the company Mom and Dad started before I was born.

The twins are too young, and Candace isn't even a factor. It's me. All of it falls on me.

And I know I've chosen to take on the girls. I could have done what it seems everyone expected, and let them go, except that was never going to happen.

I'd have to be dead for all of us not to stay together.

Even if our parents hadn't left us with a profitable business and a mortgage free house, along with money in the bank from several life-insurance payouts, I wouldn't let my sisters go.

I can't imagine living without them and the loss of our parents only makes me more determined to keep us together.

The water flowing over me begins to cool and I quickly switch it off. I can't use all the hot water. Candace will need a bath later and no doubt the twins will want to shower as soon as they get home.

I know Natalie told me not to worry about anything but getting out of the shower before the hot water runs out is something I had to do as a teen. Back then Mom would come to the bottom of the stairs and yell I'd been in here long enough.

The memory doesn't cut as deep as I expect. Instead, it brings a smile to my face and fills me with warmth.

I'm not being biased when I say I had the best parents because I genuinely believe it to be true. I've had enough friends over the years tell me they thought they were great too.

On the heels of the warm memories, sadness swamps me. No one will ever say that to me again. No one will tell Cass or Stell their parents' rock. And Candace...

Fuck!

She'll never know their love. Never experience what it's like to be loved and cared for by them. All she'll have is the second-hand stories we tell her.

I have to find a way to bring those stories to life. To give Candace a vivid picture of what they were like, how they would have doted on her.

Stepping out of the shower I grab a towel and scrub it over my hair before taking care of the rest of me. I'm still damp when I wrap it around my hips and head to my room for clean clothes.

Pulling sweatpants out of a drawer, I tug them on without underwear. I don't have the energy to go out to the basket in the hall and search through the clean clothes.

One more thing I haven't gotten to yet. At least the clothes are clean. And dry. Last time I was out of underwear they were all in the washer with the rest of our dirty clothes.

I shake my head. Forgetting to put the washing on is something I'm really good at. It's why the twins have taken over washing our clothes. Although they refuse to fold and put them away. Even their own.

That job falls to me. And just thinking about having to do it makes my shoulders slump. I can't bring myself to go out there for underwear; there's no way I'm going to fold a basket full of clothes.

Lowering my tired ass to the bed, I lie back and stare at the ceiling, think about everything that has happened this morning.

The nanny I hired didn't show up on time and when she did, the woman I thought was the nanny dispatched her in a way that was proficient and kind when it could have turned into a scene.

I made a decision about our parents' business that was the best for all of us but feels like the worst—like I'm letting everyone down.

The general manager of the newest NHL franchise offered me a contract to be their starting goalie, and I laughed in her face then cried on her shoulder.

And there's a stranger in my house taking care of things and I can't summon the energy to feel ashamed or confused or relieved about letting Natalie—the contract-offering Rogues general manager—take over.

It's been months since I've had the chance to sit.

To lie still and not worry about ten different things while doing two others.

To do nothing except breathe.

NAT

Considering there's a twenty-year-old college student in charge of the Hawkins household, the fridge is surprisingly well stocked with fresh vegetables, fruit, and meat. I don't know if Chase is responsible or if he has a delivery service.

It doesn't matter because whoever is responsible, they've given me plenty of options for dinner and Chase's lunch. Pulling out a container labeled chicken salad with a neatly printed date of two days ago, I crack the lid and give it a sniff.

Smells fine to me. Looks good too. It'll do for a quick sandwich for Chase, and I'll eat the rest while I work out what to cook the family for dinner.

I can't hear the water running in the pipes and I hope that doesn't mean Chase hasn't made it into the shower. He might not need one, but it will help him feel better after his breakdown.

And that's what it was. He broke down in my arms.

The breakdown I understand. He probably hasn't let himself feel emotions or grief, in the misguided belief that he needs to be strong for his sisters.

The twins have each other and Candace doesn't have a clue what's transpired around her. Who does Chase have to talk to?

What I can't wrap my head around is the way I stepped forward and pulled him into my arms, held him while he cracked.

Other than the girls, I've never held anyone when they cried.

And none of them cried the way Chase did.

It only takes a few seconds to make Chase's sandwich. Moving it to a plate, I shove away all thoughts of my need to support him while he cried and instead concentrate on giving his body nourishment before he has a rest.

He might be the hottest man—and I have to admit, as much as I want to focus on his age, he isn't a boy, he's all man—but he looks exhausted. Ravaged. Like he's waged a war on the ice for days instead of hours.

Plate of chicken salad on sourdough in hand, I grab a bottle of water from the fridge as I pass on my way upstairs.

The house isn't huge—not like the one I grew up in—but it isn't small either. When I get upstairs, I see the top level is split in two.

On one side are three bedrooms, on the other there's a set of closed double doors—which I assume is his parents' room—and a second door barely cracked open, a soft lullaby floating through the gap into the hall.

Candace's room. I'll peek in on her before I head back to the kitchen.

Straight in front of me is an empty bathroom. The wisps of steam and fogged mirror tell me Chase has at least done the first part of my directions.

I'm holding his second.

Turning to the left, I glance into each room until I find him in the last one. He's showered, pulled on sweatpants that conceal nothing and have my insides clenching like they haven't in years, and is laid out flat on his back on the bed.

At first I wonder if he's passed out, but as I walk closer, I hear a light snore slip through his parted lips.

Part three of my directive complete.

I look at the plate in my hand and smile. I'll wrap it and keep it for when he wakes but I'll leave the water on his bedside table.

The position he's in has me frowning though. It looks like he sat on the edge of the mattress and fell backward. His legs, bent at the knees, hang off the end, his bare feet on the floor.

Instinct tells me to move him.

Common sense tells me that won't be easy.

He's six feet four inches and while I'm six feet in heels, I admit to neglecting my exercise regimen in recent months and doubt I'll be able to lift him without disturbing him—or straining something.

I could wake him and get him into bed properly, but I don't want to risk him arguing about taking a rest—one he obviously needs.

Best option for both of us is to leave him as he is.

After putting the water on his bedside table, I lower the blind on the only window in the room to stop the afternoon sun from shining in.

He doesn't disturb and I head for the door. Before I close it, I look at him sprawled out on the bed one last time.

He really is a fine-looking man.

If I were a few years younger, and he were a few older, I'd seriously think about making a move.

I don't know what's more shocking. The thought of hooking up with him if our ages were closer together, or the fact my body is in full agreement with the idea, ages be damned.

I haven't had sex with anyone since my early twenties. My hand and vibrator don't count.

My marriage to Johnathon might have been in name only but unlike my husband, I have never stepped outside those vows.

Maybe that's why my body is reacting to Chase.

As of yesterday, I'm weeks from being officially divorced, and consciously I might not be thinking about men, but my libido must have been lying in wait.

It might not be Chase; I could have the same reaction to any good-looking man now I have the option to do something about any attraction I feel.

It's a thought to ponder later. Right now, I need to check on Candace, wrap this sandwich, and plan out the rest of the afternoon.

If Cassidy and Crystal arrive home before Chase wakes, I'll need to make sure my presence doesn't freak them out.

A strange woman in their house, cooking them dinner, is bound to have them panicking even if they don't understand why.

I mentally add to my list of questions for Chase as I check on Candace.

Are the girls in counseling?

Is he?

They should be. Together and separately.

They've experienced a traumatic life-altering event, and they should talk about their emotions to help them process the loss of their parents.

God knows I'd have had an easier time if my grandfather had taken Eli's suggestion and taken me to a counselor. Then again, my grandfather didn't care about anyone but himself.

Not even his disabled sister, the one he'd been legally responsible for since my great-grandparents deaths.

No, helping Aunt Florence had fallen on Dad and Mom, and when they were killed, I was the only one who cared about her. Took the time to visit her in the home my grandfather had shoved her into.

I'll forever be thankful to Eli for taking me to see a counselor the day I turned twenty-one and could do it without my grandfather's approval.

It had been the first day of my independence and I hadn't looked back after that first trust fund had been unlocked.

I make another mental note to look into counselors in Baton Rouge. I can get Trevor on that. We should have a list for the Rogues organization and Rogue sportswear employees anyway.

Back in the kitchen, it takes no time to find the plastic wrap.

Chase's mother has everything in logical places and I doubt he's done any rearranging since he moved back in and took over the parental role.

Putting the sandwich in the fridge, I decide on a simple meal of grilled chicken and salad for dinner. I'm not sure what any of the Hawkins children like to eat and as there is the produce to make the simple meal, I'll go with it and hope for the best.

Dinner sorted, I head out to my rental car to grab my laptop bag. I brought it in the hope of Chase agreeing to listen to our offer, which comes in handy now I'll be here the rest of the day. I can get work done while taking care of Candace and the twins if Chase isn't up by the time they get home.

First thing I need to do is call Eli. He's bound to have some information on Kent Quinn and Limitless for me by now.

I set up on the kitchen island. The space is large enough to spread out and I can keep an eye on the monitor next to the bottle warmer on the counter.

Candace is still sound asleep. And there are three bottles already prepared in the fridge, so I won't have to hunt up formula and figure out how to make one.

Deciding to video call Eli, I open my laptop and wait for it to start up. While my computer is doing that, I shoot Trevor a message to research counselors in Baton Rouge.

I get an affirmative from Trevor, and Eli answers on the first ring.

"Is he considering the offer?" he asks. No hello, no how are you.

I laugh. "Hello, Eli, I'm good, how are you?"

"Funny." He smirks at me. "So, is he?"

"Not yet."

He frowns. "Where are you?"

"In his kitchen."

"In his..." He shakes his head. "Okay, start from the beginning."

"I'm not rehashing my morning. Did you get any information on Kent Quinn?"

"Yes. He's a good choice. The best within the company to take on the role you said Chase offered him, but he might find better going outside."

"No. Chase needs to have someone he knows in the position. It's a reluctant move on Chase's part."

"Really? Why?"

"He feels as though he's letting his parents down by stepping away from actively managing the company."

"Ah, are you seeing similarities?"

"Yes. Except he doesn't have a tyrannical grandfather trying to take everything away from him."

"No, he doesn't. He's still no more equipped than you were to run the company *and* take care of his sisters."

"I learned though."

"Yes, you did. But you also found trusted people to help you. He doesn't have that. Well, he has Kent."

"And what did you find out about him?"

"Mitch Hawkins met him when he was a sixteen-year-old punk trying to jack Mitch's car."

"He's a car thief?"

"No. He *was* a thief. But only because he was homeless and trying to survive. Mitch and Sienna took him in and turned his life around."

"Thoughts?"

"Perfect for taking a CEO role in the future. If I were Chase, I'd see how he goes over the next twelve months in this new job then offer him the bigger one. Especially if I were thinking of signing a contract to play hockey in the NHL."

"Okay, so we can take the worry about the family business off his shoulders without selling it. Now the girls."

"That's going to be tougher."

"Are you saying I can't do it?"

"No. And I know you well enough to know you've taken my words as a challenge."

"You're right. I have." I glance around the room. "I think the biggest hurdle will be getting them to move from this house."

"Cassidy and Crystal are going into high school. New school. Best time there is to move them. In another year they'll have friends and outside school activities."

"Hmm..."

"I see the wheels turning."

"Our captain has a daughter."

"The secret, not so secret one?"

"Yeah. I don't know what the deal is there other than he keeps his private life extremely private. Anyway, what I was getting at is she'll be attending Hannon Grove."

"She's older than them, if I remember correctly."

"Yes, but if I could connect them, it would help them all settle into their new school, new homes." The more I think about it the more I think having a friend whose father plays on the same team as their brother would be a tick in the pro column. "

"I can find out if we can get them in. Possibly ask them to hold a couple of places just in case."

"Do that."

"If they won't?"

"The usual donation should make them agreeable."

"All right. Now what about the baby? Do you want me to look at available care for her?"

"No. Not yet. I think we can manage to juggle her to start with. She's not even six months old. I doubt Chase is going to want her in care yet."

"How are you going to do that?"

"I'll rearrange my schedule so I'm free to have her when he's training or playing."

"You're going to take care of the baby?"

My gaze meets his. "Yes."

"He'll be okay with that?"

"I'm looking after her now. Although she's currently sleeping."

"Where's Chase?"

"Sleeping."

"Nat..."

"Don't say it."

"You kept your distance from Johnathon—"

"He's a prick and I knew it going into the marriage. That reminds me. Has he signed the papers yet?" There's an idea brewing, one I've got experience with, but I can't mention it until I've untangled myself from my current husband.

"According to his lawyer, he'll be doing it sometime this week."

"Can you put pressure on him? Make it happen sooner?"

"You know what will make it happen faster."

"I did say he was a prick." I take a deep breath and hold it.

There's no sympathy in Eli's gaze. He knows why I went into my marriage and why I remained in it even though my husband stepped out on me every chance he got.

Pushing the air from my lungs in a fast burst, I keep my eyes on Eli's. "Offer a two million bonus for signing today."

"And if he doesn't?"

"Then he misses out on two million and I'll rethink the house in New Orleans."

"Natalie."

"He's fucked me around long enough. It didn't matter before, I had other things to deal with, but now it's time to deal with him. He gets two million extra if he signs today, if he waits until tomorrow I'll take that two and the house in New Orleans off the table."

"Okay, if you're sure."

"Yes."

"Want to tell me why else you want this done now when you didn't yesterday."

"Not yet."

"Do I need to prepare another prenup?"

I laugh. "You really do know me."

"I've known you since before you were in diapers, girly."

We both laugh at his words. "Yes. And if I haven't said it recently, I love you. For everything you've done for me and for standing in for Dad when he couldn't."

"I love you like my own. You feel more like mine than his most days."

"You've had me as long."

"Are we doing the usual on the anniversary this year?"

"I don't know. It'll be the Rogues first game in the league."

"I know."

"We'll work something out."

"We usually do."

A cry from the monitor has my gaze lifting over the top of my computer screen. "Looks like the little one is up."

"All right, shoot me a message or email with anything else you want me to do. I'll concentrate on the divorce then move on to the school."

"Perfect. Let me know how it goes with Johnathon."

"Of course. Talk later."

Eli disconnects a milli-second before a loud screech fills the room. Jumping from my seat, I race to the fridge and grab one of the bottles of formula. I drop it into the warmer and hit the start button before I jog out of the kitchen and up to Candace's room.

I don't need her disturbing her brother yet. I want to have her cleaned up and fed before he surfaces.

CHASE

I think it's the laughter that wakes me.

It's definitely the laughter that puts a smile on my face.

The twins are downstairs giggling, and I can hear the murmur of a feminine voice. I picture Mom teasing the girls like she always does early in the morning.

For once the girls are up before I need to head to the rink. I can't remember the last time that happened.

Although I do recall the shit they give me for not beating them out of bed and my smile grows. My sisters might be a pain in the ass most of the time, but I love them. I'll miss them when I go to college.

Smiling, I keep my eyes closed and roll over to listen. I'll get up in a minute, get my bag and head to practice.

Stretching my arms above my head and my feet toward the end of the bed, I wait for my muscles to settle into the pull. I'm aching more than normal this morning. I'll need to make sure I warm up properly before I hit the ice today.

Opening my eyes I'm met with darkness. And it's not the early morning darkness I'm used to seeing when I roll out of bed. Glancing at the window I see someone has lowered the blind.

I never lower it. It's the thing me and Mom argue about most. I hate it down.

The low rumble of voices catches my attention again, the twins and Mom…

I frown.

It doesn't sound like Mom. There's an accent I can't place.

Confused, I push up and look for my phone, but my eyes snag on a shelf holding a tower of pucks.

Images and words from the last few months slam into my head, memories flickering rapidly. Memories I don't want to have lived through, never mind think about.

"Fuck!"

I dive out of bed and race for the door. Now that my sleep-fogged brain is remembering the last few months—this morning—I tear through the house for the second time today.

It has to be after nine. I slept the whole afternoon away and left Natalie to take care of Candace.

The twins too.

They would have been home hours ago.

I don't understand why no one woke me, but I know I need to get my ass downstairs and do my job.

Look after my sisters.

When I barrel through the living room on my way to the kitchen I don't see the four females on the floor. I'm focused on one thing and one thing only.

Getting to my sisters.

"Chase?"

Skidding to a stop, I wrap my hand around the doorway into the kitchen in a last second attempt to slow my trajectory.

It works.

Sort of.

Almost face planting into the wall in the kitchen snaps my brain into focus more than it has been in the last few seconds.

"Fucking hell," I mutter as I rest my forehead on the wall, aware enough to remember not to swear in front of the girls.

"Chase? Are you okay?" Natalie's voice floats into the room. "Girls, can you watch Candace for a second while I check on your brother?"

"Sure," Cass and Stell chorus.

Pushing away from the wall, I shake my head to clear it. The last thing I want is for Natalie to find me looking confused. She'll wonder if I'm capable of taking care of my sisters.

Fuck. She's probably already questioning it.

"Chase?"

I turn to find her next to me. "Yeah. I'm good. Got a fright when I woke up and realized the time." I scrub a hand through my hair and yank on the ends.

"I let you sleep because you obviously needed it, but I should have let the girls wake you when they got home."

"They wanted to?" A grin tugs at my mouth. "Of course they did. Let me guess. They wanted to dump a bucket of ice water on my head."

Natalie smiles. "That was mentioned. I let them check in on you and that reassured them enough to let you sleep." She tips her chin toward the oven. "There's a plate of grilled chicken in the oven and salad in the fridge. We ate about an hour ago. We were just playing with Candace before I put her down for the night."

I snort. "Good luck with that."

"I didn't mean all night. I know babies her age don't sleep through yet."

"She hasn't slept longer than a couple of hours at a time yet. And like I said earlier, she's more awake at night and trying to switch that around isn't working so well."

"She might just be a night owl. Some babies are."

"You know a lot about babies?"

"Not really. But I've got friends who do. I made a few calls and when Cassidy and Crystal got home, I talked to them about what your routine is."

"I suppose they told you we don't have one because I don't know what I'm doing."

"No. The opposite."

I frown at her words. "They did?"

"Yes." She glances over her shoulder then urges me further into the kitchen. "Come on, I'll make you a plate of chicken and salad and tell you what they said."

"This I have to hear." Parking my butt on a stool in front of the island I let this woman serve me. "*Shit*. You're in my home and I'm expecting you to wait on me," I say with disgust as I bury my face in my hands.

"No, you're not. You're letting someone help you for a little while. We had this conversation already."

I look up, find her gaze, and hope she can see the genuine appreciation I have for her. "Thank you. It's not enough but thank you."

"You can thank me by hearing what I have to say when the girls are settled for the night."

"You mean the contract offer?"

"Yes."

"I can't even—"

"You can and you will. It's what I'm asking for in exchange for my help today."

She's using her no-nonsense voice again, has that steely don't-argue-with-me look in her eyes too. "Okay. Fine. But don't be surprised when I turn you down."

Folding her arms over her chest, she shoots me a smirk. "We'll see."

I don't know this woman, but I'm not an idiot. I think I've just challenged her. I'm going to hate disappointing another person, but I can't in any way see how I could possibly go back to my old world.

"Stop worrying about it and have something to eat. I'll get the girls ready for bed. When you're done, come up and say good-night to them."

"Wait. Candace needs a bath."

"She's had one."

"I slept through that screaming match?"

In the months since my baby sister was born, I've waited for the cops to knock on the door because the neighbors have called about a baby being murdered. There's no way I slept through that.

"We bathed her down here in the kitchen sink."

I blink. My gaze darting to the sink and back to Natalie. "You" —I shake my head—"In the sink?"

"Yep. Crystal warned me about bath time so we moved things down here so we wouldn't disturb you."

"She cries loud enough to wake the whole neighborhood, moving down here wouldn't have helped."

"It did. She didn't make a peep."

"Not a peep," the words whisper through my lips as their meaning solidifies in my head. With a groan, I lower my face to my hands again and say, "I'm really not capable of doing this."

"It's not you." I peek through my fingers at Natalie. "Don't look at me like that. It isn't you. It's the situation. There's too much tension in all of you. And tension feeds off tension."

I raise my head. "So what? Because I'm stressed, they're stressed?"

"In a way, yes."

"It's as simple as not stressing about giving a baby a bath?"

"Yes and no. I'm not an expert but I have done a time or two on a therapist's couch, and you're all stressed in one form or another. You more so. And that tension escalates and escalates because you aren't doing anything to fix it."

"How the hell do I fix it?" I snap. "I can't bring my parents back!"

Her eyes widen, but other than that she shows no reaction to my raised voice. I want to yell at her. Shout at the ceiling, what, I don't know, I just have the urge to scream as loud as I can.

And in the next moment I realize the reason for my outburst isn't her fault. She has nothing to do with the situation I'm in.

But I'm angry at her for making it worse with her starting goalie offer.

"Fuck!" I shove off the stool and storm to the back door. When the thing won't slide open, I slap my hand against the glass three times.

"Here." A hand reaches around me, flicks the unlock lever, and pulls the door open. "I'll take care of the girls."

Fuck! Closing my eyes, I drop my head until my chin hits my chest. "I'm sorry."

"It's okay. Go outside, get some air. I'll get the girls ready for bed then we'll come find you to say goodnight."

"I can't keep doing this," I mutter.

"You won't. It's just today. Maybe another day here or there, but you have this, Chase. You've had this for months now."

"It doesn't feel like I've got it."

"Maybe not, but from where I'm standing, under the circumstances, with what you've faced, you do."

Her vote of confidence does a lot to calm my anger. And the anger isn't at any one person or thing. It's the situation. I'm not even angry at the guy who killed Dad.

"Give me five minutes to clear my head outside then I'll be back to take over putting the girls to bed."

I don't wait for her to agree or not. I head through the doorway onto the back deck, down the stairs I helped Dad build last summer, and into the yard.

I'm heading for one of Mom's favorite spots. I can't count the number of times I found her sitting on the old chair in the back corner of the yard staring at the house or the sky.

Her thinking chair.

It's where she sat when she needed to take a moment, think a decision through, or just ponder.

I'd never seen the appeal. But right now, it holds my interest for two reasons.

I need to think about how I'm dealing with everything.

And I need to feel closer to Mom.

Out of everywhere in our home, her thinking chair is where I imagine her most. Not the kitchen, not the living room, not even her bedroom gives me the same sense of closeness.

I'm almost frightened to sit on the chair. If I put my ass in it, will it override Mom's presence?

There's so much of her already gone. Every day, my memories fade. Or perhaps I'm too busy to focus on them these days.

I stare at Mom's chair for a minute. In the end I can't bring myself to sit in it so I lower myself to the grass in front.

"Mom." I keep my voice quiet. I don't want anyone to hear me and think I'm losing my mind. "I'm sorry. I can't do this like you. Or Dad."

Blowing out a breath, I look up at the night sky.

"I've spent my whole life knowing you were there whenever I needed help or advice and the time I need it the most you aren't here. I know that isn't your fault. I'm not blaming you. I know you didn't want to go."

I don't bother holding back the tears. Although after crying on Natalie's shoulder I'm surprised I have any left.

"I will do my very best to take care of the girls. I'll make sure they get every opportunity you gave me. I don't know how. But I'll do it. For you and Dad. For them. For me."

Focusing my blurry eyes on her chair, I smile. It's probably just my mind playing tricks, but I swear I feel her hand cradling my cheek the way she used to.

"I don't know what's best for all of us, but I hope you know any decision I make that is different to what you would have done is because things aren't the same. They're so different now, Mom."

Every word is the truth. I have no idea how we're going to make it without our parents to guide us. I do know neither of them would be happy with me if I didn't at least hear Natalie out.

They'd be so disappointed to know I've turned my back on my dream even if it is to take care of my sisters.

Until this moment I haven't really thought about what our

future would look like. I've been surviving, day by day, and it took a stranger, with the offer of a lifetime, to make me think.

Natalie might believe I'm the right goalie for the Rogues, and maybe I am, but until I understand what it means, what taking a position on the team in the NHL looks like for us, I can't make any decisions.

And we all have to be okay with whatever decision I do make. It isn't just me it affects. Accepting a contract would mean relocating, and since our parents died, I've been determined to keep us in this house.

In our home. My gaze moves to the house.

Except it doesn't feel like home anymore.

Without Mom and Dad walking the floors, it's just the place we live.

Candace doesn't understand what a move would mean but Cass and Stell do. I know they're only just teenagers, but they still should have a say in how our lives go from now on.

"Mom." My gaze moves over the back of the house, taking in every window, the back deck with its outdoor seating and barbecue. "The best thing might not be staying here."

I can't get the advice I want or need but just saying things out loud, in the spot where she did her own thinking, gives me the strength to make the tough decisions.

It would be so easy to accept a contract with the Rogues, so so easy, but the logistics of signing on with them would mean moving across the country. Putting the twins in a school where they wouldn't know anyone.

And leaving the only home the four of us have ever had.

Nat

When Chase came back inside, he seemed more centered. Less freaked out and calmer than when he came barreling down the stairs after waking up.

He didn't eat, instead took over bedtime with the girls and I made a quick exit to the lower level.

Cassidy and Crystal don't need tucking in but I'm sure since their parents died, Chase has been more attentive and supportive. He mentioned the three of them reading to Candace in her room before the twins slipped into their own beds.

While Chase deals with his sisters I take a few minutes to message Oakley, Blake, and Cami.

I'll be gone more than the few days we planned for.

OAKLEY

Is he proving a hard sell? We can come up there and Walker can talk to him.

Not necessary.

BLAKE

Give him my number. Tell him to call if he's got questions.

CAMI

What do you need from me?

I smile at Cami's reply. She isn't involved with the day-to-day running of the team and insists she shouldn't be because it's not her area of expertise.

In some ways, I agree with her, but others, like planning our media coverage and press releases, I think she'd be the perfect person for it.

Unfortunately, it's not what she wants. And I'm not about to force it on her.

The four of us are KAW, but Blake and I are the only two who are employed by the Rogues organization. Oakley doesn't actually have a job with the franchise—she's the face of the owners, and she's excellent at it. Takes the pressure off me and Blake, and of course Cami.

I'll keep you updated. Just wanted to let you know I'll be working remotely for the rest of the week.

Putting my phone on silent, I tuck it into the side pocket of my laptop bag and pull out the contract I came prepared with. I also pull out a set of highlighters and a small pad of sticky notes.

Chase can mark anything he's concerned about or make note of any questions he might have to run by his agent or a lawyer.

Which reminds me. Fishing around in the inside pocket of my bag I pull out a business card.

Drake Morgan
Sports Agent

I have no idea who has been guiding Chase in the last few

years. It might have been just his father or former coach, but if he's going to seriously consider a place in the league—with the Rogues or any other team—he'll need an agent.

And Drake is a cut-throat agent. One I've gone up against several times. I'm currently dealing with him over our backup goalie.

The reason I put up with the man's shark-like tendencies is because he's good—fair—and I want my players to be happy. I'm willing to negotiate most things and Drake isn't one to ask for the ridiculous.

Setting everything up on the dining room table, I head back to the kitchen for a couple of waters. It's too late in the day for coffee. Although I'm down at least three cups on my normal daily intake, I never drink it after five.

While I'm in the kitchen I get Chase some dinner. The chicken has gone cold, but I can slice it up and make him a bowl of chicken salad instead of a plate of hot chicken and salad.

There hasn't been any noise for upstairs in a while and I can only assume Candace went straight to sleep. She was tired before I took her upstairs to change her diaper. And the twins might have said they weren't tired, but I saw the yawns they tried to hide behind their hands.

I smile thinking about the three girls. Much to my surprise, I had a good time hanging out with them today. Candace is cute and seeing her eyes widen when she focuses on something is a joy to watch.

The twins are mature for their age, and I have to wonder if that's a result of seeing their mom slowly slip away over the last few months.

Being told a parent is sick and going to die, on the heels of finding out you're going to have another sibling has to have affected each of the three older Hawkins children in different ways.

I can see the influence from Chase on the twins, but I can also see—and heard in the things the girls told me—that their parents did a good job of preparing them for Sienna's death.

Of course, no one was prepared or expecting Mitch's.

Which is why I plan to get all the Hawkins siblings into counseling as soon as possible.

The creak of a floorboard above my head tells me Chase is on the move, and I quickly put his dinner together.

I'm not one to wait on people. Sure, I do my bit when we all get together, and now that our group of four has grown to add a couple of husbands and children, I do my best to be involved.

Even when the sight of Oakley and Walker, and Blake and Branton, has me envious in a way I've never been.

I have—*had*—a husband. I *could* be a mother. Except the thought of having a child with Johnathon Whitman turns my stomach in a way I've only ever felt when being down with stomach flu.

The man was a means to an end, and he's served his purpose. And in the last few years he's become a liability. It's not public knowledge that I'm married. Although it's not really a secret either.

I've gone to great effort to keep him out of my life other than on paper, which he's been more than okay with. But now that KAW owns the Rogues, the four of us are under more scrutiny from the media, and with Johnathon's extra-marital activities becoming more and more troublesome, I can no longer remain in the marriage.

Plus, I no longer need it to access my numerous trusts. And with my grandfather dead, the only resistance to my control of the family fortune has vanished.

"Hey."

I glance up to see Chase enter the kitchen. He's pulled a t-shirt on and I'm ashamed to admit, a stab of disappointment hits me.

I don't remember the last time I ogled a man and enjoyed it

the way I am with Chase. He's over a decade my junior, that alone should dampen my attraction.

And yet, it's no less than it was first thing this morning. If anything, it's getting stronger. I'll need to keep it under wraps. I can't let my libido get in the way of what's best for him and his sisters.

What's best for the Rogues.

I'm here to do a job. And that job is getting Chase Hawkins to sign on to play for the Rogues, not wish the man would walk around shirtless.

"Are they asleep?" I ask.

"Candace is. Cass and Stell are reading for another ten minutes." He walks closer and my gaze is drawn to the thickness of the thighs his sweatpants cling to.

Yeah, going to need to work on my ogling. "Will you need to check on them? Maybe you can eat first then listen to what the Rogues organization is offering."

"I could eat. And no. They're good. They'll keep reading for ten minutes then turn their light out."

"I noticed they were well behaved, but I wasn't sure if that was because there was a stranger in their house."

"No. They've always been good." He grins. "Except to me. They're your typical younger sisters most of the time."

"That hasn't changed now you're in charge?" I ask as I hand him the bowl of salad.

The frown he directs at his food is ripe with confusion. "I haven't noticed. But now you point it out, they are different."

"How?"

"They don't tease me or pull pranks like they used to." He stares at the bowl in my hand. "Actually, I think the change started before..."

I nod. I know what he's referring to and I have no desire to make him elaborate. "That's understandable."

"Yeah. I guess. We're all different now. Well, except Candace."

I offer him a smile. "Want to eat while I tell you about the Rogues' offer?"

He leans his hip against the counter and finally takes the bowl from me. "Sure."

"I've set us up in the dining room." I don't miss the color change in his eyes; they go from warm blue to a gloomy blue gray. "Is that okay? I can move everything in here."

He shakes his head. "No. It's okay. We just haven't eaten in there since Mom and Dad."

I should have waited. Should have asked where he wanted—

"We always ate at the table." His gaze moves in the direction of the dining room and the table neither of us can see through the wall. "Always. No matter who was here. Or who wasn't. Mom never served a meal anywhere else."

"You haven't..."

"No. I've fed us here. In the kitchen. At the island."

His gaze is unfocused, and I wonder if he's remembering those meals or the ones his mother set out in the other room.

"We should eat in there again." His words are strong, confident, as he pushes off the counter and walks away. When he reaches the doorway, he glances back. "All right, GM, let's see what you've got."

He's got an almost cheeky tilt to his mouth and his eyes are alive with a light I haven't seen in the hours since he opened the door to me. He might not have woken in the right frame of mind, but it looks like he's found it now.

I follow, because there's nothing else I can do. I normally lead meetings, especially in the male-dominated industry of professional hockey, but with a few words and a smirk, Chase Hawkins has snatched control.

And I can't say I'm pissed about it.

He needs to feel in control of something. His life has been a runaway train for months now, and I'm okay with letting him lead this.

When we've taken a seat next to each other he glances at me

with an arched brow, and I laugh. He's so different when he's confident. I don't know what triggered the change from the struggling man I've spent the day helping, but I like it.

"Okay, so you know the basics. I'm the general manager of the Rogues and I would normally do this with an agent present, but in light of recent events, I didn't want to involve a third party before you had time to process what's on offer."

"Appreciate it." He forks a mouthful of salad from his bowl. He waits for me to speak again before eating.

"We're offering you starting goalie. We can talk money and other compensations if you want to consider the contract. Right now, I just want you to think about considering it."

He chews slowly, his eyes on me until he swallows. He doesn't break the connection even when he grabs his bottle of water and cracks it open.

"Do you have an agent?" I ask to break the unnerving silence.

"No."

"You had to have been looking at one in the last few years."

"They were looking at me. I wasn't interested. I've got another year of college left and I promised my parents I wouldn't go pro before I finished my degree."

"And now?"

"Now I can't finish my degree. Not full-time and I'm not interested in doing it part-time. Dragging it out doesn't appeal at all."

"Okay. So how do you feel about going professional without a degree behind you?"

"All I ever wanted was to play in the NHL. Didn't care what team, although one close to my family would have been preferable." He lowers his fork and presses his hands, palms down, on the table. "I need to forget what the dream was before. I need to think about what the dream is now."

"Is playing professionally still the dream? If you could make it happen."

"I have three young girls to raise and enough money to do it."

I wait for him to continue but he keeps his gaze locked on mine, not saying a word. We're quiet for so long I'm feeling fidgety, and I'm never fidgety.

It doesn't feel as though he's looking for my approval or my encouragement. But I can't decipher the emotions in his eyes and as I don't know him well, I can only assume he's thinking about the situation, the offer I've made, not analyzing *me*. Even if that's the way his stare makes me feel.

"What do you see happening if I accept a contract with the Rogues?"

His question surprises me because I had a similar one for him.

"Not just on the ice," he adds. "What does it look like if I sign the deal and move to Baton Rouge?"

"We've built our sportswear company around family values, we're doing the same with the hockey team. We support our employees, their families, in any way they need."

"So, someone would help me take care of my sisters?"

"Not someone. Me. I wouldn't expect you to leave them with someone you don't know or trust."

"I don't really know you."

"You didn't say you didn't trust me."

"I've spent my life honing my instincts, I know where a guy is going to shoot the puck before he does, and up until the last few months I've applied that instinct to my life." He holds up a hand to stop me from talking. "But I had Mom and Dad behind me."

"And now you don't."

"No. But what is more important than that is the girls don't have them. I'm already an adult, you could argue I don't need my parents to make decisions about my life."

"The girls have you."

"I don't know if that will be enough if I'm away all the time. Who do I leave them with? How do I parent them if I'm not there?"

"You have a partner."

"I don't and I'm not looking for one. I have plenty of things to balance without having to deal with another person."

"Before you say anything, let me finish what I'm about to ask. Don't interrupt."

"Okay."

"If you had a partner to help you raise the girls, to be there for them when you aren't, or make it so they can be with you when you travel, would you sign?"

"If that person was supportive of me playing and raising the girls, yes."

"I can give you that."

"Give me what? A partner? Do you have them ready to roll out?" He cocks an eyebrow as he speaks.

"No. It would be me."

"You what?"

"I'd be the other parental figure in the girls' lives; I'd be your partner, pick up the slack when you're training or playing or away."

"How does that work with your job as GM?"

"I'd work around their needs. And yours."

He cocks his head along with that eyebrow and asks, "What exactly are you offering me?"

This is the part that gets tricky, but I've done it before. I can do it again so both of us can have what we want, and in Chase's case, what he deserves.

"A business agreement."

"You'll be the girls nanny?" His voice is filled with disbelief and confusion.

"No. I'd be your wife."

CHASE

For the second time today I'm laughing hysterically.

And it takes me a good couple of minutes to realize Natalie isn't laughing at all.

Sucking in a breath, I stare at her.

Her mouth is tight but loose, if that makes any sense at all. Her eyes are steely, but not like earlier. There's a hint of... challenge and determination, and dare I say, you're-stupid-if you-don't-see-I'm-right, flashing in them.

This is the face I imagine she wears in board meetings or when dealing with players and agents. It's her general manager of a professional hockey team face, her billionaire business owner face.

"You're not joking," I say incredulously. *Why the hell is she not joking?*

"No." Shaking her head slightly, she keeps her gaze on mine, never once losing her confident-this-is-right expression. "I know it sounds unconventional—"

"Unconventional?" I snort. "It's fucking crazy is what it is."

"Hear me out. It would be in name only, so you have a backup for the girls. And later, when you find someone you want to be with, we'll get divorced, but I'll still be the second parental figure for the girls."

"Candace won't be an adult for eighteen years. Why would you tie yourself to us for that long?"

"You and I might not be tied that long. As I said, when you find someone—"

"I hate to break it to you but I'm not stepping out on any vows I make to a woman, in name only or otherwise, so there would be no finding someone."

"Right. Okay. Well. Let me tell you a little more about me so you can understand why I've put forward this *unconventional* suggestion."

I snort-laugh at her emphasis of unconventional but otherwise remain quiet.

"I come from money, a lot of it, but it was tied up in trusts for most of my life. The only way to unlock them was to turn a certain age or get married. At twenty-two, with billions of dollars and multiple companies at stake, I married Johnathon Whitman to secure them all. In name only. I'm in the process of divorcing—"

I jerk back, almost toppling my chair. "You're married!" Why this shocks me I don't know. She's in her late twenties—"Wait. How old are you?"

"Thirty-four."

"I'm twenty-one in two months."

"I know."

"Then you know how that's going to look."

"No one will know we're married except you and me unless something happens to either you or one of the girls, and I'll be praying nothing does and I'm not religious."

I lean back in my seat, making sure all four legs are on the floor, and study her. She's completely serious and I can't quite wrap my head around it.

Why would a woman who looks like her, who has money and success, want to tie herself to a twenty-year-old and his three underage sisters?

"If you took me up on my suggestion, we couldn't get married until I sever ties with my ex and I have to warn you, he has been difficult so far."

"Why is that if your marriage is name only?"

"Money. He has none of his own and after we divorce, he won't have an unlimited supply of it. All he will have is the amount I give him as part of our settlement."

"And how much is that?"

"Two hundred and two million. Plus, a couple of houses around the country."

"Two..." It's my turn to shake my head because what the fuck? "You're giving him that as a settlement?"

"No. I'm paying him that to sign the papers."

"You're buying him off?"

"If you want to look at it that way, yes, I'm buying him off."

"Why?"

"Because for the entirety of our marriage, he hasn't upheld our vows the way you say you would."

"Prick."

She grins. "My thoughts exactly."

"Okay. So let me get this straight. To ease my mind about the girls and their lack of a second parental figure, you'll marry me and provide them with one."

"Yes."

"And the union would be in name only and no one would know?"

"Correct."

"Huh." I scrub a hand over my head, fist my fingers in the over-long strands of hair. "I don't know what to say."

"I want you to play for the Rogues, but at this point, after spending the day with the girls, I want to give them the security of another adult in their lives. I'd treat them the way you do, as younger sisters."

"You must know that Candace is going to look at us as her father and mother. She'll have no others in her life."

"I'm aware of that. But I assume Cassidy and Crystal calling us by our names would deter that."

"It might, it might not. I'm okay with her thinking of me as her dad but I intend to discourage her from calling me dad."

"I'll take your lead on any parenting matters."

I shake my head again. "Natalie. I have to be honest with you. The offer to play for the Rogues was blindsiding, but this? This is...hell, I don't even know what this is."

"You want security for the girls. You want to be able to live your dream, the one you've worked your whole life for. I can help you achieve both of those things."

"So you say." I study her again.

It seems to be all I'm doing tonight. I can admit she's hot as fuck and I'm not sure being married to her would be a smart move when I think that.

"This would be complicated as fuck," I mutter.

"Not if we set boundaries."

"I assume we'd be living together."

"Yes. The girls would have one home with the two of us living in it—"

"Then how do you plan to keep this proposed marriage of convenience a secret?"

"I've recently purchased a house that has an in-law suite that I would reside in, you and the girls would have the rest of the house."

"We'd still be living together."

"Yes, but we'd play it as I'm helping you with the girls when you need it. And it's not like I plan to make a media announcement about our marriage or living arrangements. We don't have to tell anyone anything. I don't plan to tell the other three KAW partners."

I can't see how that would work. "How can you keep this a secret from them?"

"It doesn't affect either of us work wise. It's a purely personal business arrangement."

"I don't see how we can keep this quiet. And what would we tell the girls?"

"Exactly what we'll tell anyone else who asks, I'm helping you with the girls while you settle into Baton Rouge and your position with the Rogues."

"I haven't agreed to anything."

"No. But you want to. I can see it in your eyes, Chase, you want this more than anything."

"Not more than anything but the thing I want the most is impossible." I see it in her eyes that she understands what I mean.

"Your parents would want you to go after your dream. And I haven't had anything to do with your father for a while, but when I first approached him years ago about stocking our products in his stores, he talked about his family. He'd be proud of you no matter what you decide to do with the company or your life."

"You met him?"

"Yes. When we started Rogue sportswear. He was one of the first to take a chance on four college women with more money in their trust funds than most people earn in a lifetime."

There's a story there. I can only imagine Natalie and her friends going after what they wanted. She came through our front door and took charge. Helped a drowning man take a moment to refresh his energy and spent time with three girls she has no ties to other than she wants me to play for her hockey team.

If her friends are anything like her, they'd be a formidable team. And I can't imagine the Rogues being anything but successful.

Do I want in on that? Fuck yes. But is it really possible?

"You'll do anything to make sure the Rogues are a success."

"Not anything."

"But you're talking about tying us together for years."

"I am. But that isn't about the Rogues."

"Then what is it about?"

"You and your sisters getting everything you deserve."

"Why are you determined to help with that? You know I'm

going to do everything I can to make their lives what Mom and Dad would have. And I've got the money to do it."

"You do. And money can buy a lot of things. But it can't buy you family or a spot on a Cup-winning national hockey team."

"I'd say you've got tickets on yourself for that last comment, but I don't think you do."

"No. I have a support system and employees and coaching staff and players who all believe, or soon will, the same thing. The Baton Rouge Rogues are going to hit the ice and win. And when we lose, we aren't going to do it easily."

Her confidence is inspiring, and in some ways encouraging. She seems to be one hundred percent sure of herself and her team. And from what I know about Rogue sportswear, she's come by that confidence from experience.

She knows she can succeed, and she knows what it takes to do it too. I can't even comprehend her going into owning a national franchise without knowing exactly what it takes to make a winning team.

"Okay. I'll look at the contract. But"—I hold up a hand to stop her from speaking—"I won't make a decision on my own. The twins will need to weigh-in, and I'll need to research schools and see your house."

"I can help with the school, and I have pictures of my house on my phone but if you want, we can take a trip to see it in person."

"Is that wise? Won't that draw attention to us?"

"I can make it happen without anyone knowing."

"How?"

"Private jet."

"You have a private jet? Wait. Of course you do."

I scrub a hand over my head again. My mind is spinning but I can't deny I want to say yes to playing for the Rogues without any of the other stuff.

But I can no longer make snap decisions like that. I need to consider how they affect the girls and my need to parent them as our parents would have.

"Think about what I've said." She taps the pile of papers on the table in front of her. "Read this. Make notes or highlight whatever you have questions about."

Natalie has it all set up. Contract, highlighters, sticky notes. I hadn't even noticed it when we sat down. Sure, I saw it but *seeing* it didn't happen.

"What's that?" I point to the business card on the other side of her.

"Drake Morgan's contact information."

"The agent?"

"Yes. He represents a few of our players as well as our head coach."

"Walker Alcott, right?"

"Yes."

"And Blake Watts is assistant coach?"

"Yes."

"Can you name other players? I understand if you can't."

"I can tell you a few. Others are in final negotiations. The ones we've already signed who have been announced are, Beckett Higgison, Branton Lattimer Watts, Ryder—"

"Lattimer Watts?"

"When Branton married Blake, he took her last name."

"Lattimer married Blake?"

"For someone who has spent his life working toward playing in the NHL you aren't up on the recent media attention."

"I don't need to know about the personal lives of players or coaches to work for a spot in the league."

"I guess not." She pushes her chair back. "I'll head out. The twins said they need to be dropped off at nine tomorrow. I can be here at seven to help with the morning routine and drop off if you want."

"You"—I shake my head—"Is this what you mean about being the other parent in their life?"

"Yes."

As much as I don't want to think of myself—or Natalie—as their parent, it's what I am, what she would be if I take her up on her offer, no matter our connections to the girls.

I watch her as she gathers a laptop bag I haven't seen before. "Where'd that come from?"

"My car. I ducked out to get it when you were asleep."

"You worked this afternoon? While Candace and I were asleep?"

"Yes. And when the twins came home."

"So, you worked around taking care of them." It's not a question even though my tone suggests it is. It makes my attempts to do the same seem even more pitiful.

"I answered a few emails. Made a few calls. Nothing too detailed or urgent."

I don't need her to say she's appeasing my disgust with myself, but she is. I know she is. She's pointing out her success was limited due to the level of difficulty of the work. I appreciate her efforts, but I don't like them.

"I don't need you to placate me."

"I'm not." Her gaze locks with mine for a beat before she adds. "Fine. Maybe I was, but it wasn't intentional."

"I know the adjustment to our new life should take time. And I know I shouldn't feel guilty or inadequate or angry that I can't manage everything the way my parents did. That knowledge doesn't stop the emotions from being there."

"No. It doesn't."

"I want to say yes to the Rogues' offer. Except I can't. I can promise to give it serious consideration and thought. But I have to be honest. If the girls tell me they don't want to move, my answer will be no. They have just as much say in this as I do."

"I understand that. And I respect that. But remember, teenagers don't necessarily make decisions with logic or reasoning the way an adult would."

"I'd argue some adults don't either."

"True. I'm not going to rush any of you into this life altering decision, but I will try to talk you into it. The twins too. And I'd like you to consider taking advice from someone outside of the situation."

"Who might that be?"

"I don't know. Someone without a stake in the outcome?"

So much to think about. And I haven't even read the offer yet.

"Let's table it for tonight. I'll be back tomorrow morning, and we can discuss it more."

NAT

When I arrive at the Hawkins house for a second day in a row, I'm just as nervous about the reception I'll receive.

Last night I left right after offering Chase a marriage of convenience. Mainly because I didn't want to talk the idea to death, especially when my ex dragged his feet and didn't sign our divorce papers yesterday.

I also wanted to give Chase time to catch his breath, time to think about everything I said and did yesterday. I dumped a lot on him in less than twenty-four hours.

The offer to play for the Rogues.

The offer of a house to live in.

The offer of another parental figure for the girls.

It's the last one I think will be a sticking point for him.

He needs to prove he can take care of his sisters. Whether it's to himself or his parents or some unknown people, I don't know, and it doesn't matter. Every time I helped him, I could see the hunger to do it himself in his eyes.

It rivaled the hunger I saw when I offered him the Rogues' starting goalie spot.

He may have resigned himself to no longer playing hockey

but that dream still dwells in the back of his mind—lives in his heart.

And I plan to be the one to help him achieve it without compromising his need to take care of his family.

Switching off the engine, I grab my bag and step out of my rental. I chose a more appropriate outfit today. Linen lounging pants and a casual short sleeved summer sweater seemed more appropriate for a day at the Hawkins home.

It's a more relaxed look, and while it's not my usual armor when dealing with business, I feel comfortable and confident.

And I admit I'm hoping Chase will find me—if only a little bit—more approachable. If we're going to do this the way I've suggested, I want us—need us—to be friends.

I can only hope my position as the Rogues' GM doesn't make things harder to navigate. I'm not oblivious to the possible pitfalls of the situation. And I'm very aware of everything that can go wrong with an in-name-only marriage.

It's still the best way to ensure Chase and his sisters get what they need and want. And I refuse to examine why I'm so determined to help them this way.

Lost in thought, I barely step onto the crumbling path to the Hawkins' front door when it flies open, and Cassidy and Crystal come barreling out onto the porch.

My smile is automatic, the joy at seeing them again spontaneous and exciting.

Children of any age have never been a regular part of my life. I'm not completely ignorant about them but I'm surprised by how much fun I had with Candace and the twins yesterday afternoon.

Before they reach me, the girls are talking at once and while their voices are similar, they're saying different things and the words are a jumbled, mangled together mess and in no way understandable.

"Slow down, slow down." I laugh when they skid to a stop in

front of me and simultaneously suck in a breath like a pair of synchronized swimmers. "One at a time, please."

"Can you give us a ride to camp?" Cassidy asks with a pair of caramel-brown pleading eyes identical to her sister's.

"I can. But where's your brother?"

Crystal rolls her eyes, and I have to stifle a grin at the typical teenage action. "He's busy on the phone."

"Oh?" I glance at my watch. Who is he talking to at seven in the morning?

"Someone we don't know," Cassidy adds. "About playing hockey."

My eyebrows shoot up. "Drake?"

"No. Morgan, I think," Crystal says with a scrunch of her brow.

Chase must have made the call because I didn't give Drake any of Chase's information or even a heads up. As much as I want to give Chase a helping hand, I want him to deal with this part of his career himself.

I'm going to be in control of a lot of what happens in his professional life from here on if he decides to take me up on my offer to play for the Rogues. Letting him take care of his choice of agent will keep Chase from feeling as though I'm taking over completely.

Not to mention my position as GM makes my involvement a conflict of interest. I'm already thinking I need to hand over Chase's contract negotiations to Oakley.

"If your brother says it's okay, I can take you where you need to go," I tell them.

"He will. Candace isn't awake yet, so he has to get her up, feed her, change her, and we'll probably be late like we are every day of the week," Cassidy gripes with a pout and folded arms.

I have to hold back a smile. "Okay. Let's get inside and see what he needs help with before I take you to...where am I taking you?"

"Summer day camp." Cassidy glances at Crystal. "We didn't

want to go but Dad enrolled us, and Chase said it would be good to keep things like before."

"And it is," Crystal rushes to add. "We wanted to go. When Dad signed us up."

"Before..." Cassidy swallows, her eyes filling with tears. "Before Mom and Dad..."

My throat grows tighter, and my chest aches deeper with each word they say.

These girls have lost so much this year, and yet they're still levelheaded enough to know what their brother said is true.

Sticking to some of their usual routine, doing things the way they were always done, can give them a small amount of the comfort their situation has done its best to rip away.

"Come on, let's go inside and I'll check with your brother. Have you eaten breakfast?" I ask as I urge them back toward the house.

"No. Chase was supposed to make it before he got on the phone. I think he forgot about us."

There's another eye roll from both of them and I stifle the laugh that bubbles in my throat. I ignore the comment about their brother forgetting them because we all know that's not possible. Their words and actions are harmless, teenage melodrama.

"What time do you need to be at camp? Do we have time to make pancakes?"

"You can make pancakes?" Cassidy eyes me skeptically. "Chase's either taste like flour or nothing at all."

"If you can even eat them," Crystal mutters.

"Yes, I can make them, and they definitely taste better than that or I wouldn't keep making them." I open the front door and usher the girls in ahead of me. "I remember seeing apples in the fridge yesterday. If you've got ground cinnamon, I can make you my favorite kind of pancakes."

"We do!" Crystal takes off, calling over her shoulder, "I'll get it."

"What else do you need?" Cassidy asks, excitement lighting up her eyes. "I can show you where it all is."

I don't tell her I know they have the other ingredients I need or that I know where to find them. She doesn't need to know I spent yesterday afternoon searching through their kitchen.

I'm the interloper here. And like Chase, the girls need to feel in control of their lives, well, as much as possible for a pair of four-teen-year-olds.

"Lead the way."

The house is quiet, and as we enter the kitchen my gaze goes to the monitor on the counter only to find it missing.

Chase must have it with him. I want to find him and take that responsibility away but I stamp on the urge and concentrate on breakfast.

"Do you need to pack lunch?" I ask, trying to recall everything from my search and pulling ideas for possible lunches together.

"No. They feed us."

"It's usually yuck but if you drown it in ketchup, it's okay."

Crystal's words have me stopping in my tracks. "You don't like what they feed you?"

"It's okay." She glances at Cassidy. "But Mom always packed us lunch because you can do that if you want. Dad paid more so he didn't have to worry about it."

"Oh."

The heaviness of that implication churns my stomach. I can imagine Mitch Hawkins making that decision knowing at some point over this summer with a new baby in the house, his wife would die.

"Well, we can make you both a lunch box if you want."

Crystal claps her hands and Cassidy's grin lights up the room.

"And if we mix up enough batter, we can add a couple of apple cinnamon pancakes to it."

"Yes!" The girls shout and high-five each other and I'm reminded of how young they are even though they seem years older at times.

"All right." I put my bag down on a stool and look around. "Let's prep on the island, there's more space for all of us to help."

"What else do we need?" Crystal puts a jar of ground cinnamon on the counter.

"At least one apple. If they're small, two."

"On it," Cassidy says as she races to the fridge.

"Grab milk while you're in there," I tell her before turning to Crystal. "We'll need flour, and a mixing bowl or two, measuring cups and spoons. And something to shred the apple with."

"Okay."

I stand to the side and watch as the girls race around the kitchen, ducking in and out of the walk-in pantry to retrieve everything I've asked for.

I think they're done and ready to start when they both shout 'oh' and dash back into the pantry. When they emerge a minute later, they're wearing matching aprons and holding one out to me.

It's the look in their eyes that has me cluing in to what a momentous moment this is. For a second I debate not taking the apron, but I know they wouldn't be offering it if they didn't want me to wear it.

"Did you cook a lot with your mom?"

"Yes." I swing around to find Chase behind me. His fists are clenched and he's working his jaw side to side, his wet eyes on me. "She insisted we learn to cook. So, we could take care of ourselves when we left home."

The irony of them having to take care of themselves without leaving home doesn't escape me. I could easily make this into a difficult situation and I'm struggling with what to say or do when Cassidy takes it out of my hands.

"You need to wear it so you don't ruin your clothes. Mom never lets us cook without one." She thrusts the apron at me. "It's Mom's kitchen so her rules stand."

My gaze darts between the siblings. Each of them is fighting their own emotions and I can either stand back and keep myself separate from them by refusing to comply with their wishes, or I can put the apron on and we can cook breakfast together.

Like their mom would do if she were here.

"Thanks." I have no other words, but I know I need to tread carefully because this moment will set the stage for what comes next and as much as I want Chase to play for the Rogues, I have to admit I want this family to thrive in the face of tragedy just as much.

It takes a moment but finally Chase steps toward the pantry and asks, "What are we making?"

"Apple cinnamon pancakes," Cassidy says.

Crystal adds, "And we're making our lunch too."

Her tone is strong, laced with determination, as though she expects an argument and isn't going to let him say no.

"Is the food as bad as I remember?" Chase asks when he comes out of the pantry wearing an apron of his own.

"It's okay." Crystal looks at her brother. "But not like what Mom used to pack us."

"I remember. It's always nuggets and fish sticks. And it's never hot, which somehow makes it worse."

"Exactly."

"All right, Natalie, tell us what we need to do." My gaze meets Chase's, and I can see the swirl of emotions he's dealing with.

Determined to make this easy for all of them, I push all thoughts other than teaching them how to make apple cinnamon pancakes from my mind.

"Who's the best at shredding? We need to shred the apple and squeeze as much juice out of it as we can."

"I'll do that." He picks up an apple and small plate. "Should I do it in a bowl?"

"Do you have a strainer? I usually shred the apple into one over a bowl. That way some of the juice drips away while I get everything else together."

"I can do that."

He busies himself with the apple and I get stuck for a few

seconds admiring the way his arm muscles flex. It takes more effort than it should to pull my eyes away and focus on the girls.

It's surprisingly easy to work together. The girls take instruction well, and with enthusiasm, and Chase helps but lets them do most of the work.

He might think he's failing his sisters but from where I'm standing, he's doing a great job. He isn't taking over or telling them off when they make mistakes. And they make a few.

By the time he pulls a frypan from the cupboard, the island, their aprons, and the floor at their feet are covered in a fine layer of flour.

"Who's the best at flipping pancakes?" I ask as I move to the sink for a sponge to start cleaning up.

"Um..."

I glance over my shoulder to see one set of blue and two sets of caramel-brown eyes on me. Turning, I eye each of them hoping for an actual answer.

Chase finally speaks. "Maybe you should cook while we clean up."

"Yes. You cook, we'll clean," Crystal agrees, her elbow nudging her sister's side. "We aren't allowed to use the stove alone and Chase burns everyth—"

"Hey! I do not."

"You always burn pancakes," Cassidy says, hands on hips. "Don't lie."

"Fine, I struggle with pancakes, but I don't burn anything else."

"All right, I'll cook, you all clean." Moving over to the stove, I glance at Chase. "Can you work out how to use the coffee machine?"

"I can do it!" Cassidy pushes her brother aside. "What kind do you like?"

"Ah...surprise me. As long as it's coffee, I'll be happy."

"Okay. I'll make you Dad's favorite. He says it's the only way to start the day."

When she finishes speaking there isn't a sound. None of the Hawkins siblings move either.

It's like they're all holding their breath, waiting to see what will happen after the mention of their father.

The silence drags too long, I know someone needs to break it and I don't want it to be any of them. I want them to feel comfortable talking about their parents in any way they choose to.

"Only way? Well, how can I refuse that?" I pick up the bowl of pancake batter. "How quickly does this pan heat? You're probably burning them because the pan is too hot."

From the corner of my eye, I see Chase shake his head slightly. "I usually have the heat up high," he says as he moves next to me.

"Well, let me show you how to make the perfect pancake. It begins with a medium heat, never too high or too low. And it takes practice."

"Like hockey," Crystal says as she moves in on the other side of me. "You just need to learn how to do it right and keep practicing."

My gaze meets Chase's before he says, "Yeah, Stell, I guess it is like hockey."

"Leave the clean-up for a minute and come close so I can show you how to make the perfect golden pancake."

With the Hawkins family crowding around me, I teach them how to make the best Sunday morning breakfast. One I've had on my own too many times to count.

One I want to share with this family not just today, but many days in the future.

CHASE

I can't lie, Natalie has been a lifesaver. And not just because she dives in and helps wherever it's needed without being asked. Just having another adult around has made things seem easier, less overwhelming and out of control.

In the three days Natalie has been here the girls have smiled more than they have in the past few months.

I hadn't realized how much I missed the twins' cheeky cheerful demeanors until Natalie's presence brought a lot of it back out from under the cloud of grief.

Fuck, even I've been happier, and I've smiled so much my face is starting to hurt.

And I can't deny the ache in my chest isn't as sharp. I expected it to be worse when she first arrived with her offer. Dangling my lifelong dream in front of me when I could see no way of accepting it seemed cruel.

But as the days have passed, I realize it is anything but that. It's a lifeline. A different direction than the one I thought I had to take.

I might be determined to make sure the girls have the lives they want just as our parents would have, but now I see it's possible for me to have what I always dreamed of too. I don't have to give up the life I worked so hard to achieve to take care of our family.

Our parents wouldn't only want the girls to live out their dreams. They'd want me to as well.

Making the decision to sign or not sign a contract with the Rogues is the easiest and hardest of my life.

Easy because it's everything I ever wanted and more, and a few months ago I would have signed the contract on the spot.

Hard because it means taking us all away from where our parents are buried, from the home they made for us, the only one we've ever known.

Moving away from here isn't as simple as loading our furniture into a truck either. I need to decide what to do with the house, the business, the girls' school...

But with Natalie's help, her guidance, and the expert opinion of the agent of all agents, Drake Morgan, I think I'm ready to do it. To sign on the dotted line and change all our lives again.

There's just one final hurdle, one final opinion—or two—I need to get before I take the Rogues up on their offer and take my sisters to the other end of the country.

Natalie has agreed to have Candace for the rest of the afternoon so I can pick up Cass and Stell from camp.

My plan is to take them—at Natalie's suggestion—out for an early dinner so I can talk to them about the contract I've been offered and what signing it would mean for all of us.

I know they're aware something is going on; they aren't stupid, and any time Natalie and I have discussed things it hasn't been secret whispered conversations behind hands or closed doors.

They must know why she's here or at least suspect.

When I arrive in the camp parking lot, I stay in the car. The few times I've picked the twins up have been uncomfortable to say the least. The pitying looks, the awkward offers of condolence.

I don't need or want or have the energy to talk with anyone right now.

I know a lot of the community has tried to help over the last few months, but I don't need any well-meaning people getting in my face today. There's too much going on in my head and heart to deal with someone else's thoughts or emotions.

Honestly, it's the sympathy and pity I can't stand. And I have to wonder if the girls are noticing the difference in the way people look at us now. They leave the house more than I do, have more contact with people outside our little family, and I can only assume they're treated differently since our parents died.

Movement in the side mirror grabs my attention and I focus on it, see the twins heading my way with one of the teachers a few steps behind them. My back snaps straight and my hand darts to the door handle when I notice the expressions on all their faces.

The girls look like they've been crying, and the teacher has a pinched, angry, disapproving look. Nothing about their appearances has me feeling good.

Opening the door, I hop out and walk toward them.

"Cass? Stell?"

My voice has them rushing forward and for the first time since the funerals, they throw themselves into my arms and sob.

Wrapping my arms around them, I raise my eyes to the teacher and stiffen at what I see. Her angry gaze is trained on the twins and if looks could send daggers, this one would.

"What the fuck happened?" I can't hold the anger from my voice—or stop myself from swearing—and when the woman looks at me like I'm scum on the bottom of her shoe, I'm glad I didn't.

"Cassidy and Crystal are suspended from camp for the rest of this week and next." She folds her arms and glares at me. "When they return, they will apologize for the way they spoke to—"

"Hold up. They're suspended from camp?"

"I cannot allow them to remain when they spoke to several of my staff with disrespect."

"I can't imagine either of my sisters would do that without provocation."

"Of course they would. They've been nothing but rude and disrespectful from day one. They refuse to pair up with any of the other attendees and don't take part in group activities like the other children."

"How are they rude?"

"They're sullen and barely speak when spoken to and when asked to help with the younger children refuse to do so."

"What you see as sullen is probably sadness. I'm not sure if you're aware of our situation—"

"I'm well aware." Her gaze trails down to my feet before returning to my eyes, the sour look on her face pinching tighter if that's even possible. "And it's obvious the children left in your care are suffering—"

"What the fuck?" Nudging the girls away from me, I turn them toward the car. "Get in. Close the door."

They must know I'm about to explode or they're happy to get away from this harpy of a woman, because neither of them argues with me. And once they're in the vehicle, with the doors and windows closed, I turn back to the woman.

"Are you the head teacher here? Is there someone above you?"

Her back straightens and despite being half a foot shorter than my over six feet, she manages to look down her nose at me. "I'm the camp coordinator."

"Well, let me say this and then we'll leave, and you won't be seeing the girls in a couple of weeks because I'm removing them from this joke of a camp. You are one of the worst human beings I've met in my life. How you got your job here is questionable, and let me say, when I'm done, it's unlikely you'll keep it. Your job isn't to judge the children in your care, but you obviously have."

"I've been running this camp for over twenty years, and—"

"There's your problem. You're too old and behind the times to understand the younger generation."

"I beg your pardon."

"Nope. No pardon. You get nothing but what you've given. Those two girls have just lost both their parents and as their brother I'm now responsible for them. They are far better off being in my care than split up and put in random homes for the rest of their childhoods."

"Those homes can offer them—"

"No, they can't. What they need is family. I'm their family and I love them more than anyone else ever could. And I'm done arguing with you. But you haven't heard the last of this. I'll be contacting the camp organizers and reporting your behavior and treatment of my sisters."

She sputters behind me when I turn my back, but I ignore her and climb into Mom's car. Slamming the door, I hit the start button and after checking my mirrors, reverse out of my spot.

Ignoring the many parents and children standing around staring, I leave the parking lot before I say anything to the girls. It isn't until the camp disappears from the rearview mirrors that I speak.

"We'll talk about what happened, what's been happening, at camp, when we get home. If either of you tells me anything between here and there that will piss me off more, I don't think I'll be able to stop myself from turning around and running that woman over."

"Mrs. Bertram."

I'm not sure which of the twins speaks, the rage over the woman's insensitive comments buzzing in my ears making it hard to hear anything.

It only takes a few minutes to drive home and when I open the garage door and pull inside, I'm surprised to see Natalie waiting for us, a look of concern on her face.

With the car in park and the engine off, I twist around and peer between the seats into the back and study my sisters.

I don't see any visible wounds or injuries but have to ask anyway. "Are either of you physically hurt?"

"No," they murmur in unison, their hands clasped together on the seat between them.

"Okay. What do you want to do? I was going to take you out to eat but I don't think the conversation we need to have about camp can wait. And I'll be honest, I don't think I can sit through a meal and wait until we get home to talk about it."

"I don't want to go out," Cass says through her sniffles.

"Can I get out?" Stell asks.

Shocked she feels the need to ask, I nod my head. "Of course you can. You don't have to ask."

She's out of the car and racing across the garage toward Natalie before I finish speaking. And when she falls into Natalie's outstretched arms, I can hear her sobs echo off the concrete floor. My stomach cramps and my fingers clench so tight they ache.

"Are you really going to get Mrs. Bertram in trouble?"

I look back at Cass. Find her eyes swimming in tears and my resolve to find out what's been going on and take action grows so much stronger it just about strangles my throat.

Taking a deep breath, I try to temper my anger. "Yes. Let's go in and talk, yeah?"

"Okay." She nods, sniffs while wiping the tears from her eyes, before climbing out through the door Stell left open.

It takes me a few minutes to gain control of my anger enough that I can let go of the steering wheel. When I do and get out of the car it's to find only Natalie waiting for me.

"Crystal sent me a text." She holds up her phone. "Said they were in trouble."

Dragging in a deep breath, I hold it and count. I only get to three before I need to blow it out. "Yeah. They apparently are and after the words I just had with the camp coordinator I probably am too."

"What happened?"

"To be honest, I'm not really sure. She called them disrespectful and rude—"

"Cassidy and Crystal?" Her eyes and mouth are open.

"Yeah." I shake my head. "I can't see it either. They've never been rude or disrespectful a day in their lives."

"And you?"

"Oh, I was probably disrespectful. Rude too. Definitely angry enough to see red and want to run the woman over with Mom's car."

"Sounds like your actions might have been justified. Let's go inside. Order pizza or something and get to the bottom of what happened. We can determine if you overreacted or if the coordinator was out of line."

"Mrs. Bertram."

"Who?"

"The coordinator. Apparently, her name is Mrs. Bertram."

"Sounds like the headmistress of one of the horrible boarding schools my grandfather sent me to after my parents died."

I'm a few steps into the house before her words register. Spinning around, I have to grab her shoulders to stop her from plowing into me. "You went to boarding school?"

"Yes. Three different ones from fifteen to eighteen."

"After your parents died?"

She nods. "They were killed in a boating accident. My grandfather wanted nothing to do with raising a girl. If I'd been a boy, things might have been different."

"Sounds like a story."

"Maybe I'll tell you one day."

The smirk she gives me shouldn't lighten my mood, but it does. And if I'm honest, just being around the woman lightens my mood.

I think we're becoming friends. I know she's my closest acquaintance right now.

Despite what she'll be if I decide to sign with the Rogues, I want to continue to develop our friendship.

Her presence makes me feel comfortable, capable, when in the last few months, I've felt anything but.

"Promise me no matter what happens we'll stay friends." The

words are out before I think them but as they echo in my head, I know I mean them. "If we move in with you, if we do what you suggested to make sure the girls are looked after, I don't want me working for you to cause that to fall apart."

"I can't promise we won't have problems. If you sign with the Rogues, I'll be your boss and that could, probably will, cause friction between us, but I promise you that relationship or any you and I have, will not affect my relationship with the girls. Even if none of what we've talked about happens, I want to stay in their lives. Help make sure they get everything they, and your parents, wished for."

Her words are almost like a vow, and I know she means them; they aren't empty promises from someone wanting something from me. "Okay. I have to talk to the girls, but after this afternoon I think a move might be the best thing for all of us."

She doesn't gloat. Simply offers a nod then tips her head toward the kitchen. "Let's get something organized for dinner and sit down with the girls. Find out what happened today, what to do about it. Then we can talk about everything else."

"I'm ready to sign."

Her gaze locks on mine. I can see the excitement and the fear and wonder what evokes the second. I don't get a chance to ask though.

With another nod, she says, "Let's sort out today's problem before we make more for us to work on."

I know what she says is smart. One step at a time is the way I've been doing things since Dad was killed. Except now that I've made the decision to enter the NHL, I want to make everything needed for that to happen a priority.

Only I can't.

I still haven't talked to my sisters about the Rogues' offer, and we have to deal with what happened at camp. And I definitely want to follow through on my threat to report Mrs. Bertram to whoever runs the camp.

Trailing after Natalie, my mind is a whirl of all the things I need to do, all the decisions I need to make.

It's overwhelming but also exciting.

This could be—no, it *is*—the start of our new lives. It might not be what any of us predicted but with Natalie there with us, I think we can find a way to rise from the ashes of our parents' deaths.

NAT

I listen as Cassidy tells us about everything the girls have been dealing with at summer camp with barely contained rage.

Nobody has ignited the level of hate I feel right now since before my grandfather died. I've never wished ill of anyone other than him either.

But with every word I hear, I want to hunt down Mrs. Bertram and run her over like Chase suggested.

The woman has no place being in charge of so many young minds. Her ideas are antiquated and damaging and when I think about the hormonal teenagers in her care, I can't imagine the harm she's done over the years.

Who in their right mind suggests no one talk to two girls whose parents have just died?

I'm on the verge of calling the police when the doorbell rings. I push to my feet. "That will be dinner."

I need a few minutes to get myself under control. I don't want either of the girls thinking my anger is aimed at them. They don't need to deal with my emotions when they've got plenty of their own.

The Hawkins siblings continue to talk as I walk away. I know

I can't be involved in everything even if I want to be. I've put my hand up to help Chase with his sisters but who am I really?

A woman with a plan to put their brother on the ice for the benefit of her team.

That's what me being here boils down to.

Except I'd be lying if I said I'm not invested in this family beyond my role as the Rogues' GM.

I'm going to have to tread carefully for all our sakes. The Hawkins family have suffered enough. I'd hate to add to their situation in a negative way.

My marriage of convenience suggestion might be sound, but is it the best way to give the girls the stability Chase is looking for?

Can we do it another way?

Can I adopt Candace? The twins?

I'd be a single mother, but their brother would be their primary carer. I'd be their...what? What would that make me?

In the eyes of the law I'd be their mother, their guardian. Would Chase remain a guardian too?

I'm so stuck in my thoughts it takes me a minute to realize the person on the doorstep doesn't have our dinner.

"Hello." I force a smile. "Can I help you?"

"Yes. I'm Deanne. Melody's mom."

The woman's words shed no light on why she's standing at the door.

"Mel goes to school with the twins. I was friends with Sienna."

"Oh. Did you want to come in?" I look past her to see if Melody is with her.

"If I can. I'd like to speak with Chase about something."

"We're waiting for dinner, and the girls had a rough day—"

"I know. That's why I want to talk to Chase."

She eyes me as she enters the house and I realize I failed to introduce myself. "I'm Nat. Friend of Chase's."

"Nice to meet you." She offers her hand. "But I have to admit to knowing who you are. I'm a hockey fan. I'm looking forward to watching the Rogues play this upcoming season."

"Ah, right. Well, I'm not here to—"

"Oh, don't worry. I won't tell anyone I saw you here. But I have to say, if you're courting Chase for the team, you can't find a better goalie. The boy is a genius in the net."

I smile. "I agree."

Deanne sobers. "So, the reason I'm here."

"Right, yes, let me get Chase."

"I'd like to talk to him without Cassidy or Crystal hearing what I say."

"Is it that bad?"

"I've been hearing some things from Melody all summer, didn't think much of it until she came home today and told me the twins had been suspended. I'm a teacher at the girls' middle school. I have a lot of contacts within the teaching community, so I made some calls. Most of what I came to say they know, they've been dealing with it. But what Mrs. Bertram told the summer camp staff should not be shared with them."

"Nat? Oh, sorry. Hi, Mrs. Harper, I didn't realize you were here."

"Please, Chase, it's Deanne. I think you're old enough to drop the Mrs."

"Probably, but you've always been Mrs. Harper." He shrugs.

"Are the girls still in the kitchen?" I ask him.

"Yes." He must see something in my gaze because his head tips to the side and his brow scrunches in concern. "Why? What's going on?"

"Deanne has something to tell you about the camp coordinator. It's best if the girls don't hear what she has to say."

"Okay." He drags the word out and I can tell he's trying to decide if this revelation is going to be good or bad.

"Can we step outside?" Deanne suggests.

"Sure." Chase moves to open the door. "Do you mind if Natalie joins us?"

If Deanne is surprised by his request she doesn't show it. "Of course not. After what I tell you sinks in, it might take the two of us to stop you from tearing off in a rage."

"When have I ever gone off in a rage?" He holds the door for both of us to walk through.

"Never before this afternoon."

"You heard about that?" he asks as he follows us onto the porch, closing the door behind him. "Let's sit."

I lead the way to the end of the porch with the rocking chairs and small table between them. Chase leans against the railing opposite, his arms folded over his chest, his posture braced for whatever it is Deanne is about to reveal.

"I won't beat around the bush. Mrs. Bertram didn't want the girls to attend camp at all when she found out you were keeping them. She made no bones about her thoughts on a *child* raising three children," Deanne says.

"Yeah, I got that impression this afternoon when she told me the children in my care were suffering."

"She didn't!" Deanne shakes her head. "We've tried for a few years to have her removed from the position but her late husband's family are the major supporters of it, financially. And there hasn't been anything like this come to light that might have made it possible."

"What did she tell her staff? The thing that you came here to tell Chase?" I ask. I don't want to get us off track. The girls are going to wonder where we are sooner than later.

"Oh, yes, sorry. She told the staff at the start of summer to not include the twins, to discourage the other kids from hanging around them. When someone mentioned bringing in a grief counselor, she shut it down and told them the girls were to be left out of group activities as much as possible."

"She told me they weren't—wouldn't—take part in group activities." Chase's fists are clenched tight at his sides now and I stand, move to him.

With a hand over one of his, I say, "Take a breath. Dinner just got here. Take it inside and I'll finish talking to Deanne. We can't do anything about this tonight. Not without a plan."

"I should be in on any planning. They're my sisters."

"You will be," I reassure him. "I'm only going to gather more information, like name and contact details of the camp organizers. You and I will talk about it after the girls are in bed. Tomorrow, you will do what needs to be done to protect your sisters and anyone else this woman sets her sights on."

"I have a list of people willing to go on record. I also have the names and contact details of the camp board," Deanne pulls her phone from her pocket. "I can email them to you right now."

"Chase?"

His gaze meets mine.

"I promise you. I won't make any decisions regarding the girls without you." I lower my voice. "I know it seems like I'm taking over a lot, but I'm not, at least I'm not trying to. I only want to help."

"Hey, did you order two large pepperonis and a cheese pizza?" The voice of the delivery guy pulls Chase's gaze from mine.

"Yeah." He moves away from the railing and turns toward the front door. "Let me get your tip."

"Don't worry about that, man. It's already paid."

The look Chase shoots me has me laughing. "Sorry. Habit. I don't carry cash most of the time."

Shaking his head, he takes the three pizza boxes and thanks the guy. When he turns back, I can see he's still warring with what to do, but Deanne takes the decision out of his hands.

"I'll get going. Leave you to eat your dinner. Can I get an email for one of you before I go?" Deanne stands, phone in hand. "I'll send this list now, and you'll have my contact information if you need it. Although you already have my cell number, Chase."

"I do. And thank you. For coming over. For telling me what you found out."

"I couldn't not tell you. Those girls, you, you've all got enough to deal with as it is. And your mom was someone I thought of as a close friend. I won't lie and say we were best friends, but we were close. Hearing what that woman—" She shakes her head. "I know your mom would have done something if the situation was reversed."

Chase seems lost for words and instead of letting the silence drag out I nudge him along by saying, "Take the pizza into the girls before it gets cold. I'll give Deanne my email."

"Yeah, okay, thanks again."

I wait until he's inside, the door pushed shut behind him, before I give my information to Deanne.

"That's my personal email. I can count on one hand the number of people who have it. Please don't abuse it."

"He's going to move them, isn't he?"

Her question takes me off guard but I'm not going to lie to her because her daughter is close friends with the twins. "Probably. After today I'd say he's leaning more toward it than against."

Deanne nods. "It might be good for them all to have a fresh start. The number of times I've overheard conversations about them since Sienna died is ridiculous. And disheartening. No one has anything nice to say about that boy taking on his three sisters."

"He's hardly a boy."

"No. I guess not. But this community doesn't see him any other way. We expected Sienna's death but to lose Mitch the way we did..."

"*They* lost him."

"Yes. Yes. Sorry. I've wanted to help but other than picking up the twins and taking them with Melody I haven't known what to do."

"You did it today. You came here and told us what you knew."

"I wish I'd done something sooner."

"Hindsight is always clearer but don't discount doing what you did. Those girls won't be back at camp, and I can assure you, we will definitely do something about Mrs. Bertram."

"If they need anything else, anything at all, please, call me. I'm not sure Chase would have if it wasn't for the girls' friendship with Melody."

"No. I doubt he would have. He's determined to take care of what's left of his family."

"If anyone can do it, it's Chase. That boy has more determination and courage than most adults."

"I think we just agreed he's an adult. One his parents would be extremely proud of."

"They were proud of him. They bragged about his dedication to hockey and school all the time." Deanne smiles the first genuine one I've seen since I opened the door to her.

"Thanks again for coming over."

"Oh, don't thank me. As I said, I should have done something about what I was hearing sooner."

"Better late than never."

"I guess." She frowns. "Can you keep me up to date on what's happening with camp? I've told Melody she isn't going the rest of the week and depending on what happens, I'll probably pull her out altogether."

"Might be for the best."

"Yes." She takes a step before saying, "It was nice to meet you even if it's under these horrible circumstances."

"Same. And if you're ever heading to Baton Rouge, shoot me an email and I'll have tickets to a Rogues' home game for you."

"I would love to take you up on that."

"Be sure you do. And I'll have Chase let you know what he decides to do about camp."

I emphasize who the person in control of this situation is because those around Chase need to understand he's the adult in this family.

With a wave Deanne leaves, and I ponder how involved I've become with the Hawkins family.

I know I offered to be the second adult guardian for the girls, but we haven't discussed it since the night I mentioned it.

Chase needs help, and they all need the security of another

adult, but if he signs with the Rogues and they move to Baton Rouge, they'll have multiple adults available to lend a hand, to support them in whatever way they need.

If he doesn't mention getting married, I won't bring it up. Not that I can do anything about it if he does. Johnathon is still dragging his feet, being a prick.

Time to put the screws on that man. I want him gone and I need him to know I'm serious about severing our connection.

Pushing open the door, I head inside. The arguing coming from the kitchen has my pace increasing.

"Say yes so we can move!"

"We hate it here!"

The tearful shouts from the twins echo off the walls and when I reach the kitchen, I glance between the siblings.

It's two on one. The girls on one side of the island, Chase on the other, the pizza boxes open and spread out in front of them.

They're in some sort of standoff and while I can guess what kind from their words, I want clarification.

"What's going on in here?"

"We want to move to Baton Rouge. Live with you," Cassidy cries, her voice lower in volume but no less tear soaked.

I look at Chase.

"I told them about the offer to play for the Rogues. And your offer to move in with you."

"That doesn't explain the yelling and tears."

"They want to pack now. Go tomorrow."

Looking at the girls I want to cave to their demands, but I know I can't. For one, it's not my decision. And two, if they're going to learn to stand up for themselves, to understand Chase is there for them no matter what—that I am too—they need to face the difficulties of today's conflict.

"We can talk more about moving tomorrow." I hold up a hand when Cassidy opens her mouth. "No, let me finish."

Cassidy closes her mouth and I'm not ignorant of the way

Crystal moves closer to her sister. They aren't touching but each knows they have someone at their back.

"You need to deal with what happened today. You are not in the wrong. Although you should have said something to your brother about how you were being treated."

"If you'd told me I would have done something before now, so you didn't have to go through what you did today. Or any other day."

"She just yelled at us. A lot." Crystal's eyes dart to Cassidy, but the look doesn't stop her, the words just keep coming from Cassidy's mouth. "Most of the time it's okay. We have each other and a few of the other kids who we've been friends with since kindergarten."

Emboldened by her sister, Crystal continues to explain why they didn't mention anything to Chase. "We didn't care about talking with anyone else. When we first went, it was only a few weeks after Mom and Dad and we kind of wanted to get away from the house," she explains.

"Get away from the house?" Chase frowns at his sister's words.

"Yeah." Crystal looks at Cassidy before saying in a quiet murmur, "It hurts to be here."

CHASE

Well fuck!

It takes effort not to say the words out loud.

I promised myself I would stop swearing in front of the girls. I intend to stick to that promise no matter the circumstances.

But fuck, it's hard.

If there ever was a situation that warranted swearing, it's this one.

How did I miss the way the girls feel about being in this house?

Their home should make them feel safe—happy. It shouldn't hurt.

The guilt swamping me sinks my stomach and drags my shoulders along with it. Slumping forward, elbows on the counter between us, I force words through my constricted throat.

"Why didn't you tell me?"

The girls look at each other before Cass answers. "We feel guilty about hating it here."

"It's okay to feel the hate. And the guilt. There are no rules to grief or the emotions you feel when you suffer from it." Natalie's voice is a soothing wave of comfort.

For all of us.

"I hate that you haven't talked to me about it."

"You never talk about hockey and before you talked about nothing else?" Cass throws out.

"Yeah. Okay. I should talk to you about how I'm feeling too."

"I think you all should see a counselor. Together and individually."

My gaze moves to Natalie and the understanding I see in her gaze almost takes out my knees.

"I'll organize something after we deal with the camp issue."

"We're not going back!" Cass steps back from the island, her small fists clenched at her sides, her body vibrating with anger.

"Of course not." I straighten, gaze locked on my sister's. "Why the hell do you think I'd make you?"

"Because you said we had to do things like before."

"Fuck!"

There's no way to keep the curse in my head this time. And as I shove my hands through my hair and yank on the ends, I can't bring myself to care when there are far more important things to worry about.

"I didn't mean you had to suffer. I thought doing things the way we always have would help."

"Nothing helps," Stell mutters. "It hurts every day. Sometimes more, sometimes less."

"I know." Why did I assume they weren't thinking what I was? I need to find a way to stop my sisters' pain. "When does it hurt less? What makes it hurt less?"

As one, the twins look at Natalie.

I don't need them to voice what they're thinking—it's written all over their faces. And haven't I thought the same? Thought how much better things are with Natalie here?

"Natalie." Her name is a whisper. I'm not sure if I'm voicing the twins' thoughts or asking for her help.

"Why don't we eat, then watch a movie. We can talk in the morning about the situation at camp and once we've dealt with that, we can talk about you all moving to Baton Rouge with me." Her words settle the tension in the room with surprising ease.

Is it the sound of her voice or the promise in her words?

Or her?

I can't deny the woman has been a savior. And it's not just me she's helped, it's all of us. She's the voice of reason and calm—the stability—we've been lacking since Mom and Dad died.

And while that's a lot of pressure to put on a stranger's shoulders, she seems more than willing to share the burden of our grief and struggles.

It's unfair, and I hate that I'm relying on her so much, but I've been drowning. And I'm man enough to accept that I need help.

I might be too proud to ask for it most of the time, but she doesn't make me feel incapable or ashamed when I do.

Reaching for a slice of pizza, I say, "Candace is due to wake in about an hour. I'll grab a quick shower after a few pieces of pizza if you take care of clean up."

Natalie looks at the twins in silent question then gives them an encouraging smile. "We can do that, right, girls?"

"Yeah, we need to do a load of washing tonight."

I smile. "You don't have—shi-*oot*!" I drop my pizza and race for the laundry.

I cannot believe I forgot to start the washer.

Again.

Here I am ready to gloat about doing the washing and as usual all I've managed to do is put the dirty clothes in the machine.

The girls are laughing behind me, and I can hear them telling Natalie in halted words between their giggles about my dubious laundry skills.

It's embarrassing. Pushing a button to start the machine isn't hard. Fuck, even my fourteen-year-old sisters can do it.

I check the detergent dispenser to be sure I at least remembered that part of the process before I hit the start button.

Shaking my head I turn to find all three of them crowded in the doorway behind me.

They're matching grins and laughing eyes, and I can't bring myself to care they're amused at my expense, because the twins look happy.

And it's a far better look than the one they wore earlier.

I hate seeing them upset. I hate it even more that they didn't come to me with their worries. That they didn't give me the chance to take care of them.

"I don't care what it is or who it's about, I want you to tell me anything that worries you or makes you mad or upset or happy. Whatever. I want you to talk to me. About everything. I can't help you, or support you, or be there for you, if I don't know there's something going on."

The smiles slowly slide off their faces and with a glance at each other they come to a decision. But as usual, it's Cass who voices it.

"Okay. But you have to promise the same. We know you're an adult and we're not, but we should be in this together. You're not our dad even if you have to take on that role now."

Her words are full of wisdom and understanding beyond her years and I have to thank our parents for that. They never forced us to grow up before our time, but they taught us responsibility and never sugar-coated the realities of life.

Especially after Mom was diagnosed with pancreatic cancer.

Stepping forward, I crouch in front of them. They aren't short for their age but compared with my six feet four inches they are. Holding out both hands I wait for each of them to grab one.

"I promise. When I'm struggling with something, I'll tell you. When something good happens, I'll tell you. When there are big decisions to make about our family, I'll talk to you."

"Moving is a big family decision," Stell murmurs.

"Yes. It is. And it isn't just moving to Baton Rouge. We have to decide what to do with this house, all the furniture, the cars."

"I don't know if I want to sell it."

I lock eyes with Stell. Out of the twins she's always been

the more sensitive and I have to be aware of that, and if I want her to talk to me in the future, I need to show her I'm willing to do the same. The only way to do that is to give her my own truths.

"I don't know if I want that either, but we can't leave it empty, and I don't want anyone else living here if we keep it."

"Could we, maybe, keep it for a little while?" Her gaze darts to Natalie then back. "In case we want to come back?"

"We can. I'm sure we could have someone come in and take care of things, keep it clean, until we decide what to do." My own gaze moves from the girls to Natalie.

The quick nod from her has me breathing easier.

Looking back at Stell, I say, "But I'm betting we're going to love it in Baton Rouge. You should ask Natalie to show you the pictures of her house. It has an indoor pool as well as an outdoor one."

"Two pools!" The girls shout together, their heads whipping around to face Natalie; their hands letting go of mine as their bodies follow.

"Yes. Why don't I grab my laptop and show you some pictures while we eat dinner?"

Pushing to my feet, I shoot Natalie an appreciative smile. She tips her head in acknowledgment before ushering the girls out of the laundry room and I take a moment before following.

This whole day has given me emotional whiplash and I need a second to get myself settled. As settled as I can be when so much has happened in the last few months.

So much loss. So much pain and grief and now this weird conflict with the twins' camp coordinator.

On top of that there's the elation of being offered my dream. A position on the newest NHL team.

A *starting* position.

No one would begrudge me a minute to catch my breath.

I was fairly sure I was going to accept the contract with the Rogues and move us all south before this afternoon. But after the drama at camp, and the twins' outburst over dinner, I'm one hundred percent sure of what to do.

I'm signing with the Rogues and moving our barely patched together family to Baton Rouge.

I have to believe it's the change we all need. As much as I love this house, have wonderful memories in it, the girls are right. It hurts to be here without Mom and Dad.

We don't need the house our parents bought to raise their family in to remember them. They'll live in our hearts for the rest of our lives, and I want those lives to be happy. If that means uprooting everyone and moving thousands of miles away, we'll do it.

"Are you coming?" Natalie's voice focuses my thoughts outward. "I think Candace is stirring. I popped a bottle in the warmer and I can go up and get her while you eat something."

I stare at the woman standing in the doorway of the laundry room and wonder how the hell I survived the months before she showed up on my doorstep.

She's a straight shooting, no nonsense, somewhat brash businesswoman, and yet beneath that outer layer lies the softest of hearts. I don't know all her story, but what I do know tells me she doesn't show that heart to many.

And for some reason she's decided to share her soft center with me and my sisters.

"Yeah, I'll grab a bite then a shower if she isn't awake when I've done eating." I step toward her. "Thank you."

"For?" she asks with an arch of her eyebrow.

"Everything. For whatever forces put you on our doorstep."

"You put me on your doorstep. I was coming for you anyway. Circumstances delayed my arrival though."

"You were coming for me?" That's a revelation I didn't know I needed to hear.

"Yes. We've been watching you for a while. And I was supposed to come see you at college months ago, make you an offer."

"Why didn't you?"

I can see the war going on in her head. She doesn't want to tell me what delayed her. I can tell she knows why we didn't meet before now though.

With a sigh, she says, "My soon-to-be ex. In one of his many misguided attempts to gain my attention, he kept me from making the journey here. Until now."

"And he's still being difficult?"

"Yes. As soon as I'm back home I'll put my focus on dealing with him."

"Deal with him now. Don't let our drama pull you away from what you need to do."

"It isn't."

"It is if you're going to wait until you get home."

"Okay, I might be focused on you and the girls, but I want to be. It won't make any difference to wait. He's going to keep being a prick until I show my face. It's what he does."

"Why? You said he's stepped out on your marriage."

"He has. Since the beginning I think, although I only have proof for the last few years."

"Then what does he hope to gain?"

"He thinks he's winning when he forces me to see him." She shrugs. "Who knows what goes through his head. I certainly don't."

"But you married him?"

"I did. For billions of important reasons." She grins.

"I don't like that he's fucking you around."

"You and me both."

"What will make him stop?"

"Nothing. I'm sure even when he signs the papers and we're divorced, he'll find ways to annoy me."

Shaking my head, I say, "I don't understand that."

"Money makes people do stupid things."

"Okay, *that* I understand."

"He's getting a lot of money to sign the divorce papers but if he doesn't, he thinks he's got access to more."

A horrible thought hits me. "What if something happens to you? Please tell me you have a will that excludes him."

"I do. And most of the money is tied up in trusts preventing him from getting to it if he contests my will."

"I hate that I'm thinking about you not being here but are you sure the business, the team, is protected?"

"Yes. It's all taken care of. When we formed KAW and began operations for Rogue sportswear, we went to a lawyer and had every legal avenue looked at. Only the four of us can inherit the business. Although I guess we need to revisit that now that Oakley and Blake are married with kids."

"Something to think about."

"You need to think about it too."

I hate that I have to because that means something has happened to me and the girls are alone. "I know. I did a quick will when I signed the guardian paperwork and various other papers about our parents' estate."

"We can work on it after you sign your contract."

I grin. "Now that's paperwork I'm happy to deal with."

"You'll be negotiating with Oakley. I can't do it because it would be a conflict of interest."

"Because you're helping me? With the girls?"

"Yes. But more because you'll be living in my house."

"I thought we weren't going to tell anyone that."

"We won't. But it won't be a secret either. And I think it would be better if Oakley deals with you and your agent."

"Drake said he'd fly in to meet me."

"Get him to meet you in Baton Rouge. He represents a few of our players as well as our head coach."

"That's right, I forgot he was Walker Alcott's agent."

"He has Branton on his books too. In fact he represents several of our players."

Damn. I knew Drake was good. I've heard good things about

him over the years but knowing I'll share an agent with Walker Alcott and Branton Lattimer-Watts is like icing on top of my dream cake.

A shrill cry followed by the twins hollering, "Candace is awake," breaks us out of our conversation.

"I'll get her, you grab something to eat," Natalie says over her shoulder, already on her way to follow her own instructions.

I watch her go. The ease with which we split duties in this parenting gig makes me think I can do right by my sisters.

And I know her unwavering confidence and support has done a lot to help me see I'm capable of being the parent figure my parents would want for their daughters.

If they can't be here, they believe—believed—I'm the next best thing, and I don't plan to let them down.

For me, for the girls.

And now for the most unlikely woman to come into our lives. Natalie Redding is a hidden gem I refuse to disappoint.

If it's the last thing I do, I'll make sure she's never sorry for offering me a contract on her team. But most of all, I plan to make sure she never regrets offering to help me take care of the girls.

NAT

Today has been rough.

And I can't lie, it is not for the reasons I expected.

This morning I had to wave goodbye to Chase and the twins when everything in me wanted to jump in the car and go with them.

Last night, after we got all the girls in bed, Chase and I sat down and discussed what he should do about the camp situation.

It took considerable effort not to take control and do whatever I could to ruin the woman who made Cassidy and Crystal cry.

I hate bullies; I grew up with the biggest one, and I know I get a little more heated when I encounter one than most people because of that. Even all these years later I still can't shake the effect my grandfather has—*had*—on my life.

In the end, I knew I had to let Chase decide what to do and how to do it.

Which leaves me in the house taking care of Candace while he and the twins have a meeting with the board members of the charity that runs the camp.

The day hasn't gone to waste despite my distraction and the times Candace needs my attention.

I've gotten a few Rogues things dealt with, including ironing out the few last-minute contract changes for Ryder Perry, a rookie out of Colorado we're hoping to sign.

I also dealt with a material delivery delay due to bad weather which will affect our Rogue sportswear manufacturing line in about three weeks. We'll shift into an alternate garment production we have the materials for and push back the release of the other.

Of course, that has an impact on our advertising and order fulfillment. I've shot off multiple emails to the departments involved and handed over the follow-up to Eli. Whose semi-retirement is anything but retiring at the moment.

As COO of our sportswear brand and GM of our hockey team, I'm stretched thin. More so now with the Rogues first season rapidly approaching. There aren't enough hours in the day to get everything done.

Something has to change.

I know it. And as much as I hate to admit it, Eli is right. I can't do it all even though I want to.

Something will slip past me and who knows what that will mean for either company. I'll never forgive myself if I miss something that significantly affects either workplace.

I've already emailed Oakley, Blake, and Cami with my concerns. We need to have a KAW meeting sooner than later so we can re-evaluate our roles. Find qualified people to pick up the slack or take on a role.

Letting either business suffer because I'm too stubborn—Eli's words—to let go of the reins is not an option.

And if I'm going to follow through on my promise to help Chase take care of his sisters, I'll need to cut back my hours. Juggle my time so Candace doesn't have to go into care.

Cassidy and Crystal have places in Hannon Grove high school this coming year and I've checked out some daycare options for when Candace is older.

Although, I'm leaning more and more toward having an in-house daycare option at the training facility.

One both Rogue sportswear employees, and the Rogues players and org employees can take advantage of. I know we have an area of the mall we plan to break ground on next year designated for a childcare center, but we need something now.

We might need to run numbers and dates and push things around, get them moving ahead of schedule on the mall if we can. Although it makes more sense to have multiple childcare options across all our facilities in Baton Rouge.

If we find space to add a center to the arena and training complex, the mall can go ahead as planned. Pulling up a new email, I shoot myself a message to look into that later. Right now, I need—

The metallic grind of the garage roller door opening has me straightening away from my laptop and glancing over at my phone where it's charging on the other counter.

Chase said he'd text after the meeting. But I don't have one, and there's no missed call either. A quick look at the monitor shows Candace sleeping peacefully so I push off my stool and head for the door connecting the house to the garage.

I don't even take a couple of steps when the twins come racing in, their chatter bright and excited. The sound has a breath of relief lowering my shoulders and relaxing the muscles along my spine.

The coil of tension holding me hostage all morning unspools so quickly I need to grip the counter to stay upright.

My relief is so great I can't form words—can't move. Not that the girls take any notice of me. They're single-minded in their search for something to eat and bickering about what to have while standing in the open fridge door.

It isn't until Chase stops beside me, a grin on his face, that I'm finally about to speak.

"Things went well." It's not a question, although the inflection on the end of my last word suggests otherwise.

"Oh yeah." His grin grows. "They were very aware of the situation. Apparently, a number of parents who witnessed the incident in the parking lot yesterday questioned their children when they got home and then made complaints. A lot of complaints."

"She's fired?" It's the least I want but this isn't about me. It's about Cassidy and Crystal.

"Yes. And they're refunding the full cost of the girls' fees, including the food portion which is usually non-refundable."

"What about an apology? Not that I want them to have to face that woman—"

He holds up a hand. "The board had a written one from her; although I'm not sure I believe she's the one who wrote it, her signature is on the bottom. And they offered the refund and more restitution in the form of free camps in the future."

"They're not going back," I say, my spine snapping straight with my words.

"No. And I wouldn't be surprised if a lot of the kids don't go back the rest of this summer. If they can't turn things around, they'll find it hard to fill spots next year too."

I have to hold in my response. I want to say good. But that seems unfair when the situation was instigated by one person and now all those children and families are without a summer camp.

Instead, I ask, "Are you happy with the outcome?"

"Yes."

"And the girls?"

"I think so. They haven't said much but they held their own when questioned about the last few weeks."

"What about the other people working for the camp?" I don't like the idea of others having their reputations tarnished by one woman's actions. Although they did go along with her directives.

"They were all there. So were a lot of the other parents. The only person not in attendance was Mrs. Bertram. Camp was cancelled for the rest of the week and the board is deciding what to do for the rest of summer."

"As long as you and the girls are happy with the way things turned out."

"I am." He tips his chin in the twins' direction. "And I think they are. It might have been different if they didn't have each other. They're their own ready-built support system."

"I'm glad they have each other, that they have you."

"And now that camp has been dealt with, let's talk logistics of moving in with you."

"Oh. I... Um..." I glance at the girls. "You don't want to wait a bit before talking about it? Maybe we could take a quick trip to Baton Rouge so they can see the place first."

"No. We talked in the car. We're ready to make the move." His gaze bores into mine. "Unless you've changed your mind—"

"No. No. Of course not. I'm more than happy to help you with the girls. My house is too big for just me and I was already thinking of selling it. I'm looking forward to seeing it full of life."

"Hopefully you won't regret letting us move in."

"I doubt it. It's not like we'll be stuck on top of each other, the house is too big for that. Plus we'll all be busy with the start of the season, the new school year."

"Another reason to get things moving. As the Rogues GM, you'll want me settled and ready to play. As our Gem, you'll want us to feel comfortable before the chaos of school and the season begins."

"Gem?"

"GM. Gem."

I shake my head. "I don't get it."

"You're our GM."

"Ah, okay..." I'm still not sure I understand the reason for the nickname, but Chase's sheepish expression has me smiling.

With a shrug he adds, "Not exactly original but I doubt you want me calling you Natalie in front of other players or staff. If I call you Gem, it's a play on GM but it's got that personal connection we have weaved in. Then I won't slip up in front of anyone I shouldn't."

"Oh."

There's so much thought behind the nickname. Other than Nat, which isn't really a nickname, I've never had one. And I'm not going to lie, I like the idea of having that intimate connection between us hidden in plain sight.

With a smile I can't hold back, I say, "I can live with that."

"I promise not to make it weird at work."

"I know you won't. Besides, we won't have that much to do with each other in the day to day. I'm not planning on telling the coaches or players how to do their jobs, and I'll be in my office most of the time, nowhere near the ice, except game days, you'll see more of me before and after a game."

"Can we pack now?" Cassidy's words have both me and Chase jumping.

"Sorry. What?" I look down at her excited face.

"Pack. Can we start packing up our room?"

My gaze bounces between the girls. "You want to pack your room now? We haven't talked about moving yet."

"Why do we need to talk about it? We're moving, right?" Crystal looks at her brother. "Aren't you going to play for the Rogues?"

"Yes. But I haven't signed the contract. I'm still talking with my agent about it."

"But we're going, to Baton Rouge," Crystal's voice is full of excitement but there's a small amount of fear wobbling the edges. "To live with Gem."

I never understood the term 'my heart fluttered' until right now. Hearing Crystal call me Gem. After Chase explained how he came up with it...

I'm in jeopardy of getting choked up and I have to swallow a couple of times before I can speak. And when I do it's to reassure them all, although I direct my words at Crystal.

"Are you sure you're okay with moving?" I'm not backing out of my offer, and honestly, if they're unsure I plan to point out all the reasons why they should, but I want the girls to understand what a move like this means. "You'll have to go to a new school. Live in a place you're unfamiliar with. You'll have no friends to begin with."

"That's why we need to go now," Cassidy explains. "So, we have time before school starts and Chase's schedule becomes nothing but hockey, hockey, and more hockey."

Her words are accompanied by a cheeky grin, and I know Chase isn't offended by her comments.

"All right." I look around the room. "I guess we need to decide what's a priority and what can wait. We need to know what you want to take and what you don't, but we don't need to rush."

"Can we take some of our pictures?" Crystal asks, her gaze on the wall of family photos.

"We can take whatever you want. Pictures, furniture, clothes, anything. I can have my house cleared out before we get home so you can make it yours."

"But it'll be yours too, right?" Crystal's gaze is on mine now, her confusion obvious.

"Yes. My house has what's called an in-law suite on the lower level. I'll live there and you will have the main part of the house."

"But that's just where your bedroom will be, you'll eat with us and stuff, right?"

I'm not sure what stuff she's referring to but I'm nodding anyway. And making a mental note to talk to Chase about the best way to protect the girls. We should probably get the advice of a lawyer too.

"Yes. We'll eat together and *stuff*," I say with a grin. "Like when your brother is away playing hockey, you'll stay with me unless I have to accompany the team. But we'll work out where you will be before that happens so you're okay with it."

"Can we go with Chase?" Crystal asks, reminding me of her recent losses and how they might affect the way she feels when the people around her go somewhere.

"Sometimes, but you have school to think about." Although

if she needs to be near her brother for peace of mind, I'll do every-thing in my power to make that happen.

"Can we watch the home games in the owner's box?" Cassidy asks with an excited smirk.

"Hey, how do you know about owner's boxes?" Chase finally injects himself into the conversation.

"I watch ESPN."

Chase and I look at each other. Neither of us sure how to react to that statement.

"Dad isn't the only one interested in you being a professional player." Cassidy lifts her chin as if daring her brother to argue with her.

"I had no idea. What else do you know? What do you want to know?" Chase steps up to his sister and pulls her into his arms. "With all the shit you've given me over the years about early morning training and games, I thought you hated hockey."

"No." Her words are muffled against his chest. "It's cool having an older brother who's set to break records."

Chase leans back, a look of complete shock on his face. "You think I'm going to break records?"

"You already have."

"Well, yeah but that was kid stuff."

"Your first season in college you had more shut-out games than not."

"Huh." Chase eyes Cassidy with curiosity. "You know that?"

"She knows all your stats," Crystal says with an eye roll. "It's how Dad taught us math."

"Wow. Okay. Well, I guess it's about time I got back on the ice so you can continue to pass math."

"Don't get a big head about it." Cassidy says, shoving out of her brother's arms. "I know stats of a lot of players."

I study her a little more closely; her revelations aren't that surprising, and I don't know why I didn't think either of the girls might be interested in hockey before now.

"Would you like to tour the arena and training facilities when we get to Baton Rouge?"

"Hell—"

"Hey, language!"

"Yeah!"

Cassidy's grin says it all. Even with the reprimand from her brother she's happy. And Crystal's smiling just as big.

Moving might be a major deal, but it might also be exactly what this family needs to move on from tragedy.

CHASE

Once Gem gets an idea in her head, there's no stopping her until she achieves her goal.

In the two weeks since we made the decision to move to Baton Rouge, the girls and I have barely had to lift a finger.

First a group of women who specialize in moving families with young children turned up at our house in St. Paul and walked the three of us from one room to the next determining what to pack and ship to Gem's house, what to pack for storage for us to go through later, and what to donate.

Another group arrived to pack everything up and as each room was wrapped and boxed, I breathed a little easier—felt more in control of our lives.

The only day that caused distress was the day we packed up Mom and Dad's room. Other than a few tears shed as each piece of our parents was packed away, the move to Baton Rouge has been worry free.

And when the same women showed up at Gem's house to help us unpack and place everything in our new home as the movers unloaded the truck, I could have kissed Gem.

In less than a week, our move was complete, and I don't know about the girls, but I haven't felt one bit of homesickness. It helps to have most of our furniture and household goods, like cutlery and linen, surrounding us.

When we first arrived and I questioned Gem about the empty rooms, she told me she had no attachment to any of her furniture and didn't see the point in keeping it.

I'm not sure I believe her, although she did have a few pieces moved to the in-law suite on our arrival.

After our somewhat dramatic exit from St. Paul, our arrival in Baton Rouge has been smooth sailing. There were no tears, only happy smiles, the afternoon we closed the door on the only home we've ever known for the last time.

I think each of us, in our own way, was ready to leave that chapter of our life behind.

We have so much to look forward to. The first, our new home. And Gem was right about her house. It is far too big for one woman. Even with five of us living here it seems too big.

There are seven bedrooms including the one in the in-law suite. Two living rooms, two dining rooms, and a huge kitchen with a butler's pantry you could easily mistake for the actual kitchen with its extra dishwasher, oven, and cooktop.

The girls have settled into their new rooms without a blip too.

Candace has proven the easiest of us to relocate though. Her routine remains unchanged, she's still a night owl, but we're seeing more and more of her during the day which means our nights aren't as sleep deprived, and fingers crossed, that trend continues.

Cass and Stell have thrived since we arrived. They're like their old selves again, the ones I remember from before Mom's diagnosis, from before Dad died. Their smiling and joking around increases with each day.

Their biggest smiles were when Gem pointed them up the stairs and told them to pick any room. They chose two bedrooms connected by a large bathroom.

Although they're still sharing one room. They plan to eventually have their own space but for now their beds are in one room and their desks in the other.

I have to admit, it's a cool set up, and their excitement over Gem's promise to go shopping for new furniture when they're ready made my heart ache—in a good way.

Seeing them how they were before Mom got sick is a balm to not only my heart, but it also boosts my confidence.

Moving was the right decision.

Signing with the Rogues was the right choice.

There's no doubt we would have made it if we'd stayed in St. Paul, but it would have been a struggle. One I'm glad we no longer need to go through.

Not that being here will be free and easy.

I know there's bound to be issues. But the different surroundings—even with a lot of our own furniture in Gem's house—has lifted all our spirits.

"Hello."

Looking up from my seat beside the pool where the twins are finally getting their wish to go swimming, I find Gem in her usual business attire towering over me.

She's still in her ever-present heels which I know are one of the first things she takes off when she gets home so she must have just come through the door.

"Hey." I lean back and shield my eyes from the sun. "I didn't think you were coming home this early."

"I wasn't, but my last meeting was canceled and there isn't anything I need to do I can't do from here later."

"Oh?"

She drops into the chair next to me with a heavy sigh. "I thought it would be good to spend time with the girls. And you. Maybe take everyone out to one of my favorite restaurants. Show you more of what Baton Rouge has to offer."

"We cooked, but I can put it in the fridge for tomorrow night."

"What did you make?"

"Lasagna." I eye her, and with a grin say, "Good thing you weren't here an hour ago. The kitchen was a disaster zone."

"It looked spotless when I walked through."

"I bribed them with a dip." I nod at the twins. "They've been nagging all day to get in the pool and I know they don't need supervision, but I can't leave them out here alone."

"What were you doing that stopped them from swimming earlier?"

"Ah, well…" I'm not sure how she's going to take what I organized. I know she told us to make ourselves at home but it's still her house.

"Out with it. What have you been up to?"

"I had a fully equipped gym set up in the basement." The words rush out of me, and I wait, breath held, for her to say something.

"Hmm…"

She's got her thinking face on. She'd probably hate to know I've been studying her so closely I can tell what's going on in her head most of the time.

The silence drags so long I fidget. I'm not normally nervous around her, but for some reason this has me holding my breath and bracing.

"You look like I'm going to kick you out for doing exactly what I told you to do," she murmurs, her gaze on the girls as they crawl out at the deep end of the pool and grab hands, ready to cannonball back in.

"I wasn't sure if I'd overstepped. When I first had the guy out to show him the space and tell him what I wanted, I didn't think it would look like it does," I explain.

"You don't like it?"

"Oh, no, I do. It's just…" I swallow. "I didn't realize how much space it would take up."

"The basement isn't big enough to put in a practice rink so a gym with all the bells and whistles seems a good use of the space there is down there."

"Maybe you should take a look before you decide it's okay. If it's too much I can have it ripped out."

"Chase." She turns toward me, her gaze locking with mine. "This is your home now. And if we do what I suggested to give the girls the extra security you want them to have, it will be their home until they go to college, or we decide otherwise. And where they are, you are."

"About that. You got a delivery today. It's from a lawyer's office."

"Finally!" Gem shoots to her feet and takes off for the house.

How she manages to move that fast and stay upright on those heels is a miracle. I know I move around on slippery ice on razor sharp blades, but I doubt I could pull off the speed she does in those shoes if I tried.

"All right, girls," I call. "Time to get out and shower off before dinner."

"Aw, come on," Cass whines. "We're not hungry."

The fact Stell's head whips in her twin's direction, a look of surprise on her face, tells me they are not in accord with Cass's words.

"Gem's home early. She wants to take us out for dinner."

I'm playing dirty, I know the second I mention Gem the girls will do whatever I ask. The bond they formed with her in the first few days back at home has only strengthened since moving here.

Gem has breakfast or dinner, sometimes both, with us every day, even though she's been back at work full-time since we arrived. Most days, it's me and the girls in the house sorting through our things, because school hasn't started, and I haven't had any team commitments yet.

That changes next week.

The first of which is a meet and greet for all the Rogues players and staff.

I worried about taking the girls, but Gem assured me they'll be fine. She's organized activities and care for anyone who wants or needs it because the meet and greet is not only for players and coaches, it's for everyone working for the Rogues.

Partners and children are encouraged—expected—to attend as well, to help build a support network for those who have relocated to Baton Rouge.

Which pretty much means everyone.

I'm looking forward to meeting my teammates. Speaking with my coaches. I haven't had any kind of exercise routine since Dad died and I know I've lost physical strength. It remains to be seen how much.

With the new gym I can start training sooner than later. I hadn't planned on it taking as long as it has to set up, but now that it is, I'll be taking advantage of any free time I have around caring for the girls.

"He signed it!"

The shout from behind makes me jolt upright and I spin around. Gem is standing in the doorway waving a big wad of papers. It doesn't take a genius to know what they are.

"You're divorced?" I say as I push to my feet.

"Yes. Finally." She lowers the bundle and fans through the pages. "I think the threat of taking away all the money did it."

I haven't been privy to the negotiations with her ex, but I have overheard enough to know she drew a line and forced him to it. "Are you sure this is what you want?"

She stops moving, her eyes zipping up to meet mine. "Why would you ask that?"

"It cost you a lot of money and property to get his signature."

"Not as much as it would have if he hadn't been a prick and tried to squeeze me for more. It took a while, but he finally worked out I wasn't fucking around when it came to reducing his payout by five million every day he didn't sign."

I don't like seeing the effect her ex has on her. It makes me want to hunt him down and remind him how to be a gentleman. I might not get into fights during a game—my position leaves me out of ninety-nine percent of them—but I know how to throw a punch.

To take our minds off the man and put it squarely on the happy part of her relationship with him, I say, "Dinner will be a celebration then."

"One between you and me, right?"

"Of course. But aren't you going to tell Oakley, Blake, and Cami?"

I've only met Oakley so far, and only because I had a meeting with my agent and the Rogues' owner when I signed my deal the second day we were in Baton Rouge.

"No. Not yet. I'll probably mention it next week at our monthly cocktail hour."

"Cocktail hour?"

"Once a month we get together like we used to before we started Rogue sportswear."

"A business meeting with alcohol?"

"No. A best friends get together. For a few hours we try not to talk about work at all." She shrugs. "Sometimes we don't have a choice, but most of the time we stick to the rule of no shop talk."

"I assume Oakley and Blake leave their husbands at home."

"Yes. Their kids too. Although baby Drew came for the first few months of his life."

"How old is he again?" I think he's around the same age as Candace but I'm not sure.

"Um...eight months?"

I laugh. "Is that a question."

"Kind of. He was born at the end of last year...so no, he's seven months?"

I can't hold in a second laugh. "Let's leave it as a couple of months older than Candace for now."

"Oh. I never even thought. They're almost the same age."

"Where are you taking us for dinner?" Cass interrupts us, stopping beside us, dripping water all over the ground.

"Where's your towel?"

"I'll get it in a second. So?" She ignores me and looks at Gem. "How do burgers sound?"

"With fries?"

"Of course. Who eats a burger without fries?"

Stell has joined us, and both the girls look at me. With a sigh, I raise my hand. "Me. It's me. I eat burgers without fries."

"Are you even human?" Gem asks, the twitch of her lips telling me she's struggling to hold back a smile.

"Yes. But only in the off season. And no more than a couple of times."

"Whoa." Gem shakes her head. "I'm always surprised by the weird dietary restrictions you players have. They're never the same."

"I don't have many, but I hate weighing my body down with carbs, so I make sure I don't eat many."

"Well, you might want to make an exception tonight. Where we're going has the most amazing duck fries."

"Duck fries?" Cass takes a hasty step away, shaking her head. "I'm not eating duck!"

Gem laughs. "They're called duck fries, but they're not made of duck, only cooked in duck fat," she explains.

"I'm not sure that's any better," Cass pouts. "Do they have normal fries?"

"Yes." Gem palms Cass's shoulders and turns her around. "Now go grab a towel, head upstairs, and shower so we can get going."

Stell follows her sister although, unlike Cass, she's already dried off and wrapped in a towel. I wait until the girls have gone inside before I ask the question that has been plaguing me since Gem first came home.

"Are you sure it's okay for me to take over the basement with gym equipment?"

"Yes. Stop worrying about it. I won't change my mind." She waits for me to acknowledge her words before saying, "I'll go get changed—how long do you think it will take the girls to get ready? I might do some work before we leave."

"I have to wake Candace." Glancing at my watch I see it's time to do that anyway. If she sleeps any later, getting her to sleep tonight will be a struggle. "Will half an hour work for you?"

"Perfect. But I won't do anything that can't be interrupted so come get me if you're ready before."

I nod. "I'll send the girls in."

One thing I haven't done is intrude on her personal space. We've taken over her house, basically pushed her into a couple of rooms, and I don't want to infringe on her territory any more than we have.

I might be curious about her space, but that's because I'm curious about her. She's such a different person when in work mode.

It will be interesting to see how things go once we're working together. And I know she said she isn't in the training facility and only around on game days but she's still my boss.

And we're living together.

And as off today, we're free to follow through on her suggestion to give the girls more security and get married.

NAT

It begins.

Months—no, *years*—of hard work and stupid amounts of money have come down to this.

Today.

The Rogues' first game in the NHL.

Game one of pre-season.

On home ice.

I don't know if the league did it to appease us after the debacle of our franchise announcement or if it was luck of the draw, and I don't care because games one and two of our first pre-season are here, in Rogue Arena.

The crowd is pumped. So are the players. And the excitement levels of the Rogues staff this past week has been a living breathing thing in every hallway, every room. From basement to rafters, Rogue Arena has been vibrating with anticipation for days—weeks.

"Hey." Oakley bumps her shoulder into mine. "Ready for this?"

"Been ready for months."

"Have you watched them train?" Her gaze remains on the

empty ice below us. "They look really good. Walker thinks they're one of the most in sync teams he's seen."

"He'd know."

"Yeah. And when pushed, Blake agrees."

"Pushed?" I glance at her.

"She doesn't want to 'count her goals before they're scored'," Oakley mutters with a roll of her eyes.

I smile. "Sounds like old times."

"Doesn't it?" Her gaze moves away from the ice to the children in the corner of the owner's suite who definitely weren't part of those old times.

Cassidy and Crystal are entertaining Micky, while Candace sleeps in her stroller off to the side of them. She's due to wake around the time the first puck drops.

"You going to let her sleep or wake her up?" she asks as if she can read my mind.

"Not sure yet. I'll decide after the team hits the ice for warmup."

"I'd wake her." Blake bounces over beside us. "This guy is fussy as hell tonight. We don't need two babes distracting us."

"You should be down with the team." I fold my arms, and stare at my best friend and business partner—the Rogues' Assistant Coach. "There are plenty of us to watch Drew and your parents will be here any minute."

"I know. I know. But..." she glances at her boy. "I hate it when he's like this and there's nothing I can do to soothe him."

"He wants his daddy," Oakley murmurs. "Micky was the same when I told him he couldn't go with Walker."

We all look over at her and Walker's adopted son. "He seems okay now," I say.

"Ice cream."

"What?" I shake my head and look at Oakley.

"Pa promised him a triple scoop cone if he spent the game up here with me."

"And where is Pa?"

"Who knows. He loves having full access to the arena. He's probably in the locker room." She eyes Blake. "Where our Assistant Coach should be."

We're interrupted by Crystal. "Candace is stirring. Did you bring the warmer?"

"Yes, it's plugged in behind the bar and her bottle is in the fridge with the water."

I might be the person taking care of Candace while her brother does his job, but the twins are just as hands on with their little sister as he is. I think it's because they feel the loss of their parents deeply and subconsciously know Candace will never have a memory of them.

"The twins are good with the baby," Blake comments. "I've seen them looking after her sometimes when Chase is training."

"They are. We try to balance how much they help though. Chase doesn't want them to become adults before their time."

"He's good with them too." Oakley's gaze meets mine. "How's it going at home?"

My gaze darts to Blake but she's too busy bouncing around with Drew strapped to her chest to take notice of our conversation. Oakley is the only one who knows Chase and the girls are living in my house.

"Good. Surprisingly good." I don't like the speculative glint in her eyes so I change the subject. "Did you talk to Laken about the possible trade?"

Oakley sighs. "Yeah. Neither of us wants to make it but we're both aware of how an unhappy player can affect the whole team so she's open to considering it."

"Should we see if Lindberg will give it a few months? Maybe wait until mid-season, or later in the season." I hold up a hand. "And yes, I'm aware neither option is ideal but if Lindberg is that unhappy here, we owe it to him to see if we can make things better without making him move again."

"I'm not sure how open Byrd will be to a trade either."

"Laken hasn't asked him?"

"No."

"Huh."

Our conversation is cut off by the rise in volume of the crowd filling every seat in the arena. And when I look out at the rink I see why.

Players are skating around. None of the Rogues yet, just the Vancouver players. But everyone knows our guys are moments away from taking the ice.

"Here they come," Blake yells right as the door to the suite flies opens and people pour in.

Oakley's grandfather leads the way. The grin on his face is so wide you'd think this was his team. Then again, Pa has been instrumental in helping us see this dream come true.

Behind him are Blake's parents, her brother Mason and his boy, Cash, with them. I'm surprised to see Mason here. With everything that's going on with his son's mother I didn't think he'd make it even after my personal invitation.

He tips his head at me before ushering Cash to the seats in front of the windows. I don't miss the frown on Blake's face. Or the calculating look that quickly follows.

I'll wait to see if she comes up with anything, but at our next meeting I plan to broach the subject of bringing Mason on board as player liaison—possibly Assistant GM. I think a move will do him and Cash good. It has certainly benefited the Hawkins siblings.

Glancing over at the girls, I see the twins are giving Candace her bottle. I love seeing them all take care of each other. Except I'm supposed to be watching the three of them while Chase plays.

"I'll be back. Need to check on the girls."

I don't wait for either of my best friends to answer, just head across the room to the girls and Micky. It's a small area I plan to expand now that the number of little ones who might be at home games this season has grown.

"Hey, how's she doing? Want me to change her?"

"Yes. But I think we need to wait..." Crystal eyes her baby sister laying between her twin's legs. "Almost done..."

When I look at Candace, I see what Crystal is talking about. The girl is loading her diaper. "I swear, we put it in, and she pushes it out."

"Right?" Cassidy's voice is nasally due to the fingers pinching her nose.

I laugh. "I'll grab her bag and come back for her."

"Take your time. She's got some milk left in her bottle so when she's done with the scrunchie-face thing I'll see if she wants it." Crystal holds up the one third full bottle.

"Okay." On my way to the bag, I detour over to where Mason sits with Cash. "You guys doing, okay? Need anything?"

"We're good for now," Mason says, holding up a bottle of water.

"Help yourselves to the food and drinks behind the bar."

"I'm surprised you don't have a server in here."

"They're in the other boxes. This might have owner's box on the door but it's more of a family room."

"Don't you have one of those as well?"

"Yes. But with everyone adding to the team this last year or so, we don't want this to be a traditional owner's box."

"I get that." He glances at Cash. "We're staying in town for a few days to spend time with Blake, Branton, and Drew—mind if we use one of the practice rinks while we're here?"

"Of course not. Time it for when the team is practicing, and you can pick up some adult players if you want. If the coaches will let you." I grin.

Mason knows as well as I do how much Walker and Blake have been single minded about practices.

"She's annoying. Can you make her go down there?" Mason points at the Rogues bench.

"I tried. I doubt she'll make it long once the game starts."

"Good. I always hated seeing her amped up for a game, but I think this is worse."

"Probably because she has no control over the outcome. She has to sit back and let her players do their job."

"Yeah, pretty sure that's why she said no to coaching the Canadians for a second run at gold."

"I can't deny or confirm that."

"But you know the answer?"

I glance around before bending to talk closer to Mason's ear. "She chose to push for this."

"Ah, right." His gaze moves back to the ice where our guys have just stepped out to warm up. "Damn, this crowd is hyped."

"It's a good sign."

"It is."

"Do you miss it? Playing? Coaching?"

"Yes and no." He glances at Cash who's leaning forward, elbows on knees, watching the players. "Had other things I didn't want to miss more."

I lower my voice and ask, "He doing okay?"

"Better. He's better."

"Good. I'm glad." A squeal from Candace has me twisting my head to see if it's a good or bad cry. "Oops, gotta go. Someone is not happy about the state of her diaper."

Mason grins. "Never thought I'd see you taking care of a baby."

I want to be affronted by his comment but it's not far off my own thoughts. I always wanted children. But after the debacle of my union with Johnathon I didn't think I'd be in this position either.

"I'm not opposed to it, just never had the opportunity."

"Until now."

I look back at Mason. "Yes. Until now."

It's the closest I've come to admitting to anyone I'm going to mother Candace. I might not be her mother or even married to her guardian, but I plan to make sure that little girl *and* her big sisters know they're loved and cared for by someone other than their brother.

Leaving Mason, I walk behind the bar for the diaper bag then go get Candace.

"You two want fries or burgers?" I ask the twins. "I can order anything you want."

"No. We're good."

"I fed them up earlier." I turn to find Pa beside me. Arching an eyebrow, I prompt him to continue. With a sigh he says, "We had fries and ice cream before you all came in."

"No wonder Micky was bouncing around when we got here."

"Don't tell Oakley." He presses a finger to his lips. "It's a secret between me and my partner in crime. Except we had a couple of tag-alongs on this latest adventure."

I love that Pa is taking an interest in the girls. He's pulled them in the same way he did Micky. I have no worries about them staying with him if I'm unable to remain behind when the team has an away game.

"What on earth is that—" Pa blocks his nose the same way Cassidy did. "Never mind, I think I know." He bends down and uses his free hand to poke Candace's belly. "You, little miss, need a diaper change."

"I'm on that now."

"Good. We've got a puck drop to watch."

Scooping up a squirming Candace, I head for the suite's private bathroom and its change table. I left Blake in charge of deciding how to set this up because at the time she was the only one with a baby.

Now we've got Candace, who's only a couple of months younger than Drew.

I hate rushing through diaper changes. I like to give Candace a chance to stretch and kick her legs but there's a puck drop happening that I do not want to miss.

And I don't want any of the girls to miss it either. Crystal might not care that much, but I'm betting Cassidy will be glued to the glass for most of the game.

After discovering her interest in hockey, I started involving her in more of my conversations with Chase.

I don't talk to him about running the team, but we do discuss how he feels the team is meshing, if there are any areas he sees that could use improvement, and as he's just made a move like every other player wearing a Rogues jersey, I have an insider's perspective on how everyone is settling in.

And for the most part, excluding Lindberg, the players and their families are happy.

The roar of the crowd has me quickening my movements. "Sorry, baby girl, I know I'm rushing. I promise to give you some naked time later. But right now, we need to get back out there."

Candace makes a bit of noise, whether agreement or not doesn't matter, it still puts a smile on my face and fills my heart with joy.

She's a delightful baby. Other than her night owl habits, she's easy. She rarely cries and her protests are usually ones of hunger or needing a diaper change.

Pressing the last strip of the clean diaper into place, I snap the crotch buttons of her onesie together then pull her legging up over the top of it before lowering the cute mini jersey with Chase's name and number on the back.

I know it's not cold in the suite, but I don't want her little limbs freezing when we head down to meet her big brother after the game.

Tossing the soiled diaper in the bin designed to reduce smell, I pick up Candace and leave the bag. I have no doubt I'll be back in here before the end of the game or she takes another nap.

Which reminds me. We're going to have to rethink her sleeping schedule. It might pay to let her stay up late instead of the early bedtime we've been aiming for because nights like tonight are going to disrupt her sleeping pattern.

Entering the suite, I see everyone crowded toward the windows.

"Just in time. They're about to announce the team." Oakley slips her arm through mine. "I was just coming to get you."

"Sorry. This one was a little on the stinky side."

"Lord, am I glad I didn't have to deal with that when we got Micky."

"You'll have to when you and Walker have another kid."

"Yes, and I've changed Drew a few times and if you'll let me, I'll handle some for Candace. I need to get used to the idea." Her gaze moves to where Blake is standing, Drew still fussing in the carrier strapped to her chest. "Although I'm not sure I'm ready to deal with that."

"He doesn't want to be in the carrier. As soon as she pulls him out and lets him roam, the better."

"Then why the hell is he still strapped to her?"

"Because she's nervous and antsy because she wants to be with the team."

"Dammit. We need to make her go down there."

"We will. Give her a few minutes of game time and I bet she'll be racing out of here. Especially now Drew's second favorite person in the world is here."

Oakley grins. "He really does love his grandpa."

"Grandpa loves him right back."

"You know, I never saw us doing this with kids."

"Me either, but here we are."

"And I definitely didn't see you with three of them!" Oakley laughs.

"I don't have three."

"Yeah, you do. I don't know what's really going on, but you definitely have three kids."

"The twins aren't kids."

"Can they drink? Vote? Drive a car?" She arches an eyebrow at me. "No."

"They're still not mine."

"I beg to differ and when the time comes, I'll be happy to say I told you so."

I don't have to argue because the first Rogue, team captain Beckett Higgison, is announced. He steps onto the ice to thunderous applause.

If ever there was proof that pushing for an NHL franchise based in Baton Rouge was worth the hard work, this is it.

The town loves their team. Now it's up to the team to show their appreciation of that support by winning our first game.

CHASE

Five games into pre-season and it's the first away game the girls haven't traveled with me. And I don't like it.

Gem is here too, so the fact they're not at home with her is more unsettling.

Although they're staying with Pa, Oakley's grandfather, who has adopted my sisters as his own grandchildren with open arms, I can't shake the worry.

Except I need to concentrate; this game is tight. Thankfully we're holding. Playing well. Even with the small section of crowd booing us at every opportunity—especially when I stop a puck— as a team, our focus is solid.

For the most part I've managed to push my concern for the girls aside. I'm not going to lie, it's tough to travel without them and not worry, tougher than I thought it would be, but I do it because there's no other choice. And I need—the team needs— my head in the game one hundred percent of the time.

But when I barely clip a puck edge enough to divert its trajectory, I realize I've let my mind wander. Again.

Refocusing on the players zipping around me, the puck whizzing over the ice away from me, I think of nothing but what I need to do to guard my house.

We're up by one and I refuse to be the man who changes that score. The only change I'll accept is an uptick in our goal count.

Magnus Lund skates past, one eyebrow raised beneath his furrowed brow. I know what he's asking, he's worried my head isn't in the game. I give him a nod and his face smooths out before he offers me a smile then turns to watch the play happening down ice.

Our front line has the puck up by Detroit's goal and I can see the move before it happens. I've watched them do it multiple times during practice.

Bran takes the puck up the right side, but not all the way even though he's got the space. In a quick flick, he passes it off to Bex who appears to line up a shot at goal but sends it across the goal to Mikkel Vinter instead.

And Vin sends that black disc straight through the Detroit goalie's legs.

The goal light flashes, the buzzer sounds, and the crowd behind me boos, but the Rogues fans spread out through Detroit's arena drown them out with their cheers and applause.

A minute later, the horn sounds ending any hope of Detroit catching us, and we put another win in our pockets.

Everyone is jubilant, our spirits high as we leave the ice and head for the visitors' locker room.

I'm not expecting to see Gem—she usually waits until after the team is showered and changed before making an appearance, and it doesn't take a genius to work out something is wrong.

I'm just not sure if it has to do with the girls or something else. And I can't ask. If she doesn't single me out, which she doesn't do without at least one of the girls with her, I can't do more than tip my chin in acknowledgment. Hope she sees the concern in my eyes.

Making a beeline for Walker, she leans in to whisper in his ear and my curiosity and concern increase. She's only in the locker room a minute more. Just long enough to call out a congrats to the team before slipping out the door.

The churning in my gut is at vomit level now. Gem looked angry, but I could see the underlying distress and it takes everything in me to follow my normal after-game routine instead of following her.

My concern has me rushing through my strip down and shower. Once I'm in my suit, I shove my stuff in my bag and leave it for the equipment team to collect and load on the bus.

I'm out of the locker room, checking both directions of the hallway trying to decide which way to go when Walker comes out behind me.

"The bus is waiting if you're ready to head out."

I raise a brow. He doesn't get the hint, so I ask, "Which way? This isn't our arena, and I didn't take notice of how we got to the locker room when we arrived."

"Oh, right. I forget some of you don't know the arenas like I do. That way." He points right. "Turn left at the end, you'll see a couple of security guards by the exit door. Bus is right outside in the parking lot."

"Okay. Thanks." I start off, pulling my phone from my pocket as I go, but there aren't any missed calls or messages.

Either from Gem or the twins.

That eases some of my worry but not much. The more I think about it, the more I don't like Gem's demeanor.

I'm sure to anyone else she would have appeared her normal self. But I've been making a study of Gem's expressions. She fascinates me. Yes, some of that is I'm attracted to her, but who the hell wouldn't be?

She's hot as fuck with her non-nonsense buttoned-up businesswoman look and attitude.

Except my fascination runs deeper than her looks and work persona. She's so different at home, with the girls, with me. And the few glimpses I've had of her with her fellow team owners and their partners have been enlightening too.

She comes off as brisk and unapproachable, the unbending in-charge leader of many, but there's this soft underbelly. One she doesn't expose to anyone but her closest circle.

And I've somehow found myself inside that circle.

I want to stay in it more than anything. Which is why I've been extra careful when we interact at work. The last thing I want to do is compromise her in any way.

Stepping out into the night, I scan the area to see if I can locate her. There's no sign of her or anyone else except the bus driver and a couple of security guards.

Nodding at them as I pass, I board the bus and head for the back. I want to put off having someone sit next to me as long as possible. I need to message Gem and don't need anyone looking over my shoulder when I do it.

> Hey. Everything okay?

It takes almost a minute for the bubbles to appear in our text thread. And I hold my breath waiting for her words to appear.

> Yes. I need to go to Atlanta in the morning. I'm making sure the girls are covered just in case I can't get back by tomorrow night.

Atlanta? What the hell? I don't get a chance to ask why—and really, do I have the right to ask?—when another text pops up.

> He who shall not be named is causing trouble at one of my family's companies. I need to sort it out in person.

My fists clench and my gut cramps. I thought she was free of him. Then again, she did warn me he probably wouldn't leave her alone once their divorce was final.

Which it is. The court signed off, or stamped, or whatever it is it has to do, weeks ago. If we'd done as Gem suggested I'd get off this bus and find her, tell her I'll be beside her for the trip to Atlanta.

But we're not married. And I have the girls to think about. It might feel like I should support Gem like a partner would, but we only live under the same roof, share the care of my sisters. We're not together.

And I don't know how she'd feel if I went all caveman and beat the shit out of her ex.

"Hey." Casio Lindberg drops into the seat next to me.

I glance around, see only a few other guys have boarded the bus and wonder why he's chosen to sit beside me. I don't have to wait long to find out.

"Can I ask you something?"

Putting my phone away, I turn to look at him. "Sure."

"How do you leave your sisters behind?"

I laugh. "Not easily. And this trip is the first. They've been at all our other away games."

"Hmm..."

"Why do you ask?"

With a sigh, he rubs a hand over his face. "I have a sister. She's six."

"Oh?"

"Yeah, not something I talk about much. She's the product of my old man having an affair. My mother acts like Bella doesn't exist and since my dad is dead, she only has me and her mother."

"And you're involved in her life?" I'm not sure why Casio has decided to confide in me but I'm not about to shut him down. I wish I'd had someone to talk to when I'd gotten guardianship of my sisters.

"I am. Was." He blows out another breath. "Her mom wouldn't move with me. I've offered to support her and Bella, but she refuses. Fuck, my old man never gave her anything but sperm, so I get why she doesn't want me helping her."

"But she's let you spend time with your sister?"

"Oh, yeah, she's all about that."

"What's the age difference?"

"Twenty-four years."

"You could be her dad."

"Same as you and yours." He eyes me. "The baby could be yours."

"She could." A lightbulb lights up in my brain. "Ah, that's why you're talking to me about this."

"Yes. I figured you'd have some insight in how to cope with being away from her. We FaceTime and any break I get, I fly to New York to see her."

"Did you want to come to Baton Rouge?"

"No. And I want out as soon as I can." He shakes his head. "No, I'm not going to play shit to make them dump me."

"Never even thought that. Why the hell would you think it?"

"I didn't. Someone on my old team told me to do it so I can get back to New York."

"You came from the Knights, right?" At his nod I say, "So you played with Coach."

"I did. The man was a genius on the ice. He's one off it. I loved playing with him, love working under his guidance too, but…"

"You miss your sister."

He nods.

"And her mom won't move here?"

"No. She's got a good job, with benefits, and she's worked her way to where she is without help. Although, once I knew about Bella, I've been making sure neither of them go without. I even bought an apartment, wanted to give it to her but she refused." He snorts. "She pays me market rent on the damn thing."

"You don't need the money."

"I don't. That's why I'm funneling it into an account for Bella's future. Or a rainy day if something goes wrong."

"Sounds like you've got it all worked out. Except living close."

"Yep." He leans into the aisle before turning back and lowering his voice. "I want a trade. I might have someone willing to swap but we haven't spoken to anyone about it. You're close with the GM, right?"

"Ah... She's helping me with my sisters." I don't elaborate. And it's ridiculous to deny because everyone has seen Gem with the girls. Mainly Candace.

"Do you think she'd listen if I could convince the guy from New York to trade places? Our positions are the same, deals similar, and I'd take a cut to go back home."

"Shit, man, you need to talk to someone about this. I think Gem would be open to the suggestion, but it can't be a simple swap. The New York GM would have to agree."

"I know, I know." He shakes his head. "I'm just testing the scenario."

"Casio. If you hate it here that—"

"Don't hate it. Kinda love it actually. But I feel guilty about that too."

"Look, I'm cool with talking to you about this, but I think you need someone who can help fix the situation. And that isn't me."

"I get it. I just wondered how you deal with being away from your sisters. Didn't mean to dump all that on you. Sorry."

"Don't be sorry. I'm happy to talk. Whenever you want or need."

"Thanks."

"I mean it, talk to Coach or even Gem. What does your agent say?"

He snorts. "He thinks I'm an idiot for wanting to go back. New York is still struggling after the drama from last season."

"That was bad." I'd spent a few weeks refreshing my knowledge of the league after arriving in Baton Rouge and read all about the ex-husband of the owner taking her to court to try and wrestle the team from her.

"It looked bad from the outside, the inside was a little easier, but still not good for the players."

"Explains how you ended up at the bottom of the standings when the year before you almost made it to the cup."

"Losing Walker didn't help. And I don't know what happened, but Landon Watts wasn't playing at his best."

"They're looking good this year though."

"They are. But then so are we." He grins. "I might want to live in New York, but I want to play for the Rogues. I think we're going all the way this year."

"It's our first season."

"Wouldn't matter if it was our tenth. The team is playing fantastic hockey."

I shake my head. "And you want to leave that?"

"No. Not really. But Bella is more important than a career that's going to be over in a few years."

"Would you retire early?"

"No. Although I have thought about it."

"Maybe play this season out and see how you feel then."

"If I can't get traded, that's the plan."

"I wish I could do more. Be more than just a guy you can talk to."

"You and me both, but getting traded is a given in this job, right? And I know how lucky I was the last eight years. I played for one other team before the Knights, and that was only one season my first year out of college. And Bella wasn't around then."

"Would her mom be open to coming down here for visits or does her job make that difficult?"

"I don't know. I kinda lost it on her when she wouldn't move here when I suggested it. We haven't really spoken since."

"Sounds like you've got some apologizing to do."

"Yeah, I guess I should start with that."

"Moving back might not be the best thing if you're fighting with Bella's mom."

"Probably. Maybe some time without me there will show her they need me."

"They?"

"Ah, yeah, I might have a thing for my father's one-night-stand baby momma."

I can't hold in my laughter.

"Yeah, I know, laugh it up. I'd laugh too if I wasn't living it."

When I get myself under control I ask, "Does she know you have a thing for her?"

"No. I can't see how we could be together with the connection we have. And my mother would never speak to me. Then again, that might not be so bad."

"Are you living in a soap opera?" I grin. "I swear, you're reading the script for one of those daytime shows."

"It feels like it. Unfortunately, I have the hots for my sister's mom."

"Ah, maybe don't say it like that. It's sounds super seedy, like a porno script, when you put it like that."

For a second Casio looks confused and I'm about to explain it when he says, "Holy fuck! No! That's not what I mean."

By the time he finishes talking I'm laughing, and he quickly joins in.

"Oh God." He chokes on a laugh. "That would really be a fucked-up life."

"It would. Maybe lead with her being your *half*-sister's mom before you tell people you have the hots for her."

"I don't know if I'll tell anyone else. Not sure why I told you."

"I'll pretend I never heard it."

"Thanks. And thanks for listening."

"Any time."

"You having a drink with us when we get to the hotel? I heard talk of them opening the bar just for us."

"Probably. It's too late to call my sisters." I spoke to the girls before the game and even though I worry about them, I know they're in good hands with Pa.

Besides, having a drink will mean a chance to see Gem. Maybe get a few words with her before going back to my room—Baton Rouge—without her.

The thought of letting her deal with her ex by herself has my chest tightening. I know she's capable, but it doesn't sit right letting her. Everything in me wants to help her, protect her.

It seems Casio isn't the only one with a thing for a woman he shouldn't.

NAT

Climbing into the backseat of my ride share, I lean back and breathe a sigh of relief. My plane out of Atlanta was delayed and after spending most of the morning dealing with the latest Johnathon debacle, I'm more than happy to be home.

They say home is where the heart is, and I have to agree. My heart is definitely here. And I don't mean Baton Rouge. I mean the Hawkins siblings. I smile and close my eyes. I can't wait to see them.

My phone vibrates in my pocket, and I debate ignoring it. Except I can't. It's been in flight mode for the last couple of hours and there's bound to be something—or someone—needing my attention.

When I tap the screen and see the message, I jolt upright, the seatbelt digging into my shoulder.

AMOS POWELL

> Cami and Whitney Higgison accosted by a
> reporter at school

Amos's text is light on details but the fact he's messaged at all tells me he thinks the situation is serious. He has no reason to contact me otherwise.

I've barely left the airport pickup zone. I still have to drive all the way across town. Unlocking my phone, I pull up Chase's contact and hit call.

It rings three times and when it connects, I don't wait for him to speak before talking. "Are the twins home from school?"

"Yeah, they just got here, they're telling me something happened to Whit—" I can hear the girls talking in the background. "And Cami?"

"Can you leave them at home with Candace? I just left the airport, and I don't know if anyone is with them."

"With Whit and Cami? The twins said Bex is supposed to pick Whit up today."

"I know. And Beckett is probably on his way from training but can you—."

"I can run down there. I left training early because Candace was fussy. She's asleep now. If you come straight home, I can go to the school now and see what's going on."

"Yes. Do that. But tell the girls to stay inside, not to open the door for anyone. And arm the security system before you leave." Fear is tightening my chest, making it hard to draw breath.

"Hang on a sec..." There's some noise, a few muffled words, a loud thump, then a couple of clicks and Chase is back. "You're on Bluetooth. The girls are safely locked inside and I'm heading down the street now. Do you have any idea what's going on?"

"No. Just that there was an incident at the school, something about a reporter accosting Whitney and Cami."

"Shi-oot!" His breathing grows sharper, faster.

"Are you running?"

"Yes."

"Why didn't you take your car?"

"No. Time," he pants.

"I'm about five minutes from home now." I want to lean

forward and tell the driver to hurry up but he's already pushing the speed limit.

"On, school, street."

"Don't hurt yourself getting there," I warn. The last thing I need—or want—is Chase sustaining an injury.

"All. Good."

"Can you—"

"Bex is here." His breathing evens out. "EMTs and the cops too."

"Oh, okay, that's good." I breathe easier knowing Cami and Whitney aren't on their own. "I'll stay at the house with the girls if you can find out what's happening."

"Give me five and I'll call you back."

"No!" I reach for the door handle as the car turns into our driveway. "Keep me on the line."

"Gem, let me call you back."

He hangs up before I can argue, and I can't hold in a growl of frustration. Which isn't like me. I rarely show my emotions. Then again, I've been doing a lot of things I don't normally do since Chase and his sisters came into my life.

Like now.

Instead of heading to the office after flying in from Atlanta, I'm going home. To spend time with Chase and the girls.

I miss them.

It's only been forty-eight hours, and I miss them so deeply I can't think about anything except seeing their smiling faces.

And now I need to figure out what the hell is happening with Whitney and Cami.

I waste no time getting out of the Uber, don't even throw a thank you over my shoulder before slamming the door. Lugging my carry-on behind me, I race toward the front door, smile when I see Cassidy's and Crystal's faces pressed to the window either side of it.

Hopefully Candace is still asleep. If she was fussy today, she probably didn't have a morning nap. Or she's teething again. I wish those damn teeth would just cut through already. The poor little thing has been plagued by them for weeks now.

Pleased the girls don't open the door for me, I pull out my keys and slide the right one in the lock. They might not have opened the door, but the second I do, they're disarming the security system.

"Is Cami okay?"

I stop, turn my head to look at the girls. "Cami?"

"Yeah, she fell down the stairs when a man tried to grab Whitney," Crystal explains. "We raced straight home to tell Chase."

"You didn't go back into school to tell someone?"

"No. We were already out the gate, and there were a few teachers and the principal in the parking lot. They all ran over," Cassidy adds.

"And the guy ran." Crystal's eyes grow so big I worry they'll fall out of her head until her next words stop my breath and flush away any relief I felt knowing Cami and Whitney aren't alone. "At us!"

I can't form words. I'm too busy conjuring up all sorts of horrible images in my head. A cold sweat snakes its way down my spine. Shaking myself to erase the distressing thoughts from my mind, I slam the door and reach for them.

If they're shocked by my actions they don't show it, and if the way they cling to me is an indication, they need this hug as much as I do.

"You're both okay, right?" I swallow, fear thick in my throat, constricting my chest. "Other than being scared, you're not hurt, are you?"

"No." Cassidy leans back, tears in her eyes. "But I think Cami is."

"Maybe, maybe not. We have to wait until your brother calls me back." I ease up my grip. "Let's go to the kitchen. Get a snack and a drink."

"He ran to school."

I smooth a hand over Crystal's hair. "I know. I was on the phone with him."

"Should we go there?" Cassidy asks.

"No. Best if we wait until we know what happened, what we need to do. Plus, Candace is asleep and your brother said she was fussy today."

"She was fussy last night too. Pa gave her some of that stuff for her gums."

Crystal's words confirm my thoughts. Candace is teething again. I make a mental note to check our supply of gel and pain reliever.

"Come on. I need a drink." Wine would be good, but I'll stick with water in case I need to drive once I find out the situation. "Do you know if your brother planned anything for dinner?"

"No. We just got home."

Entering the kitchen, I check my phone. The screen is dark, and the damn thing is quieter than a church mouse. I don't like not knowing what's happening. I'm not used to letting others take control of difficult situations. It's usually me who takes care of things, fixes what needs to be fixed.

Except I'm here, watching the girls. Trusting Chase to find out what's happening.

It's a strange sensation. I've only ever put my faith in Eli, Oakley, Blake, and Cami. Eli more than the girls, but only because he's been in my life longer. It's why he was the first person I thought of to take charge—with Chase's approval—of Limitless.

And just this morning Eli reminded me we still haven't found anyone to take over some of our tasks within Rogue sportswear and the Rogues' org. And right now, with this latest Rogues' issue and the work that waits for me, I'm feeling the stretch of too many roles more than ever.

I really need to stop finding fault with every candidate Trevor presents us with.

"Can we have some figs, are they ripe yet?" Cassidy asks, a fig in her hand.

"They should be. What do you want with them? Yogurt? Cream? Melted chocolate?"

The sound of the front door opening, followed by several beeps from the alarm, has us all turning around. And when Chase ushers Whitney into the kitchen I take the first deep breath I have since the message from Amos popped up on my screen.

Except no one follows them. I turn to Chase, an eyebrow raised in question. He tips his head toward the butler's pantry, and when I nod, he heads that way.

Grabbing three glasses from the cupboard I shove them, one after the other under the cold-water dispenser in the fridge door then place them on the counter. "Here. I need to talk to your brother, can you get yourselves something to eat while I do?"

The twins eye me like I'm stupid and I laugh.

"Of course you can. Why don't you decide what to have for dinner while you snack?"

"Take out?" Crystal asks, as she comes around to open the cupboard where we keep the chocolate.

"Probably the best option tonight."

She grins at me, and I turn to go only to swing back again. "And if Candace wakes, can one of you go up and get her if I'm not back, please."

"Sure." Cassidy is already busy cutting up the figs.

"Thanks."

Leaving them to organize their snack, I head in the direction Chase went only to find the butler's pantry empty. But the door at the other end is open which only ramps up my concern.

Whatever he has to tell me can't be good. He's obviously taking no chances on the twins or Whit overhearing it.

Stepping into the wine cellar, I don't wait for the door to close or my eyes to adjust to the dimness before demanding, "Tell me."

"A reporter tried to grab Whit. Cami defended her by getting between them and throwing her laptop at him. Unfortunately, she lost her footing and tumbled down the stairs."

"Is she okay?"

"Yes. I think so. Bruised, mad as hell, but from what I could tell, and no, I didn't ask, she hasn't broken anything. Bex is staying with her while she talks to the detectives, then he'll bring her here."

"Okay." I let out a breath, the tension in my shoulders easing, Cami can't be hurt too badly if they're not taking her to the hospital. "We should organize dinner. Something they can take with them if they don't want to eat here."

Chase grins at me. "I told Bex we would. Did you call Oakley and Blake? Cami's parents?"

"I'll message the girls, call Fenton. I expect to see them all here if Bex brings Cami and they stay for dinner."

"He has to for her car. I drove it here."

"Cami's car?"

"Yeah. Whit has her handbag too."

"Which means we probably have Cami's phone."

Chase shrugs. "I guess."

"All right. Let me make sure the girls have a decent snack and get them to do their homework now. If everyone descends on us, and I'll lay money on that happening, they won't want to do it later."

"Definitely not."

"So, pizza?"

"That would be easiest."

"Although I told the girls to decide what they wanted. They might pick something else."

"Not likely. Pizza is their favorite."

"Anything else I need to know before I start making calls?" I ask, referring to the reason we're hiding in the cellar.

"No."

"Good. Let's see what happens when Beckett and Cami get here."

"Should we offer to have Whit overnight?"

"Only if he's comfortable leaving her. He might not be after what happened."

"True. But it would be a good distraction for her to spend time with the twins."

"Also true. Let's wait and see."

A faint cry from Candace filters into the room.

"That's my cue." Chase goes to step by me but stops when our shoulders are aligned. He turns his head my way and says, "We need to keep a closer eye on all the kids associated with the team."

It isn't until now, with our faces inches apart, that I see the worry in his eyes. And even though that was on my list of things to talk to the head of Rogues' security about, I know Chase needs me to ease his mind now, even if I don't have any solid plans.

"We will. I just need to speak with Ray and his security team."

"Good." He nods once. "And thank you."

"Don't thank me. Depending on what Cami tells me about today, we may need to overhaul all our security measures."

"You don't think the interviews she's doing are putting everyone in the spotlight? Drawing unwanted attention?"

"No." I shake my head. "This thing with Beckett and Whitney seems to be from her being kept from the public eye so long."

"I haven't done my interview yet."

It takes a moment, but I quickly work out what Chase is really worried about.

"I will protect those girls with my life. I'll tell Cami to hold off on interviewing you until last. That way we can make sure we protect the girls from unwanted attention and hopefully, this thing with Beckett and Whitney will have died down and the only interest the media shows is for the team and the games we're winning."

"Okay." Candace's cry is louder. "Sounds like someone got grumpy pants up for me."

"I asked the girls to do it before I came in here."

"Thanks." He turns to go but I stop him with a hand on his arm.

"Chase." I wait until his gaze returns to mine. "Stop thanking me. I told you I would be your partner in caring for the girls and I meant it."

"I know. But it still seems like you're doing me a favor, that I'm taking advantage of you."

"I'm not and you're not. I wanted you on the team. I wanted you and the girls to have the lives your parents wanted for you. I could easily have thrown money around to make it all happen."

"To be honest, I'm kind of surprised you haven't."

"I don't want to." I swallow over the lump in my throat. "I don't have any family. They're all dead and I never counted my ex as family. The women of KAW and their families are the closest relationships I have besides Eli. And none of them are blood related to me."

"I—"

"No, let me finish. I know I'm not family to you or the girls, but I want to be there for you like family would be. Well, not my family, there was no love in my family or my marriage, and maybe that's why I'm so determined to make sure the four of you stay together. And I want to be part of that if you'll let me."

"You mean the marriage of convenience you talked about when you first came to St. Paul?"

"Yes. If that's what you want to do. But there are alternatives. I could adopt the girls, you would still be their guardian," I rush out. "But I'd be a second parent without you having to tie yourself to me."

"Why wouldn't I tie myself to you if I'm willing to tie the girls to you?"

"Well, you're twenty-one and I'm thirty-four for a start."

"So what? Isn't Coach younger than Oakley? And I know Coach Watts is older than Bran."

"You would consider a marriage of convenience?"

"It's the only option I'd consider to protect the girls."

"Oh." I'm not sure why I thought he would prefer the other option.

I'll admit I'm shocked he's open to it. We've been taking care of the girls together for weeks and he's never mentioned getting married. Of course, I was still married to Johnathon for half of that time.

"You work out the details and I'll do what I have to to make it legal and secure the girls."

"They're secure now. I promise you. A marriage between us won't change the way I treat them."

"I know. But it might change the way you treat me."

I don't get a chance to process his words, never mind question them, because he leaves me alone in the cold cellar.

He wants me to change the way I treat him?

What's wrong with the way I treat him now?

CHASE

The Rogues just won their first game in the regular season ever and instead of celebrating, I'm pacing our hotel suite.

The girls are in bed. Candace is asleep but I'm not sure about the twins.

And there's no way I can go to bed yet. Gem isn't here.

Whatever went down with Cami after the game tonight wasn't good. All I know is what Whit told Cass and Stell.

Cami collapsed in the hallway leading to the visitors' locker room.

That's where Gem is. I think. I do know wherever she is, she's doing what she does best, fixing things, and I'd be lying if I didn't admit I want to be with her.

I offered to take care of Whit because Bex is also there—with Cami—wherever there is, except Dana and Fenton Barnes, Cami's mom and dad, took her back to their room. And as much as I wanted to ask Whit for more information, she was visibly upset, and I didn't want to cause her any more distress.

Despite what was happening, everyone was ushered back to the hotel after the game to celebrate our win in the first round of the season as planned.

No one was surprised we won. We're playing stellar hockey

right now and I don't see that changing. The mood at the hotel was jubilant to say the least. Rogues' staff and players and families, all piled into multiple rooms with food and drink and replays of the best plays of the game rolling on screens spread throughout the rooms.

I did my best to enjoy the moment, to celebrate with the team—the girls. But there was no stopping my gaze from searching out Gem. I saw her a few times. Fleeting glimpses that did nothing to soothe the agitation of not knowing what was going on.

Surprisingly no one other than a select few seemed aware there was an issue. And with Oakley, Blake, and Gem making appearances it looked as though nothing was amiss because Cami rarely attends any Rogues events.

The coaches were tight-lipped too, and I'm positive Bran knows more than he said but I'm not going to force him to break confidence with his wife because I can't stand not knowing what's happening or where Gem is.

Or Cami.

To anyone looking in on our celebration they wouldn't see a problem, wouldn't notice the owners flitting in and out in an attempt to hide the situation. And they succeeded. Most in attendance were clueless to the drama unfolding behind the scenes.

But I knew.

The girls knew.

Their concern, for their friend, for Cami, for Gem's absence, showed on their faces and in their searching eyes. It was torture for all of us to pretend we weren't worried, so I made excuses about the girls' bedtime and brought us up to our suite.

It took forever to convince the twins to go to bed. And in the end, I resorted to bribery. A day out to do anything they want, go anywhere they want.

We'll probably end up in New Orleans. We haven't ventured that far from home yet and I know they're keen—I'm keen—to explore more of our new home state.

They wrangled an extra promise to take Whit with us too.

I smile despite the tension holding every muscle rigid.

Cass and Stell have blossomed into confident young women in recent weeks. And it's not only the move that has been good for them, allowing them to come into their own.

It's Whitney Higgison.

It's their relationship with Pa.

It's the found family the Rogues have given us.

I might have had a small bit of doubt over the move. A teeny-tiny niggle of regret in not keeping us in our family home. But I can't argue with the way we've all come out from under the cloud of grief.

Yes, we miss our parents. Every day. But Gem has helped with our sadness by talking about them, by hanging their pictures on the walls of her house—*our* house.

There's no denying her house is now our home. We're more comfortable there than we were in the last few months we lived in the home we'd grown up in.

I'd go as far as saying the girls love it in Baton Rouge. Love Gem.

Fuck, after what I let slip the other day, I think I'm in love with her!

She fascinated me from the beginning but after my chat with Lindberg, my subconscious must have been pulling all my emotions together and forming a conclusion I've been too blind or stupid to see.

I'm falling for Gem.

Maybe I've already fallen.

The anxiety I feel right now could only be because I love her. It's the same way I feel when any of the girls has an issue. Cass usually. She's been the one to struggle the most with my parenting, at least outwardly.

Not that we've had a lot of issues, just the occasional explosion of emotions when she doesn't like what I'm telling her to do.

It's expected, and if Gem wasn't living with us, I'm sure

things would be worse. She manages to calm us all when things get unsettled. Just her presence, her clear—

The beep of the door lock has me spinning around and lunging for the handle. Yanking the door open, I stare at the woman using her keycard to get in.

"You're here." The relief I feel is bone dissolving. And I'm helpless to stop myself from reaching out and pulling her inside—into my arms.

"What—?" Air bursts from her when she slams against me.

"You're here," I repeat, whether for her benefit or mine, I'm not sure.

"Chase?" She tries to pull free, but I don't let her and a second later she sighs, her body relaxing against me. "Damn. I didn't know I needed this."

I don't know how long I hold her. Long enough to reach out and shut the door then slowly shuffle us backward to the sofa.

When I have her back to the couch, I ease up my grip and lower her to the cushion. "Do you need a drink? Water? Wine?" I ask, slipping to my knees in front of her.

"No. I'm—" I unbuckle one shoe. "What are you doing?"

"Taking your shoes off. You don't have to go back out, do you? You're home now, right? Finished for the night?"

"No. Yes, I'm done for the day, but I'm expecting a call at some point." She glances around the room. "I need to charge my phone."

With her second heel removed, I hold out my hand. "Give it to me, I'll plug it in."

Pulling it from her pocket, she holds it out but doesn't let go when I grab it. "Are you taking care of me, Chase?"

"Yes." I give the phone a tug. "Now give it to me."

"I don't need taking care of."

"I know you don't. Doesn't mean I don't want to do it, or you should stop me from doing it."

"I can take care of myself."

I don't know why the sudden stubborn streak to be an independent woman, but she's not alone, not anymore. If we're going to take care of my sisters together, then we're a team. "You can. And you will. But I'll also do things to make sure you're looked after. It's what people do when they're partners."

She eyes me suspiciously.

"I swear, I don't want anything." I do. I want her to fall for me like I'm falling for her, but I can't tell her that. "All I want is to give you a few minutes where you don't have to think, don't have to be the one in charge, getting everything done."

Closing her eyes, she leans her head back on the couch. "God. That would be nice."

"Then for the next ten minutes the only thing you have to worry about is if you're hungry or thirsty, telling me what you want so I can get it."

"I want a cheeseburger."

Her words have me going still. "That's very specific."

"They were on tonight's menu except with everything going on I didn't get one. And I really wanted one."

"I'll order one now. Water or wine?" I ask because I know they're her usual choice.

"If I have wine, I'll fall asleep. And now that we're talking about food my stomach is rumbling, and my mouth is watering. I really want that burger."

"I'm on it." Tugging the phone from her grip, I stand and head for the desk where my phone is currently charging. Switching the devices then picking up the hotel phone, I glance back to see Gem hasn't moved.

If it wasn't for the continuous tapping of her fingertips on her thigh, I'd think she was asleep. Those tapping fingers tell me she's still thinking, probably worrying too.

"Room service."

The voice in my ear snaps me back to what I'm doing. "Yeah, can I get a cheeseburger? With fries." Gem might not have asked for them, but I know how she feels about eating a burger without fries.

"Is that all?"

"Yes."

"Okay, Mr. Redding, we'll have that up to your room in ten minutes."

"Ah, thanks." I lower the phone to its cradle and contemplate Gem's last name.

I know she didn't change it when she married her ex. And I suspect she won't change it when she marries me. Except now all I can think about is making her a Hawkins.

If this thing between us was real, if she had feelings for me like I do her, would she change her name if we got married? It would make taking care of the girls simpler if they shared a last name.

I want to ask her to do it. It's dumb, I know that. We're getting married on paper only—if we do—and we're not telling anyone...

Yeah, dumb. Changing her name would be a huge banner proclaiming we were married.

We've spent weeks getting to know each other, sharing care of the girls, the joys of a winning season so far, and neither of us has mentioned her original suggestion until the other day.

Since then, it's all I've thought about. If we go through with it, do I stand a chance of getting her to fall for me? In all the years she was married to her ex she never fell for him.

Then again, from what I know, they never lived in the same house, barely stepped into the same room together.

"What are you brooding about over there?" Gem's voice jerks me out of my thoughts.

"What happened tonight? I know it had something to do with Cami."

"Fucking motherfucking reporter." Her words are soft, no force in them, which shows how tired she is and makes me more determined to take care of her.

"Eh..."

She lifts her head, her gaze locking with mine. "Remember the guy who outed Whitney?" I nod. "Well, it seems that fucker isn't happy with the drama he already caused. A few days ago, someone broke into Cami's apartment, the night she went home with Beckett and we had Whitney, and the police believe it was him."

"Sounds like it was a good thing she didn't go home that night."

"Definitely. But tonight, he attacked her." Her voice has gotten stronger—more fierce—with every word, the anger simmering inside her firing up again.

"Attacked her? I thought she collapsed on the way to the locker room."

"She did." Gem pushes herself off the sofa. "Let me get out of these clothes, get a quick shower before my food gets here, then I'll tell you everything."

"I don't know if I can wait that long," I mutter.

"Then come with me, I'll tell you while I shower."

I choke on my own spit.

She glances over her shoulder, her forehead scrunched in concern. "You all right?"

Shoving my hands in the pockets of my sweatpants, I pull them away from my groin in the hope of hiding the insta-boner I'm now sporting. Clearing my throat, I say, "Um, yeah."

"Hmm…" It takes her barely a second to decide not to question me more. "Can you get me some ice water?"

"Sure." The switch in subject gives me a reason to turn away and more time to mentally think of the most disgusting diaper Candace has ever produced to rid myself of my unwanted erection.

It's not the first time Gem has had my body reacting this way. Although it is the first time it's happened so quickly and right in front of her.

By the time I have two glasses of ice water in hand, I can hear the shower running in her bathroom. We're in a three-bedroom suite. The twins have one room, me and Candace are sharing another, and Gem has the master with the attached bathroom.

Entering her bedroom, I ignore the open bag in case her underwear is visible and place one of the glasses on the bedside table.

I can't ignore the open bathroom door though. And in spite of every breath I take being filled with the scent of Gem, I somehow don't walk through it.

Instead, I lean on the wall beside it and take a moment to get myself under control.

"Can you hear me clearly?"

How the hell does she know I'm standing here? I haven't made a sound she could hear over the running water.

"Yeah."

"What we know so far is Cami and her dad were walking through the public area of the arena when someone pushed her from behind. Video footage shows it was the reporter who outed Whitney."

"Didn't they have security?" I ask, my voice raised a notch higher than normal so it travels into the bathroom.

"Yes, they had an escort. After Cami almost fell, security hustled them into the restricted area. What nobody knew until she passed out and we re-ran security footage, was that she wasn't pushed, she was stabbed with a syringe."

"What the fuck?" I jerk off the wall, take a step forward only to stop when I remember where Gem is. "*Shit!*"

"I'm waiting on a call from Ray. He, along with Beckett and our medical intern, have taken Cami to a private hospital he has access to in an attempt to keep the media from getting a whiff of what happened. The last thing we need, or Cami would want, is for this to be splashed across the country's tabloids."

The water switches off as she speaks the last few words and my imagination pulls up vivid images of naked, dripping wet Gem. And my dick decides that's the cue to rise again.

Clenching my jaw, I try to focus on the conversation. "What was she injected with?"

"We think a sedative. I'll know for sure when Ray calls."

There's rustling on the other side of the cracked door and I'm so tempted to push it open wider that I need to move away.

Several steps back don't curb the urge, so I call out, "I think room service is here," and make a hasty retreat to the living room.

I glare down at my hard dick. If I'm going to have this reaction to Gem from now on, it's going to make our marriage of convenience very uncomfortable.

Maybe I need to get laid. Take up one of the many offers from the bunnies who hang around after an away game. I can't do it at a home game. Too many people to see, and more importantly, I have the girls to take care of.

It's a good idea even if I'm not feeling it. At all. In fact, my dick has deflated.

"Huh." I stare at my groin.

I guess the easiest and quickest way to get rid of an unwanted erection inspired by Gem is to think about fucking someone other than her.

"What are you doing?"

I jolt straight. "Shit!" Spin around. "I didn't hear you."

One eyebrow is cocked—no, arched, it's arched. I don't need to be thinking about anything cock related right now—and she's looking at me with concern. Again.

"Sorry. Was thinking. About tonight. The girls. You and me." I'm not lying. Those have all crossed my mind in the last few minutes. The context of those thoughts isn't something I plan to reveal though.

"Yeah." She tugs at the oversized Rogues jersey she's wearing over leggings. "Tonight has been something else."

"If Ray hasn't called before you finish eating, will you wait up?"

"I'd like to say yes, but I'm exhausted and will probably nod off if I try."

"Want me to wait up with you?"

"No. Go to bed. Get some sleep. Candace will be up in a few hours, and we all need to be up early for our flight home."

She's right. It doesn't stop me from wanting to argue. I manage not to voice my objections and take a seat on the couch instead.

I'll sit up with her while she eats, then go to bed.

I doubt I'll sleep, there's too many thoughts swirling in my head for that, but I'll at least lie down and pretend. Gem doesn't need to be worrying about me too.

Nat

After what happened to Cami three weeks ago, everyone is walking on eggshells. No one knows if there will be another attack—and at this point, that's how I'm referring to the incidents plaguing my best friend.

Even with the beefed-up security measures, no one is taking any chances.

Especially with the children.

It's causing tension, on and off the ice, and with another tough game coming up, we need the players to focus on their game, not the dangerous antics of a scandal monger reporter.

The other thing on my mind constantly is the very real possibility of something happening to one of the girls. Or Chase. And how powerless I'd be if it did.

Those thoughts are why I'm currently waiting for Eli to call me. I need to have a legal way of looking after Chase and his sisters and the fastest, easiest way to do that is to marry Chase.

He's been distant since Cami's attack, and I put it down to fear of something happening to one of his sisters.

He's not the only one feeling it. I need to talk to him about it, about how scared for my friend I was when I saw her pass out and how that fear has transferred to him and the girls.

When my phone finally rings, it scares the shit out of me, and I fumble it trying to bring the damn thing to my ear. "Hello."

"Natalie. What the hell is sitting on my desk?"

"You know what it is. Can you get everything worked out this week?"

"You want to marry your star goalie this week?"

"Yes."

"Why? You've gotten what you want already. Chase is playing for the Rogues, and he and his sisters are living in your house."

"I've got no say if something happens to any of them. What if one of the girls is hurt and needs medical attention, serious medical attention, and Chase isn't here, and because I'm nothing to them but a roommate, I can't authorize anything?" Even I can hear the fear strangling my voice. It chokes my throat just thinking about the possibilities.

"Is this about what happened to Cami?"

"Yes. No. Maybe." I sigh and lean back in my chair. "They've lost so much."

"Nat."

I hear the sympathy in Eli's voice, the love he's given me my whole life. Even before my parents were killed in a boating accident, Eli was part of my life. He was Dad's best friend. Mom's stepbrother.

There's no blood connection but blood means nothing to me. I shared blood with my grandfather, and he was an asshole. A vindictive, manipulative, mean asshole. Without Eli there to look out for me, my teenage years would have been far worse than they were.

"I know it doesn't make sense. I know it's probably not necessary. But I want to take care of the girls, and I want the connection to their brother beyond having his signature on a contract for the Rogues."

"Are you worried he'll take them away from you once he's on his feet?"

"What? No. He'd never do that. To me or them."

"Then what is it?"

It takes me a minute, but finally I whisper, "I've got no one. If something happens to me, everything goes to Oakley, Cami, and Blake."

"I know." And he does. He helped me draw up my first will at twenty-one, and every amended one since.

"I want them to have it."

"Natalie, I'm in the backend of their family's business, they don't need your money."

"It's not about the money."

"Then what is it about? Talk to me. I know a decade ago I convinced you a marriage of convenience was the best option, but that was to gain access to your trust funds and control of your Redding stocks but if there had been another way I'd have pushed for that."

"You aren't to blame for Johnathon. We chose him because Grandfather would approve of him. And we knew I could function without his interference because all he wanted was money. It gave me a small amount of freedom to do what I had to to get out from under my grandfather's thumb."

"And it gave the old man someone other than you he could control."

"Yes."

"What you want to do is about you being in control. Of four lives. Think about that. Think about what you're planning, who you're behaving like."

If Eli had slapped me, it wouldn't have stung more than his words. "I am *nothing* like my grandfather. I would *never* use my connection or money to control them. I'm giving Chase the choice. Marriage or guardianship or adoption of the girls."

"I don't have anything about guardianship or adopting the girls on my desk."

"No. Because if he agrees to a union between us, what we do about the girls will change."

"I don't like it."

"I don't care!" I suck in a breath, lower my head. "Sorry. I didn't mean that. I do care what you think, but this isn't like Johnathon. You said yourself, Chase isn't going to say yes for my money. Did you know he's paid me ten thousand a month for expenses since he moved in? And that doesn't include the takeout and groceries he's paid for."

"Okay, so this isn't about money. It could still blow up like—"

"No. Chase is nothing like Johnathon. If you came down here and spent time with him and the girls, you'd see that."

"I've been busy spending my time digging into Limitless." I open my mouth to say thank you when he goes on. "And I think I do know Chase, a little. He emails me every day to check in on the business. To ask my advice on what he should do with the company long term. He isn't as uninvolved as you planned for him to be."

"He what? Since when?"

"Since you asked me to handle things for him."

"Wow. I didn't know that." I put Eli in charge of Limitless so Chase could concentrate on the girls and hockey. Obviously, he's far more capable than I gave him credit for because he's still involved and his game is almost perfect and the girls are thriving.

"Natalie, I'm not trying to talk you out of doing what you and Chase think is best, but I want you to really think about the repercussions of a second marriage of convenience. Don't you want a family? Children of your own?"

"I kind of have them." I can't help the smile that curls my lips. "They might not call me mom, and the plan is to make sure Candace doesn't as she grows up, but that's the role I have in their lives."

"And you want to make that legal. For you as well as them."

"Yes. I want them to have the security of me as a guardian in whatever way we make that happen."

"Chase is onboard with this?"

"I think so. We've talked about it." Eli doesn't need to know it's only been a few words here and there. "But we need to iron out the details. There has been so much going on with the move, start of the school year and season that we haven't done it yet."

"Then do it. Today. When you see him next, hash out what you both want and then get back to me. I won't do anything with this paperwork until I hear from both of you that this is what you really want."

"You're being a pain."

"No. I'm doing what I have no legal right to do. Being a parent to a child that isn't mine."

Eli hangs up before I can say a word past the lump in my throat.

I know he tried to get custody of me after Mom and Dad died, and I know my grandfather put a stop to it, threatened to ruin him if he pushed for it.

There was no love for me in my grandfather's heart. Some would say Albert Redding didn't have a heart at all, but he loved himself, so there had to be something in that cold chest of his. And it didn't matter that he didn't, or couldn't love me, he would never give up anything he considered his.

And I was his.

Even if I was a disappointment because I didn't have a dick. My life would have been so different if I did and while my childhood wasn't the best, especially after my parents' deaths, it would have been so much worse if I had been a boy.

"Hey, got a minute?"

Glancing up I see Chase has poked his head into my office. "Of course. Is something wrong?" I ask with a frown.

"No, no, all good. Just wanted a few minutes of your time without the girls here to distract or interrupt."

"Oh. Well, come in, close the door." Neither of us speaks until he's in a seat across from me. "What's up?"

"I want to talk about your suggestion for giving the girls security if something happens to me. The marriage of convenience one."

It appears we're in sync with our thoughts today. Come to think of it, we're in sync a lot.

"What about it did you want to discuss?"

"I know it seems like this is out of the blue because we haven't talked about it since you first mentioned it. Not seriously, anyway. But I think, no, I *know*, it's the best option for the girls' future. I also want you to adopt them if I can remain their legal guardian as well."

"I..." I close my mouth.

Does he realize if I adopt the girls, we don't need to get married?

The thought of adopting the girls without marrying Chase has my stomach sinking. But I can't let him believe both are necessary to achieve what he wants.

"Either option would give you what you want. We don't need to do both."

"We do."

I eye him. He seems certain—determined. The expression on his face is the one I've seen close-up numerous times on the Jumbotron when he's in goal guarding it from all comers.

"You want to tell me why you want both?"

"I want all of us to have a connection."

As explanations go, it's simple. But the complexities behind it are not. "Why?"

"Because you don't have anyone either. You should have someone."

"I have Oakley, Blake, and Cami. And Eli."

"Yes. But you should have someone who's just yours."

"I have Eli."

He nods. "You do. But he isn't in your life every day. He won't be sharing the parenting of a couple of teenagers and a baby."

"We don't need to be married to do that."

"We don't. But it's what I want."

I don't understand why a twenty-one-year-old would want to

tie himself to me even with his sisters as a strong motivator. "Chase. What if—"

"Don't say it. It isn't going to happen. My focus is the girls and hockey. Our co-parenting partnership."

"Is that how you're looking at it? A partnership?"

"Yes. We'll be partners in parenting the girls and ensuring they get every opportunity in life our parents would have given them."

"And you're okay with keeping it a secret?"

"Yes. But I think we should tell the twins you're adopting them and Candace, and why. They're old enough to understand."

"They are and I agree, if we do that, they should know."

"Good." He pushes out of his seat, towers over my desk. "So, you'll do whatever you need to for us to get married and you to adopt the girls?"

"I can. But don't you want to do it? Make sure I'm not—"

A bark of laughter cuts me off. "You're the most capable and honest woman I've ever known, I don't need to make sure of anything. Just do what needs to be done and tell me what I need to do."

"I'll find out and let you know." He doesn't need to know I already have the information or that I started the paperwork to make him and the girls my beneficiaries in the event something happens to me. "Are you getting Candace now?"

"No. I've got an extra session with Coach Watts and Kallan Larsson."

"How's he doing?" Kallan is the youngest member of the team. It's how he got the nickname Young.

"Good. He's training well and he's getting out and exploring his new city. More than most of us actually."

I study his frown. "Do we need to get out more?"

"Yeah, I think so. The girls should see more than school, the house, and the arena."

"What do you have in mind?"

"We all enjoyed the day out in New Orleans with Whit the other week. Maybe we could do something like that again? Go somewhere different of course." He shrugs. "I don't know, this isn't my hometown or state."

"It isn't mine either, but I can ask Oakley and Cami for suggestions."

"I know the other guys' kids are younger than the twins and Whit, but do you think we should organize something for the whole team? Some kind of outing for the guys with their families?"

"Yes. That's exactly what we should do." A team family day will help bring everyone together, remind them they aren't in this alone. "Let me get together with the girls and work something out."

"I know we're heading into winter but maybe a barbecue?"

"Oakley could host one..." I say, the idea already taking shape in my head, Pa would love to have the team at his house.

"Not us?"

I have to bite back a sharp no. And he knows it.

"Right. Not us."

"No one knows we live—"

"Actually, they do. It's the Rogues' worst kept secret. Nobody has questioned me about it. It's just accepted, and I think it's because they know you're helping with the girls. They know we're *friends*."

"Are we?"

"What the fuck, Gem?" His spine has straightened, and his fists are clenched at his sides.

"I don't know. I've never had guy friends. Until Oakley and Blake got married, it was always just us four girls. Occasionally Blake's brothers, but those times were less and less as Rogue sportswear took off."

"Okay, but what do you think we are if not friends?"

I can see he genuinely wants to know what I think, but I don't have an answer for him. In a few days, a week at most, he'll be my husband. He's already my partner in parenting his sisters. We share a house, so roommates?

Except I'm also his boss. He's my employee. I might not tell him what to do day to day but I'm still in charge of the team he plays for. As GM and owner.

"You think about it because if we aren't friends, we can't do what we're setting out to do with the girls. We can't be partners."

"Of course we can."

"No. We can't. Look what happened last time you tied yourself to someone you weren't friends with. If you can't accept me as your friend, then we have to rethink this whole thing. I'm sure it will be easy enough to find a place for me and the girls."

"You'd move out?"

Ignoring my question he says, "I gotta go. I'll be late and that means suicides."

He doesn't give me a chance to protest, to question him again, keep the discussion going. He's out the door, and it's closing softly behind him before I can get my brain to come unstuck and tell my body to stand.

But it's too late.

He's gone.

And if he's serious, my office isn't the only thing he'll be gone from in the near future.

CHASE

I didn't mean to give Gem an ultimatum. Except that's exactly what I did.

And now we're barely talking. Walking on eggshells. Tiptoeing around each other as though we're afraid to break the fragile connection we have left.

The strain between us didn't stop us from getting married or submitting the paperwork for her to adopt my sisters. Nope, it was full steam ahead on both fronts.

Three days after I walked out of Gem's office, she came home with paperwork for me to sign and an appointment the next day for us to go to the courthouse where a judge joined us in 'holy matrimony'—his words, not mine—and while our vows were simple, I meant every word of them.

I never thought about being married, what it would be like, and I only have Mom and Dad's as a benchmark, but I can say without a doubt my marriage to Natalie Redding is nothing like what my parents had.

It's like two enemies being forced to work together for a common cause—my sisters. There are days when I wonder what the hell I was thinking to go through with it when there was conflict between us.

Not that looking back helps. We *are* married, have been for almost a month, and I will honor my vows. Because even with this fractured weird relationship we have right now, I love her.

It seems impossible. Half the time I don't believe it. But I can't deny the way I feel about her. And I'm at a loss as to how to turn things around. How to show her I'm in this for the long haul, and not only for my sisters.

I'm in it for *her*.

I have no idea when I made the decision to make Gem my wife for real, probably before I brought up the subject of us getting married to secure the girls' futures.

I've discovered I've lied to myself, or stuck my head in the sand and ignored things concerning Gem for most of our acquaintance.

Hard to believe we've only known each other five months, lived together for less. It seems like a lifetime since we lost Mom and Dad, forever since I made the difficult decision to move us all to the other end of the country to live with a stranger so I could give the girls a good life and follow my dream.

And it is a good life.

All the girls are thriving.

The twins love school and have made friends other than Whit, although she's their closest one. Candace goes to the Rogues Arena childcare a few mornings a week and is growing so fast it's hard to believe she's the baby I first held.

But it isn't just the girls who have benefited from the move south.

I'm having a blisteringly good season. Like my first year of college, I'm having more shutouts than not and the Rogues are at the top of our conference and on a trajectory for the Cup.

I know we all talked a good game back in August when we first hit the ice together and then during pre-season when we won our first game, and again at the beginning of the regular season. But I'll be dammed if we aren't following through on our boasting.

The media is having a field day with the way the Rogues are carving up the opposition. Not that we're mopping the rink with all the other teams. Miami has given us stiff competition, and the Knights are finally getting their shit together and pulling off some wins.

Every part of my life is coming up roses except my relationship with Gem.

It's annoying and frustrating and I want to fix it as much as I want to hold the Cup my first season in the NHL.

Both of those things seem like a pipe dream. Except we're winning and playing the best hockey, and the girls are doing better than well. Why can't I have the Cup and Gem?

In two weeks it will be Christmas, and I haven't done anything about it. I don't remember where we put any of our Christmas decorations.

Every other year of my life, now would be when Dad would load us up in his truck and drive out to the farm to chop down a tree to bring home to Mom, who would be waiting with boxes of ornaments ready to hang, hot chocolate with marshmallows and cookies.

I can't decide if I should try to replicate other Christmases or start new traditions.

And I haven't a clue what Gem normally does. It's a subject I need to discuss with her. If I can get her to talk to me that is.

Speak of the devil...

The door to the garage opens and Gem steps through it, her hair a mess and what looks like streaks of mud are on her skirt, her hands, and chin.

"What the fuck?" I'm in front of her, running my hands up and down her arms before cradling her face. "Are you hurt? What happened?"

After the last few months with Cami, Bex and Whit, and those reporters, my first thought is someone attacked her.

"I'm fine. Dirty but fine." She shrugs out of my hold and

steps around me. "I need a hot shower, clean clothes, and a bottle of wine. In that exact order."

"I'll get the wine." I walk toward the pantry and the cellar on the far side of it. "Any preference?"

I might have learned a thing or two about wine, but I can't drink it. Not that I drink anything really. I've had the odd beer and Magnus Lund bought me a scotch one night after a particularly hard game we lost in overtime. But when it comes to wine selection, I leave it to Gem.

"Whatever. I don't care." She disappears down the hallway that leads to her rooms without looking back.

I'm torn between following her to find out why she looks like she's been dragged across the ground or going to get her wine. In the end, the wine wins out because in the months I've lived in this house I've never stepped foot inside her personal space.

The space she's spent more and more time in since the day I threatened to take the girls and move out.

I can admit, even if it took me a while, it was a dick move. I should have just told her why I thought we were friends. That I wished we were more.

I should have taken into consideration what she said too. Because we might not have been talking like we did at first, but I haven't stopped studying her. Learning about her.

I've asked Eli a few questions too. And surprisingly, he's answered them. In fact, the man has given me some valuable insight into who Gem is. How she became the powerhouse Natalie Redding, COO of Rogue sportswear, and owner and GM of the Rogues NHL franchise.

She's worked her ass off.

All the women of KAW have.

They deserve every success because they've earned it. Despite a few digs in the media from years ago about them all being 'trust fund babies', there is very little about how they've worked to build their globally successful business.

It's shocking really. And maybe they wanted it that way, less chance of people—and by people, I mean the media—coming after them to drag them down.

Except now, with the Rogues, there's no going under the radar. They're in the spotlight every day we play. And if any of that attention has to do with the way Gem just came home, I'm going to...

Fuck! I don't know what I'll do.

I want to protect her, support her, love her, and I can't do any of them. Not in the open. The only avenue I have is to love her in secret and support her by playing my ass off so the Rogues win—bring home the Cup.

Inside the cellar is cool, the room specifically designed to house thousands of dollars worth of wine. Not that the shelves are full. When I asked about it after we moved in, Gem said it was already in the house, and it seemed a waste of money to rip it out.

Her explanation was sound and after I took over the basement for my home gym, I wasn't going to point out the area could be used for other things.

I've tried not to change anything else in the house. It's my home—feels like my home—but I don't feel as though I have the right to change anything else.

Hence, my procrastination over Christmas decorations.

But I can't keep doing that. This is our life. I need to be all in or get out.

And I'm not going anywhere unless she asks me to.

Scanning the shelves, I think about her request. If Gem wants a bottle of wine, she isn't planning to return to the office today and I've already gotten in a workout this morning and don't have to return to the arena until later to pick up Candace.

It's rare that none of the girls are around and if we're both free of responsibilities for the rest of the day, I'm going to take advantage of the time and use it to connect with my wife.

If she'll let me.

Grabbing a bottle, I don't bother looking at the label, I won't know if it's good or not anyway, but I'm assuming if Gem has it on the shelf, she likes it.

Passing through the kitchen, I collect a stemless wineglass from the cupboard before I do something I've never done before.

I walk down the short hallway and let myself into Gem's rooms.

She's in the bathroom. I can hear the shower running. I hope she's taken a change of clothes in there with her because I'm about to make myself at home on her bed.

Placing the bottle and glass on her bedside table I kick off my shoes, and sit on the bed, position my back against the wooden headboard.

Her room is plain. There are no pictures or artwork on the walls, or books cluttering surfaces waiting to be read. It's almost hotel-like in its plainness.

The only color in the room is the bed cover. It's a dark burgundy, the pillowcases a slightly lighter shade.

I'm not sure what I expected, to me she's soft and welcoming —well before I fucked things up she was—and I guess I thought her space would reflect that.

But this is so bare of personality it could be anyone's room, and while there is some color, it doesn't scream Gem.

"Oh good. You brought the wine." Her voice has my head snapping around and I all but swallow my tongue. "Is it a screw top or cork?"

I haven't a clue. I didn't even look at it. Not that I can say that. Not with my tongue tied in a knot and no air in my lungs.

She's wearing a pair of...workout shorts? Is that what they are? Whatever they are, they hug her body like paint. And they're short. Like barely below her pussy short.

"You don't want some? Wait. Of course you don't. You don't drink during the season." She undoes the bottle cap and pours herself a full glass. "Not that you drink anyway. God, you're barely old enough to do it legally."

I hardly register her words because I'm too busy checking her out and my brain isn't exactly functioning right now, what with all the blood rushing to my dick.

Which is standing at attention, tenting my running shorts like the center pole of a circus tent. And I'm too lust fogged to think to do anything about covering up.

It's no surprise when Gem turns toward me and her eyes skim over my groin that she bobbles her glass and spills wine down her chin.

I don't like wine. But I'll be dammed if I don't want to jump up and lick every drop off her skin.

We're caught in this weird, stunned silence for what feels like hours and the whole time my brain is spinning scenarios of how this might be different. How *we* might be different.

How if she were my wife for real, I'd pull her down on top of me and ravage her mouth, fill my hands with her ass, and yank her against the part of me that's throbbing with a beat so hard and fast it borders on painful.

"Chase."

She says my name like a whispered prayer and I'm powerless to stop from reaching out and running a fingertip down her flat belly.

Her skin is soft and warm against my callused finger, and I wonder how it would feel against my lips.

I'm not a virgin. Although I haven't been with many women —girls really—I'm not new to sex despite the nervous jittery sensation filling my gut.

"Chase," she says my name again, louder this time, and I bring my gaze up to meet hers.

"Yeah?"

"What are you doing?"

"Touching you."

"I..." She swallows, the pulse at her throat fluttering like crazy, and I'm pleased to see I'm not the only one unsure of what's happening.

"Is it okay?" I spread my hand, trail all my fingers across her torso from hipbone to hipbone. "Me touching you?"

"It's fi—" She sucks in a breath when I place my whole hand over her bellybutton, slide up until my fingertips hit the bottom of the sports bra she's got on.

I smile. I like that I make her speechless. And I'm not referring to the no talking we've been doing for the last month. "You're so soft."

Her belly quivers beneath my hand and my smile grows wider.

"You know, I've imagined you like this, so many times I've lost count, and yet nothing I thought was right, or did you justice."

"Chase." There's a plea in her voice, a tremor of something I can't place, and when my eyes land on hers again, I know whatever this is has to stop.

Something happened and had her coming home dirty and disheveled, left her shaken and unsure, in need of a breather and a bottle of wine and there is no way—no matter how much I want to fuck her—I will take advantage of her vulnerable state.

Pulling my hand away, I roll off the bed and stand beside her. I study her a few seconds more before I cup her face with one hand and brush my thumb over the wetness still on her chin.

"When you're ready to tell me what happened to bring you home in this state I'll be in the kitchen. We've got a few hours before the twins are home and Candace is still at the arena daycare. I'll stay out of your way, let you work your way through whatever you need to on your own. But if you want to talk, want someone to listen, I'm your man and I'll be waiting."

I don't stay in her room. I do exactly what I told her I would. I go to the kitchen and, to keep myself busy while I wait to see what she'll do, pull out the ingredients for dinner and hope she'll come find me.

Hope she'll let me in.

NAT

Something changed between me and Chase the day I came home after changing a flat tire. I'd been on my way from a meeting with the construction company contracted to build the mall when it deflated. Obviously, I'd picked up something at the worksite.

It wasn't the first time I had to change a tire. Eli made sure I mastered that skill years ago. But for some reason the tire represented everything in my life that was out of my control.

Or more specifically, my relationship with Chase.

The nuts on the wheel weren't the only things that gave and by the time I'd switched the flat for the spare I did something I so rarely do that I can count the times on one hand.

I retreated.

I went straight home thinking I'd have the house to myself only to find the man causing most of my anxiety right inside the door.

I'm pretty sure we haven't let our animosity—if that's even what it is—affect us outside the house. And the girls haven't picked up on the tension between us inside the house, so I have to assume the only people caught in the spiraling tension are me and Chase.

And since we called a kind of truce, things have shifted again.

We are back to how it was before all the drama with Cami happened. Back to being two people who share a house and the parenting duties of three young girls.

It helps that we both aired our troubles, mine being I hate that we were at odds. And unsurprisingly, his being the same.

Once we worked out that we were on the same side of this marriage of convenience, things smoothed out and our interactions got better. Life got better.

They're so good I'm currently waiting in the bigger of the two living rooms in our house, the lights of the Christmas tree flashing rainbows all over the room, wondering if I'm going to have to go upstairs and start waking people up.

I haven't been quiet either. I made sure to bang around in the kitchen when I made pancakes—now keeping warm in the oven—cutting up fresh fruit to go with them, and making myself three cups of coffee.

That was almost an hour ago. It's just shy of nine and I can't stand waiting any longer.

Shoving out of my seat, I put my empty coffee mug on the side table and head toward the stairs. Fingers around the railing, I take the steps two at a time, making sure to stomp my feet as much as possible.

I'm grinning when I get to the top. And not because my burst of energy—probably the three cups of coffee—makes me feel good.

No. I'm grinning because in front of me are two sleep-rumpled heads, with identical sleep-encrusted caramel-brown eyes, and bodies encased in matching green Grinch pjs.

It takes them a moment but when their eyes focus, they widen, their mouths opening in shock.

"You wore them!" Cassidy rushes forward and throws her arms around me.

"I said I would."

"I know but I figured—"

"What's all the noise out here?" Chase comes out of his room, a matching pair of pjs on, and the twins burst into giggles.

"Ah, yeah." He tugs on the bottom of his shirt where it only just covers his groin which is shrink-wrapped in green pants that only go to his shins. "They're a little small."

I have to cover my mouth to hide my grin.

"Don't you laugh." He points a finger at me. "You look like you're a little girl wearing your mom's clothes."

I do. When I let the twins shop for our matching Christmas pjs—which is a Hawkins tradition they wanted to continue—I didn't think to tell them what sizes to get. It didn't even enter my mind until we opened them last night.

They got their own and Candace's sizes right. But me and Chase? Yeah, their guesstimates were off. Way off in their brother's case. I've already made a note in my calendar to go with them next year.

"The top's not so bad." Chase tugs on his shirt again. "But I'm going to grab sweatpants before we open presents."

With a collective gasp, the twins let go of me and take off for the stairs.

"Be careful," I call after them before turning back to Chase. "Want me to get Candace or should we let her sleep?"

"Let her sleep. She was up at three." He yawns and scratches his head. "Took me an hour to get her settled again."

"Teeth?"

He nods while scrubbing both hands over his face. His shirt lifts, giving me a glimpse of washboard abs and my insides clench. "I'll, um." I point over my shoulder. "Go make sure the girls don't tear everything open before we get down there."

I spin on my heel and walk away from him, even though everything inside me wants to head toward him.

That's the other thing that's changed since we talked. I'm back to seeing him as a sexy, I want to jump him man. And with how intense my lust is, I've obviously been suppressing my attraction because there isn't a day I don't want to jump Chase—don't think about jumping him.

It makes it difficult to keep our marriage platonic. And the hardest part is I know he reciprocates my feelings. I vividly remember how it felt to have him touch me. I can't remember the last time a man touched me.

But we promised to be friends, and I can't go around wishing he'd break that promise and kiss me. I can't break it either. We have the girls to think about. They are the most important part of our patched-together family and I won't risk hurting them.

"Look at all the presents!" Crystal runs up to me the second I reach the living room. "There wasn't this many last night!"

Cassidy is busy moving presents into two piles. "I don't believe in Santa."

"Ah..."

"Then where did all this come from?" Crystal asks her, pulling things out from under the tree beside her sister now.

"Gem and Chase of course."

Cassidy is so adamant she's right. And she is, in a way. Except some of the presents wrapped beneath the tree weren't purchased by me or Chase.

They were discovered hidden away in boxes inside their parents' bedroom. The service I hired to help pack and unpack their house found them and brought them to my attention.

Chase doesn't even know about them.

And I hope I've done the right thing by wrapping them. Since I met them, I've tried to make sure none of the Hawkins children forget their parents, tried to make sure the siblings keep their memories alive and have everything their parents wanted them to.

These presents are tangible evidence of that want—of Mitch's and Sienna's love for their children.

"Hey, what's all this?" Chase asks, stopping beside me, nudging my elbow with his. "Did you buy more stuff?" he whispers so the twins don't hear.

"No." I turn to look at him, make sure his gaze is on mine

before I say, "I found them in your old house. They're from your parents."

His eyes go wide, his head whipping around to look at the brightly wrapped gifts. "You wrapped them?"

"They would want you to have them."

His hand bumps mine, then turns and grips. The hold is tight, but not painful, and I give him a reassuring squeeze.

"I can either be here with you all when you open them or make myself scarce."

The fingers laced with mine tighten. "Don't you dare go anywhere."

I can hear the emotion in his words, see it on his face, in his eyes, and when he tugs me with him toward his sisters, I go because there isn't anywhere I want to be than here with them.

Chase clears his throat. "Cass. Stell." The girls glance up and instantly stop what they're doing. "Can you guys come sit for a minute? I need to tell you something about the presents."

It's easy to see they understand the gravity of the moment. Crystal in particular, is very sensitive, and picks up on a lot of emotion in others.

And that makes me wonder if they were aware of the friction between me and their brother after all. Not that it matters now. We've moved past that and found our footing again as co-parents.

"Is this about Gem adopting us?"

Cassidy's question has Chase and I looking at each other. We told the girls of our intention when we filled out the paperwork— asked if they would be okay with it. But they haven't mentioned it since.

"No." Chase lets go of my hand and holds out both his to his sisters. "Come here."

Once they're settled on the couch either side of him, he keeps their hands in his and takes a deep breath. His gaze meets mine and I lower myself to the seat across from them. Apart but here in case they need or want me.

"When we packed up the house, Gem found some things in

Mom and Dad's room. Things they'd put aside for us." He raises an eyebrow at me, and I nod. "She knows they would want us to have those, so she kept them aside."

"Where are they?" Cassidy looks between me and her brother with curiosity, but Crystal has tears rolling down her cheeks, her glassy eyes on mine.

"You wrapped them," she whispers.

"Yes."

"And put them under the tree."

I give her a nod. I can't speak. My throat has gone tight, my gaze blurry.

"Thank you." She slips her hand from her brother's and stands up. "Will you sit with me when I open mine?"

"Of course." I hop up and move over to her. "Where do you want to sit?"

"There." She points to the pile on the left of the tree. "They're the ones with my name on them."

I put my arms around her, pull her in for a hug. "Want to unwrap now or eat breakfast first."

"It'll take too long to make—"

"I made pancakes." I cut Chase off. "They're in the oven keeping warm."

"Oh." He frowns. "Why didn't you wake me?"

"Because it was your night to get up with Candace."

"It's my night every night," he argues.

"Yes. But it's Christmas." I grin. "Merry Christmas, Chase."

His frown deepens before he says, "You better not lift a finger to clean up after we eat. You cooked so I'll do the dishes."

I don't have the heart to tell him they're mostly done. It'll just be our dishes and the platter the pancakes are on. Instead, I nod and ask, "So unwrap presents or eat?"

"Presents." The twins speak as one, but their earlier exuberance is muted now.

Pulling Crystal with me, I lower myself to the floor, legs

crossed, in front of her pile of gifts. "Let's see what you got," I say with an extra punch of excitement.

It wasn't my intention to dampen their Christmas spirit. Although I should have known getting gifts from their dead parents would. I should have waited until later, or even tomorrow to give them to them.

"Okay." Chase rubs his hands together. "Where's mine?"

"Under the tree."

"What do you mean they're under the tree?" He plants his hands on his hips and frowns. "You pulled all these out."

"Yeah, I got mine and Stell's." Cassidy shrugs.

"I see how it is." He drops to his knees and shuffles over to the tree. "I'll get mine and Gem's out while you two open yours."

"No." Cassidy grabs his arm. "Sit with me."

Crystal slides her hand into mine and holds on. I don't know if she thinks Chase will refuse her sister's request or if she just wants the connection. I'll give her comfort however she wants it so I squeeze her hand gently and reach for one of her gifts with my other hand.

"Okay, what have we got here?" I ask and place it in her lap.

"Is this one from them," she asks.

I shake my head. "No. This one is from me."

"Oh!" She lets go of my hand and rips into the wrapping.

Under the paper decorated with elves and snowmen is the newest workout gear from the Rogue sportswear for teens range. They aren't in the shops yet and when her smiling face looks up at mine, I know she recognizes them.

"You got them for me!"

"Of course. Can't have the assistant designer not having the first ones off the production line."

"Thank you!" Her arms are around me, almost choking me, but I don't care.

Today was always going to be hard. It's their first Christmas without their parents and while I've managed to keep a little bit of them here today, they are all well aware this will be the last time they will ever receive a gift from their mom or dad.

My gaze catches Chase's. He stares at me for a moment before mouthing 'thank you'. I give a small nod, it's all I can manage with Crystal's arms still wrapped around my neck.

"Hey! I got them too!" Cassidy is on her feet and the next thing I know I'm flat on my back with the girls wrapped around me.

I can't hold in my laughter. Despite the somber start, I'm positive today is going to be the best Christmas Day I've had since my own parents died. And I know, with the Hawkins siblings, every one for the rest of my life will only get better.

"Come on. Get off her." Chase tugs at his sisters. "There are more presents to unwrap, and I haven't even started yet!"

The girls are giggling now. Their joy infectious. It isn't long before the three of us are laughing and trying to tickle Chase into joining us.

When we finally give up our efforts, we're all out of breath and lying on the floor.

And when a hand brushes mine and I look down, I see Chase reaching out. Taking his hand, I look up and find his eyes on me. There's so many emotions swirling in the deep blue depths. Too many for me to decipher. But it doesn't matter what he's feeling right now.

What matters is that we're in this together.

CHASE

If I wasn't in love with Gem before Christmas I certainly am after.

She made what could have been a very difficult few days into a happy time even if there were tears shed.

Mom and Dad had obviously been preparing for her not living to see Christmas because with each of our gifts was a letter. They are written in Mom's hand, but I can tell they both had input. And I think if we were given the notes and presents before, when Gem first became aware of them, it would have torn us all to ribbons.

But with the months between us and losing them, with Gem at our sides, we were able to accept the heartfelt words and gifts from our parents with as much happiness as sadness.

And it's her thoughtfulness, her ability to understand and know what we need, that has me more in love with her.

But the holidays have been and gone months ago. It's now mid-February and life is great. Except for one thing.

I'm in love with my wife and she doesn't have a clue.

"Hey!" With a big grin on his face, Gannon Byrd pops in front of the treadmill I'm running on.

I'm breathing hard, too hard to talk, so I tip up my chin in greeting.

"Can I ask you something?" His grin doesn't slip exactly but he's definitely unsure about his question. Or maybe it's the answer.

Reaching up, I press a few buttons, and the treadmill begins to slow beneath my feet. I've been running for over an hour, which is more than my usual daily run, but after the indulgences of the holidays I need to work a little harder to burn off all those extra calories.

Besides, the extra exercise has helped my game. In the last few months, I've only let in a handful of goals. Which puts the Rogues firmly in the top spot in our conference.

Gannon waits until I'm at a brisk walk before talking again. "So, I heard something, and I'm not sure if you're aware of it or not or if maybe I've misinterpreted the situation."

"Okay."

"I thought you were taking care of your sisters."

I frown. "I am."

"Yeah, I get that but..." His frown matches mine.

"Just spit it out." My tone is a little harsh, but I don't have time for this circling around what he wants to ask thing.

"I heard you live with the Rogues GM, Natalie Redding."

"We do."

"So, you're what?" His left eyebrow rises, his face twisting in confusion now. "Dating the GM?"

"No." I don't elaborate. I want to say no, we're married, have been for three months, but that's a taboo subject, even between me and Gem.

"But you live together?"

"We share a house because she helps me with my sisters."

"Like friends?" Confusion is still written all over his face and I want to laugh except the situation isn't funny.

It's become downright depressing if I'm honest. The woman I'm in love with, the one I'm married to, is nothing more than...

"Yes. We're friends."

"Huh."

"Do you have a problem with that?"

"What? No! It's just, the way Lindberg talked I thought maybe you two were together."

"We're raising my sisters together." When his eyebrows rise into his hair, I explain. "We're all that's left of our family. I'm the only adult the girls have to take care of them. Gem offered to help me by becoming their second guardian."

"Ah...okay." He shakes his head. "Sorry. It's just that I've seen the two of you since I was traded in and I have to say, as a stranger, it looks like more than that."

"Is Lindberg the only one talking about it?" I'd hate it if the team was talking behind my back. And Gem would...I don't know how she'd react if people were gossiping about us, but I know she would not be happy.

"Yeah. He told me all about the players and staff. Before the trade. Before I told him I'd be interested in playing down here."

"That makes sense." To change the subject I ask, "So how do you like it here? Happy you made the move?"

"Yeah." He reaches up and fingers the ring that hangs from a chain around his neck. "I left some things behind, but I'll get those here soon enough and then there's nothing tying me to New York."

"Things?"

"Just a few. One." He turns away and swallows and I don't know if I should push him but before I can he turns back and offers me another grin. "I'll catch you later."

He's gone before I can switch off the machine. "Well, that was weird."

"Who are you talking to, Hawkins?"

Stepping off the treadmill, I spin in Coach Alcott's direction. "No one. Just muttering to myself."

"Did I see Gannon in here?"

"Yep. He just left."

"Dammit. I was hoping to catch up with him." He rubs at his jaw. "He's been here weeks and other than yelling at him on the ice, I think we've said four words to each other."

"Oh?"

He eyes me. "Oh, you probably aren't aware. He's my best friend. Since college. Not sure why he's avoiding me."

"Probably finding the shift from best friend-teammate to best friend-player-coach hard."

"Yeah, I guess that could be it. Although it feels like he's avoiding me."

My watch beeps. "Is there anything you need me for? I need to get changed and pick up Candace."

"No. Only came in to see if I could catch Gannon."

"Okay. I'll see you tomorrow."

"You ready for it?"

"As ever."

"Can we expect another—"

"Don't say it." I shake my head. I'm not superstitious but I know a lot of guys are. "You know better than that."

He grins. "I do. But you know I'm wishing for it."

"You and me both. And, like always, I'll do my best to make both our wishes come true."

"Thanks." He claps my shoulder then heads off the way he came.

I grab a towel and wipe the sweat from my face. I'm about to get another to clean the equipment when one of the equipment guys rushes in.

"I've got it."

I smile. It's so different having people clean up after me. I've always done it myself. Even in college when some of the younger guys were assigned the job of keeping the school gym clean, I preferred to do it myself.

Of course, as Gem pointed out when I mentioned it to her, doing it here means I'm taking someone's job. "Thanks."

"There are fresh towels in the locker room." He holds out his hand for the one I'm slinging around my neck.

"Yeah, okay." I lower my arm and drop it into his outstretched hand. "Didn't want to drip over the floor on the way there."

"Don't worry about that. Cash has that job this week."

I smile.

When Gem told me Coach Watts' nephew was going to be working for the team the rest of the season while staying with his aunt and uncle, I was confused. He's only a year or so older than the twins. But she quickly pointed out he's homeschooled, and it doesn't matter where he is, he can still attend school.

He's a good kid. Works hard when he's here. Keeps to himself though. I don't know the story, but I heard his mom recently got sick—too sick to care for her teenage son—so he's spending a year with his dad.

Mason Watts is a legend. Like his father before him and his brother Sutton after him. Actually, the whole family are legends. Coach Watts has Olympic Gold and now she owns a team in the NHL. The same league her younger brothers play in.

Yeah, the Watts family is hockey royalty and I'm sure Cash being here is part of his grooming to follow in his family's footsteps.

My watch beeps again and I quicken my pace. I need to get that shower and change so I'm not late grabbing Candace.

The locker room is empty when I get there and I strip off in front of my bag, leaving my gear on the floor, and head for the showers. It's always weird being in here alone. The quiet. It's rare too. Working out extra these last few months means I'm often the only one using the facilities in the afternoons.

Unless it's a home game day. Then the guys are in here prepping for the game.

Aware of how close I'm cutting it, I don't waste time washing off. I want to get Candace and be home before the twins get there. We're quickly heading toward the final weeks of the regular season and at this point there's no way we're missing a spot in the playoffs.

Which means less time with the girls because there isn't a chance in hell I'm going to sit on my ass and cruise through the games. Nope. I'm going to pull out all the stops and that means extra training.

Shutting off the water, I grab a towel and rub myself dry. I'm so used to being in the locker room without clothes on that it doesn't even occur to me to wrap the towel around my waist when I'm done.

That's why I find myself walking, dick swinging, through the middle of an empty room when the door opens.

Gem, head down, gaze on her phone walks in, talking as she lifts her eyes. "Hey, I've got to stay—"

Her words stop. Her feet stop.

As the door swishes shut behind her, she stares at me like I'm a alien who's here to abduct her.

And my dick gets hard instantly.

It always does when she's around, or I think of her, so most of the time I'm sporting at least a semi. But in the interest of keeping us on the track we set months ago, before Christmas—the friends track—I brazen it out and pretend like I'm not standing in front of her naked, dick now at full attention.

"Hey. What's up?" I keep walking to my bag, bend over and rummage around for my underwear. I come up with my shirt first. That'll do.

I've got my arms in the sleeves, above my head when I realize she still hasn't spoken. I glance at her, find her gaze glued to my bare butt, and try to hide my smile.

Oh, yeah, we might say we're just friends but the way she's looking at my ass as though she wants to take a bite out of it says different.

"You okay?" I ask. Keeping my arms above my head, eyes on her, I turn. "Gem? Did you want something?"

"I, um," she stammers when she's faced with a full frontal,

and I sink my teeth into the inside of my cheek to keep from grinning.

There have been days when I thought the only thing I'd ever have with this woman is what we have now. A marriage on paper only and parenting responsibilities of my sisters. But seeing her speechless as she checks me out—stares at my dick—tells me there's hope.

Hope I never imagined was more than wishful thinking—and a million fantasies envisioned while getting myself off.

But that look, the way she's swallowing repeatedly and can't seem to get a word out says I can do more than hope.

I can plan.

"Gem?" I duck my head and slip my shirt over it. Pulling it down my torso I don't care that it gets caught up on my hard dick. Or that she can't take her eyes off it. "Did you want something?"

"Um. Yes. I..." She swallows again, then licks her bottom lip and my dick twitches at the thought of her using that tongue on me.

I turn and dive back into my bag, this time coming up with my underwear. And because I'm more than happy to torture us both, I drop them on the bench next to my bag and go searching for my shorts.

"Do you, um." In my peripheral vision I see her shake her head. "Sorry. A lot on my mind. Do you want me to get Candace? I have a conference call later that I'll take at home so I can have dinner with the girls."

Shorts in hand, I turn to face her. "I was going to get her and be home when the twins are. I want to spend some time with them before playoffs start."

"That's weeks away."

"Not many." And because I'm enjoying this moment, I put my hands on my hips, my long fingers pointing to my erect dick. "And we both know we're making them."

She holds up a hand, fingers crossed.

"Don't need that."

Her mouth turns up in a small smile. "So confident."

"Shouldn't I be? We're playing great hockey. *I'm* playing great hockey. The best of the season. Things seem to have gotten better since Byrd came on board."

"Yes. You are. The team is. Especially Byrd."

"I hate saying it, but Lindberg getting traded back to New York was a definite win for us."

She looks at her phone when it rings. "I need to take this."

I nod. I still haven't put my pants on and at this point I don't think I will until she leaves the locker room. "I'll get Candace."

"I'll still be home early."

"All right. Maybe we can head out for dinner. Give the girls a treat before we get busier than busy with the end of season and the playoffs."

"Sounds good." Her gaze drops and I realize since she started talking again her eyes haven't dipped below my chin. "I'll, um... Okay, I need to go."

She spins on her heel and yanks the door open. And just because I'm having more fun and feeling more hopefully than I have in months when it comes to my wife I call out, "Hey, Gem?"

When she twists her head around her gaze is already angling down and I grin. "Y-yes."

"Thanks for offering to pick up Candace." It's a bullshit state-ment. I stopped thanking her for helping with the girls at Christ-mas, but it's all that comes to mind to get her attention on me again.

"Of course." She frowns, her hand on the door handle. "You're enjoying this, aren't you?"

I grin full on now. "Oh yeah, totally loving it."

She lets out a huffed laugh. "Put some pants on and go get our girl."

My laughter follows her into the hallway. And I'm still smiling when I'm dressed and shouldering my bag.

My wife is not unaffected by me.

It's a revelation and a salvation. Because if I had to keep living with this unrequited attraction bullshit, I'd die from blue balls.

Now, instead of sneaking in a tug session with my wife as inspiration making me feel guilty, I can do it with the knowledge that she's probably—hopefully—doing the same.

NAT

I have never considered myself a coward. I would even go so far as saying I'm fearless.

But even I have to admit my belly has been yellow in recent weeks.

Six weeks to be exact.

Six weeks since I got the show of my life and saw Chase—my husband—in all his spectacularly naked glory.

And obviously my cowardliness has started to attract the attention of others because right now Oakley is in my office, a scowl on her face, hands on her hips.

Everything about her posture says she's here to do battle.

Except in the minute she's been in the room she hasn't said a word. Not one. She's just stared at me through narrowed eyes.

And I'm starting to squirm.

Again, not something I would have done before now.

"Are you here to just stare at me or are you working up to whatever it is you want to yell at me about?" I ask, the urge to stand strong, but I keep my seat.

She might be one of my closest friends, one of a few I can be vulnerable in front of, but I'm not ready to admit anything to anyone yet. I'm barely acknowledging my lack of spine to myself.

The only response I get is an arched eyebrow.

With a sigh, I lean back in my chair. "Come on. I don't have all day to play charades or guess what or whatever the hell this is, Oakley."

"Sorry I'm late! I had to pee!" Cami rushes through the door, her rounded belly barely noticeable to anyone who doesn't know she's pregnant. "Oh, I'm not the last one here!" She grins.

"Nope. That's me." Blake rounds out this little pow-wow I wasn't warned about. Closing my door behind herself, she heads for my desk.

I watch as my three best friends—my business partners—line up, shoulder to shoulder on the other side of my desk. They're a unit. It doesn't escape me that normally I'd be standing right next to them.

"Okay. What's going on?" I lean forward, press my forearms to my desk and eye each of them. "I'm unaware of a meeting…"

I let the words hang to see if any of them picks them up but all I get is varying degrees of emotion.

Oakley seems the most irritated. Blake is more disappointed, I think. And Cami? Well, she isn't angry at all. If I had to guess I'd say she was happy with the situation. Whatever the hell that is.

"Out with it!" I tip my chin up, ready to take whatever they throw at me.

"You know what I'm going to say." A flash of disappointment fills Oakley's gaze before she goes on. "I don't need to tell you what your role in this organization is. *You* chose it."

"General Manager. And yes, I chose it. And I'm doing it." I indicate the papers spread out on my desk.

"No. You're hiding behind paperwork to avoid a certain player." My gaze darts to Cami. "You forget, I might not be here day to day, but I have insider knowledge neither of these two get."

She grins. Actually grins!

"I have no idea what you're talking about." I try the ignorant route, it seems the best course of evasion at the moment.

"Ha!" Blake points a finger at me. "You may as well have said, yes, Cami, you are correct. I am avoiding a certain player."

"How do you figure that?"

It's Oakley who answers my question. "Because you didn't *ask* what she was talking about, you said you had no idea."

I stare at Oakley. "I fail to see the difference."

"The difference is not wanting to talk about it and not knowing what it is." Cami's words have me shaking my head.

"I'm sure that makes sense to you but I—"

"Cut the crap, Nat. And get your ass out of this office. I want to see you at the games, home and away, in the locker room, the occasional drop in at training," Blake says.

"I don't need to—"

"Wrong. And it isn't about you anyway, it's about the team, and everyone, players to the front receptionist, knows you've pulled away."

"Pulled away from what? Getting in the way of everyone trying to do their jobs?"

"You never got in the way."

"That was in the beginning, when we were building the team. Now we're established, winning more than losing, and I don't need to be as hands on."

Oakley looks to the side, Blake and Cami turning her way. "She's not going to break."

"Then we'll make her." Blake's words have me sitting straighter.

"What does that mean?"

"You will be at every game for the rest of the season. Every game of the playoffs. And you will bring Chase's sisters with you."

Oh. The tension in my shoulders dissolves as the true meaning of her demand falls into place.

"Yeah, now you're getting it." Blake's smile is soft. "This is a season for the record books. Our inaugural season and we're going to the finals, and Chase and his sisters deserve you to put whatever has you holed up in here aside so they can experience it together."

"And don't forget, they have to get through the anniversaries soon," Cami adds. "The twins told Whitney they are worried Chase might not be able to concentrate because of them."

I glance at the calendar on my desk. "Dammit," I mutter. The anniversary of their father's death is only days away. Their mother's right behind it. I can't believe I've been so wrapped up in my own problem I forgot about this important—gut-wrenching—milestone the Hawkins' siblings have to face.

"This isn't like you, Nat. What's really going on?" Oakley asks.

I could tell them, reveal the reason I'm hiding out is because when I'm not, when I see Chase—think about him—my brain turns to pile of lust slush. But I can't. "I don't want to be a distraction."

"Or you don't want him to be a distraction?" Cami asks. She puts up a hand. "Don't say it isn't about Chase. The twins might not fully understand the undercurrent running between you and their brother at home, but they aren't blind to it."

My back straightens, my stomach churns. "What are they saying?"

"You and Chase are weird around each other. It's not like the weird you two had going on before Christmas but it's not the family vibe you had going after it either."

I'm sure what Cami is saying makes sense. And to a pair of teenagers, young teenagers at that, they wouldn't—shouldn't—be able to tell the weird behavior is sexual tension.

Since the day I walked in on Chase in the locker room wearing nothing but a smile, my libido has kicked into overdrive. I don't go a day without thinking about jumping him.

Who am I kidding?

It's an hourly struggle.

"Okay, now that we have you thinking, and have reminded you what we expect the GM of the Rogues organization to do, we can get out of your hair and let you do it." Oakley grins at me. Then with a wink she says, "And if you need to *do it* to get things back on track, do that too."

Cami snickers behind a hand.

Blake's lips twitch but she spent so long keeping her thoughts off her face so the opposition couldn't read her that she holds firm.

Oakley though, is cackling like a loon.

And I can't help it. My lips tug up and I'm smiling wide as I watch two of my best friends attempt to hold in their mirth while the other lets it run free.

These women are my people.

It's been the four of us against the world for over a decade and in that time, we've gotten degrees, won gold medals, taken a start-up company from the ground to global success, and shaken up the male-dominated arena of professional hockey with a winning team.

"Is this intervention over?" I ask. "Do you all have time to go get lunch?"

"A working lunch?" Cami asks.

"No. Just lunch. Maybe a bottle of wine...okay, no wine for you," I say, my gaze on Cami's midsection.

"Yeah, so, no wine for me either." With a frown, Oakley raises a hand. "I think."

"What?" "You're pregnant?" Cami and Blake lunge for Oakley as they speak.

I take my time getting out of my chair and moving around my desk. "You think?" I question.

"I haven't done a test. But I'm late. We've been trying. We love Micky so much and watching him with Drew and Candace..." She shakes her head. "We want him to have siblings. We never want him to be alone again."

Tears shimmer in her eyes and like we've done too many times to count we move in for a group hug.

"He'll never be alone again. He has all of us. Just like Whitney, Cassidy, Crystal, and Candace, he's part of our family now. We might not share blood, but we share something better. We chose to love each other." Cami's voice is coated in tears.

"We know. We still want him to have siblings. Cousins are fun too, but we want him to have brothers and sisters."

"Hell, woman, you don't even know if you're pregnant for sure and you're talking more than one? Of each?"

Oakley laughs. "I want at least four."

"You do not!" Blake says.

"I do. I always wanted a sister and brother. I have you girls but when I was younger, it was just me at home. I want the big family I never had but always envied." Her watery gaze lands on Blake.

"Well, as the only one of us qualified to talk about what it's like to grow up in a big family, I can say it's a love-hate thing. But yes, I want what I had growing up, Bran does too. I'd like Drew to be out of diapers and sleeping through the night before we try for another, but I'm not getting any younger and Mom and Dad are talking about staying down here more often now that Mason is thinking of moving to Baton Rouge permanently with Cash." Blake shrugs.

Cami pulls back with a gasp. "I just realized, well except for Nat and she kind of is, we're all moms now!"

"Er..." Three sets of eyes land on me. I haven't told them I adopted the girls. Didn't even mention I was doing it.

Cami raises a hand, index finger out, and draws circles it the air in front of my face. "What's that?"

"What?"

"That look on your face."

"I, um..."

"You're pregnant!" Oakley grabs my arm.

"Oh lord." Blake's eyes pop wide.

"No! I'm not pregnant." I roll my eyes and laugh. "Unless it's an immaculate conception."

"Oh." Oakley pouts. "I thought we could have babies together."

"No. I have a baby. She's almost one."

"You..." Cami tips her head. "Wait, wait, something the twins said... Oh! I know! You're their legal guardian, same as their brother."

"Kind of. He's their guardian. I adopted them."

"All of them?" Blake asks. "Not just Candace?"

"All of them. Chase wanted them to have security. And with no other relatives, if something happens to him..." I shudder.

"The only thing happening to that man is he's going to keep our goals against low and get us through the Cup finals." Blake's fierceness blazes in her eyes. "We will play for the Cup. I feel it in here." She palms her chest.

"Beck is pretty sure they've got what it takes to go all the way to the finals."

"Walker agrees. Although he doesn't talk about it much. I don't think he wants to jinx anything."

"I've been studying the other teams. We've got a better than most shot at the Cup. Although, like Coach, I'm not ready to proclaim we're getting it. I'll be happy with making it to postseason," I say.

"We're already guaranteed that," Blake says. "Even if we lose—"

Oakley slaps a hand over Blake's mouth. "Hush!"

"I know." I grin. "So, lunch?"

"Let's do it. I'm starving." Cami rubs her belly. "And I'm eating for two now so not somewhere with healthy salad. I want a burger and fries."

"Frankie's!" The rest of us say.

"Oh, yeah." Cami looks down at her hand where it rests on her unborn child. "Little Bit, you're going to love Frankie's."

"Little Bit?" I ask.

Cami chuckles. "Yes. Whitney keeps asking how big her baby brother is, and Beck kept saying 'a little bit bigger than last time you asked', and I thought it was the perfect way to refer to this one seeing how we are not finding out what we're having."

"So, she's not asking about a brother because you found out?" Oakley asks. "But I thought you were going to find out."

"Changed our minds. Life has so few good surprises. This one is the goodest of the good."

"Is goodest a word?"

Cami eyes me with a raised brow. "Does it matter?"

I shake my head. "No. What matters is getting you and Little Bit fed."

Sliding her arm through mine, she says, "Let's go. We can take my car seeing how I won't be drinking any wine."

"I can drive too." Oakley grins.

"Nope, I'll drive." Cami steers me out of my office. "We've got a stop to make on the way."

"Oh?" Oakley follows us, Blake behind her.

"Yes. You need to know for sure, so first we head to a drug store for a pregnancy test. If you'd told me before I drove here, I could have brought you one of the ones I have at home."

"Why do you have them at home?"

"Because once I figured out I could be pregnant, Beck bought every brand the drug store had on the shelf."

"Bex bought them?" Blake laughs. "Lord, I can see it. That tall streak of serious standing there trying to work out which one to get. It would have taken him a good ten minutes to give up making a decision and toss them all in his basket."

"Yep." Cami grins. "According to Whitney, that's pretty much how it went down."

We're all laughing as we leave my office. And even though I'm still worried about how I feel about Chase, I'm glad my best friends pushed me to confront my behavior. It doesn't matter that I haven't figured out what to do, because regardless of what I do do, I know these three women will be at my side.

Like they have been from the day I met them.

CHASE

Game six in the last round of playoffs. Win this and we win the series—and play for the Cup.

I'm not surprised we're here, or that we've dominated every series in postseason before this one. I don't know if it's the hunger in us to prove we've got what it takes to reach the finals or if the chemistry between us is just that good.

We've hardly made a mistake. Our games have been flawless and that says a lot about our coaches as well as us players.

Nobody wants to slack off. We're training harder than we have all year, and we trained hard from the beginning.

All season we've been under the microscope. Every member of the team—the org itself—has received a lot of attention. Conversations with a Rogue have added to the usual media frenzy around a winning team.

We were dealing with it—I was comfortable with it—until it was my turn to have a conversation with Cami. When that episode aired, when I talked openly about the death of my parents and the choice I made at twenty to raise my three younger sisters, the media went stupid.

At one point I thought we might have a repeat of the craziness surrounding Whit and Bex. But thankfully, the worst we had was a couple of photographers trying to sneak pictures of the girls coming and going from school and the arena.

I'm pretty sure Gem had something to do with them stopping. She and Cami's father, Fenton Barnes, had their heads together at the Rogues end of season party far too often for me to ignore the timing of our sort-of stalkers stopping.

I can't lie. Playing through the anniversaries of our parents' deaths wasn't easy. And I had to remind myself repeatedly that I was living the life they always wanted me to live. It helped.

It helped even more when the twins decided to celebrate our parents by cooking their favorite meals and talking about good times spent together every night for the month of April.

We cried. How could we not?

We laughed. Because we'd had a great childhood with wonderful parents.

And we felt so much better than we would have because Gem, with her calm and understanding, her insightful words of wisdom, was there every step of the way.

Honestly, dancing around my attraction for my wife when I know she's not oblivious to my appeal has been the hardest thing to deal with in the last few months.

Whatever had her pulling away back in February—and I'm fairly sure it was the locker room incident—ceased to be an issue by the end of March. A few days before the back-to-back anniversaries of our parents' deaths, the Gem who guided me and my sisters through the first Christmas without our parents was back.

Every game, home or away, she and the girls cheered from the box or seats behind the bench. It was surreal to have them rink-side. And hilarious because Gem bought Candace a pair of pink fluffy noise canceling headphones to wear. Of course, my baby sister spent most of the time yanking them off.

And the twins weren't to be left out. They convinced Gem they needed matching pairs. Although they never actually wore theirs either. They spent the games with them wrapped around their necks instead of on their heads. Not that I care. Those bright pink puffs make it easy to find them in the crowd.

Crouched in front of the net, my gaze darts to where I know the girls and Gem are. They're jumping up and down, yelling out who knows what, each of them—except Gem—with my name and number on the back of their team jersey, pink headphones around their necks—including Candace—and I grin.

I love having them with me my first season in the league.

And Gem has made sure they've been on every step of this history-making ride with me, homeschooling the twins with the help of Deanne Harper of all people.

She hired Mrs. Harper to homeschool the children of any players who wanted their families traveling with the team for the playoffs. It's working so well she's talking about offering her a full-time position for the entire school year.

Pulling my gaze back to the game, I focus in on the play. We're a goal up but only because Vegas scored for us. Caron's attempt to clear the puck hit the back of his own teammate and ricocheted into the very place he'd been trying to avoid.

That was two minutes ago. And the puck has been up and down the ice non-stop for those two minutes. Back and forth, back and forth, no one able to make a break and get it close to either goal.

Which is fine with me. Although, I know I can't get complacent. They'll be gunning for me, hungry to even the score.

Especially Caron. He's got a point to prove now.

Even as I think it, Caron breaks free with the puck and heads my way. One of the league's top scoring centers, he has a look on his face that says stopping him is going to take everything I have. It's crazy, but I know this one is going to test me like nothing else has all game.

It's in the way he moves, the way he seems to vibrate on his blades.

Byrd gets in his way, and at first, I think he's got him, but then the puck shoots out and Caron zips around Byrd like he's standing still and with what looks like a gentle sweep of his stick, collects the puck and has control again as though he never lost it.

The guy is a master, and I heard a rumor he signed with New York for next season. But right now, he's playing for Vegas and like the rest of us, he doesn't care what team's jersey he wears as long as he wears one and gets to play. And in this second, his sole focus is keeping his Cup dreams alive this year.

He's closer now, a bunch of Rogues and Vegas players closing in as well. The puck comes at me, and I deflect, only for it to come back again. And again.

It's almost too fast for the eye to follow and I know I'm barely keeping ahead of the play because I'm good at guarding my goal.

There's a tussle for the puck, two Rogues and a couple of Vegas wingers. Bodies are contorting and one is going down...

And before I see it, the puck is behind me, the light on the top of my goal going off and the crowd going wild.

My gaze zips to the Jumbotron above center ice and I watch the replays while Vegas celebrates evening up the game. I study every second of those clips and once they finish showing them, I know there was no way I could have stopped that one.

It was a brilliant goal. I might be disappointed I let it slip past, but I'm not mad at myself. Even if I was perfect, I didn't stand a chance against that one.

Both teams are over by their benches, the game stalled to allow for a commercial break, and I look down the ice to see my counterpart has his water bottle in hand and is skating toward his teammates.

My gaze goes to our bench—to Coach. He's shaking his head. And I don't understand until things get moving again.

Vegas pulled their goalie.

I search out the clock, see we're less than a minute out from the end of the game and I know why the goal I'm staring at is unguarded.

Vegas doesn't want to win in overtime. They want to score

now. Put them one up tonight and even the series. Force us into another showdown.

The play is crazy, Vegas is pushing up, all players with only one purpose, to sink the puck they have control of into my net.

It. Isn't. Happening.

I don't need to see the looks on any of the Rogues' faces. I know they're all set with determination. Single-minded resolve. Keep the game even and go into overtime, or if the chance arises, get the puck down to that open net.

Every man on the ice is converging on me and I'm sweating more than I have all game. But I'm not going to be the man that forces us into another game this series.

The players are bunching up, to the side against the boards, then right in front of me, and I hold my breath and concentrate on the little black disc no one seems to be able to get control of. It's like watching a group of five-year-olds trying to work out how to use their sticks.

Bodies move as one until they separate just enough to leave a gap barely big enough to see the other end of the ice. Then it gets bigger. A split second later that black disc appears.

And I don't think. Just react.

Pulling back, I slap that thing out the far side of the gap.

I should get back in position. Guard my house. But I'm standing straight. My gaze aimed down the ice, following a puck that is making a beeline for the other end of the rink.

And that open goal.

I don't think I hit it that hard. But it's traveling so fast the players in front of me haven't even worked out it's gone.

Half a second later the goal lamp lights up and I've done something few goalies do.

I've scored a goal.

In the dying seconds of game six in the last series of the play-offs, I scored a goal.

Giving the Rogues a ticket to play for the Cup.

"Holy fudge sticks!"

Bex is on me. Yelling, "We're playing for the Cup!" in my ear. The weight of him sends me off balance and we topple to the ice.

Then everyone in on us. Bran, Mikel, Tasman, and Gannon. More weight piles on and I think the whole team is on top of me.

Bex's face is in mine and next thing I know, he's grabbing my helmet and giving it a shake. "We're going to the Cup!"

"Holy fudge sticks!"

"I think you can say holy fucking shit right now, Chase," Bran laughs. "The kids aren't out here yet but they're coming."

I turn my head and through the arms and legs and torsos and gear, I see what he means. Everyone is pouring onto the ice. Is the game even over? I don't remember hearing the horn.

It has to be though. No one would be out here if it wasn't.

I see the girls before Gem. The twins have Candace with them, and I push up, shoving guys off me so I can get to my feet—get to them. I don't want any of them slipping on the ice.

Out from under my teammates I see the ice is full of people. And the crowd on the other side of the glass is going crazy. I can't hold back the grin. Don't want to. I just put us in the Cup final!

This is why we moved. Why I trusted a stranger to help me make my dream of playing in the NHL a reality.

Cass launches herself at me and I catch her. Spin her around. Stell, with Candace on her hip, arrives at a slightly more sedate pace but she's still moving faster than I want on the slippery surface.

"Here. Give her to me."

I reach for Candace, scoop her against my side and throw my other arm around Stell. Lifting her off her feet, I give them the same treatment I gave Cass. And when I put Stell back on her feet, Cass presses against my front.

"You won!"

I nod. Because suddenly the moment is sinking in. I scored a goal. Won the game that puts us within touching distance of the Cup.

"You scored a goal!" Stell looks at me with astonishment and I have to admit, I'm feeling the same.

"Crazy, right?"

"I told you you'd break more records."

Cass's words have me turning my head and that's when I see Gem. She's a few steps away, congratulating each member of the team as she draws closer to us.

Every instinct I have wants to kiss my wife. It's insane how sharp the need is. Except I can't. She's the reason I'm here. The reason I was able to make that record breaking, game winning goal, and I can't do more than say thank you.

Maybe give her a hug.

It sucks.

And when she's right in front of me and I see the desire in her eyes I almost say fuck it and crush her to me.

But I know it wouldn't be a good move. Especially with the media capturing everything.

In spite of the gnawing need in my gut, I reach out and pull her close for a hug. Candace is between us, her small body blocking mine from Gem's and that's probably a good thing.

"Congrats! I'm so proud of you, Chase." Her words are a whisper in my ear, and I tip my head so I can whisper in hers.

"You have no idea how much I want to kiss you right now."

Her body jolts but she doesn't pull away. She doesn't speak either. But her arms around me tighten and I take that as a good sign. An acknowledgment of the want and need brewing between us.

It's been building for weeks. Months.

Less than a year ago I had no idea who this woman was. Now she's my boss, my co-parenting partner, my housemate—my wife.

Without her I wouldn't be standing here. Wouldn't be heading for the Cup final.

And I wouldn't be surrounded by hundreds of people sporting a hard on beneath my uniform.

NAT

Three a.m. and the party doesn't look like it's winding down any time soon.

But the players deserve to celebrate. They put their all into the Rogues from the first day they strapped on skates and stepped out onto the practice rink in Rogue Arena.

My gaze lands on Chase.

He has had a few too many drinks and it's obvious he's not used to drinking alcohol. He looks confused a lot, especially when he stumbles or sways. And he's come close a couple times in the last hour to outing our marriage.

Right now, he's talking with a couple of the younger players, the ones that appear to have also had a few too many in spite of the fact I know they're underage. Not that any reasonable law enforcement officer would charge them. Not tonight.

Chase shakes his head, his gaze moving in my direction. His face lights up with a grin and he heads my way. As he gets closer the twinkle in his eyes has me on alert.

When he's close enough to speak, he murmurs, "My whiff," and I know it's time to extricate ourselves—him—from the room.

Oakley is still here with Walker. Hours ago, after Pa left with a sleeping Micky over his shoulder, they promised to stay until the last person wobbled back to their hotel room.

Blake's already gone, slipping out with Drew, leaving Bran to celebrate with his teammates. Not that he lasted more than thirty minutes after she left.

Two hours ago, Whitney convinced the twins to leave with her. She's staying with Cami's parents at the house they own here in Vegas. And Candace is tucked up in bed. Deanne Harper and her daughter Melody volunteered to babysit and took her back to their room right after the game.

I told Chase I'd take care of the girls tonight, let him enjoy the celebration with his teammates. He protested, said I had as much right to celebrate as he did, but I promised I'd have a drink with my three partners another night.

Tonight is about the players and their families. Management can have their own gathering once we return to Baton Rouge.

I notice the older Rogues have taken it easy, while the younger ones are no doubt going to feel it in the morning.

Good thing Coach Alcott gave everyone tomorrow off.

They'd better take advantage of it too. Because he and Coach Watts are planning to push them harder than they have so far. And that's saying something because I think they've been training all day, every day since the final games of the regular season weeks ago.

The smile on my face widens when Chase leans toward me making him sway.

A dopey grin on his face, he says, "I tinks I dunk."

Laughing, I say, "Yes. I tinks you dunk too."

"Lie down?" His knees bend and I jump forward, lift his arm and tuck myself under it. His face press into my hair and I go still when he sucks in a breath causing air to rush by my ear, and murmurs, "Yum."

He drags out the word and a shiver trickles down my spine, warmth pooling in my core. "Come on, let's get you to bed."

We're sharing a suite—as we usually do when I bring the girls to away games. Except tonight there aren't any children to play buffer. Good thing he's stumbling drunk. It'll be easy to resist him when he's under the influence.

And after the heated looks he's been sending me all night, I'm surprised nothing in the room has caught fire.

I'm on fire, I know that. Every glance my way has left a scorching trail of desire in its wake.

"Need help with him?"

I turn my head to find Beckett and Cami beside me, and sigh with relief. "Would you? He's heavier than he looks."

Cami laughs. "He looks heavy, Nat."

I send her a smile and move out from under Chase's arm as Beckett positions himself under the other one so he can take over. "Thanks. We're on the same floor as you."

"Are you going to stay down here?" Cami asks.

"No. Oakley and Walker agreed to supervise the rest of the night." I glance at my watch. "Not that there's much of it left."

"This lot will keep going until they fall down like this one," Beckett says with a smile as he gives Chase a little shake. "All the smarter guys have already gone to bed."

"Good thing no one needs to get up early. I rescheduled our flight back to late afternoon, so they can celebrate for as long as they last." I push the ballroom door open so Beckett can drag a passed-out Chase through. And at this point he is dragging him. "Should I see if there's a wheelchair or something?"

"Nah, I've got it." Beckett glances at Cami. "He's not that heavy, even if he is a dead weight."

The elevator is right outside the ballroom, so it's relatively quick and easy for us to get him inside and up to our floor. The walk down the corridor is a little slower. Mainly because both Chase's shoes come off at different times as Beckett drags him toward our suite.

By the time I get the door open and we maneuver him inside, we're all laughing because his socks are now hanging off making his feet look comically long.

"Do you think the hotel would give us the security footage of our trek?" Cami asks grinning. "I'm sure Chase would love to see how he got back to his room."

"No." I frown at her. "We are not acquiring hotel security footage."

"Shame. We could have used it to embarrass him at the party the twins are planning to have this summer."

I stop short. "What party?"

"Oh. Um..." Her gaze bounces around the room.

"*Cami...*" I give her the look that gets the twins to spill when they're trying to hide something.

"Fine. But don't tell them I said anything. Maybe pretend you found their notebook with their planning lists."

"Okay, this is sounding worse by the second."

"No. It's not. It's really sweet actually."

I eye my friend. "You think what they're planning is sweet?"

"Yes. They feel bad because Chase didn't get a party to celebrate signing with the Rogues. Or for his twenty-first birthday. Their parents would have put together a big bash for both. Cassidy and Crystal want to do it for their brother because they can't."

"Well, shit." I completely overlooked Chase's birthday last year. It was right before preseason and everyone was getting used to the new facility and team, new routines, their new city.

"We should get that footage."

"No! And I'm surprised you of all people are suggesting it."

Cami's face flushes red. "I thought it would be funny."

"Have to agree with Natalie. Not sure why you came up with the idea. One of the guys, sure, but you." Beckett shakes his head. "Nope."

"Is Chase in bed?" I ask Beckett.

"Yeah. Threw a cover over him." He pointedly looks at my hands. "Didn't need to remove his shoes."

"No." I drop the shoes beside the couch. "He took care of that. Thanks for helping."

"I'm sure you would have managed without me." Beckett reaches for Cami and slips his arm around her. "I'm going to get these two to bed, but if you need anything, help with Chase, let us know."

"Thank you, I'm sure we'll be fine. Hopefully he'll sleep until morning."

"He should. Although, I'm not sure he drank all that much. Everyone kept handing him a drink to toast his series winning goal, but I never saw him actually finish one of them."

"Hmm..." I glance over at the room Beckett put Chase in. My room. I guess we're switching. "Hopefully he won't be too hungover tomorrow then."

"Buzz when he's awake. I want to do a quick interview with him," Cami says.

"I'll ask him."

"No. I want the rough edges. The rawness of the morning after a big win and celebration." She smiles. "I plan to grab a few words with all the guys tomorrow."

"Okay. But maybe start with the one you're sleeping with."

"Come on, you." Beckett tugs her toward the door. "No more work tonight."

Once they're through the door, I say, "Thanks again. See you both later." And when it closes behind them, I take a deep breath and turn to face the room.

Beckett mistaking my room for Chase's shouldn't be an issue, it's not like I have to sleep in the main bedroom. But it does offer a logistical problem when it comes to me showering and getting ready for bed.

All my toiletries are in the bathroom attached to the room Chase is currently in. I could pack everything up. Move it over to the other bathroom. My clothes too.

Except I don't have the energy for that. All I want is a quick rinse off before slipping on my comfy pjs and climbing into bed.

Checking the door is locked, my gaze sweeps the room and

lands on the bottle of champagne I'm assuming the hotel delivered after our win.

I didn't order any and while I refrained from having a celebratory drink tonight, I no longer need to be *on*. I no longer need to be the in-charge owner and GM. Here, in the privacy of my suite, I can drink from the bottle if I want.

That thought brings a smile to my face.

When was the last time I drank wine from anything other than a glass? College?

The small rebellion against manners holds an appeal I don't want to resist. And I'm already walking over the table where the ice bucket is.

There's a couple of glasses beside the stainless-steel tub stamped with the hotel's logo, a puddle of condensation spreading out from its base. And the ice has long since melted, making me think it's been here a few hours. At least. But when I pull the bottle from its water bath, it's still ice cold.

With practiced ease, I remove the wrapper and pop the cork. It shoots up, bounces off the ceiling and lands somewhere on the other side of the couch. The sound echoes through the room and my eyes dart across to the open doorway I can see Chase through.

He doesn't stir and a rush of air leaves me, making me laugh at myself.

What does it matter if he wakes?

It's not like I'm doing something I'm not allowed to do.

I'm an adult. I'm thirty-fucking-five. If I want to drink champagne from a bottle, I can.

I will.

It can be a belated birthday celebration for myself. Chase's isn't the only birthday I overlooked. Candace's is the only one we acknowledged and had a cake and presents for.

Lifting the cold glass to my lips, I tip it up and relish the burst of bubbles on my tongue. And because obviously I'm doing all the things polite society would frown upon, I guzzle the cool liquid instead of sipping.

I've never been a huge fan of champagne. It reminds me too much of my childhood and the man who insisted on strict rules that were appropriate for our station in life.

Shuddering, I repress the memories that threaten to fill my head.

Albert Redding is dead. He can't do anything else to ruin my life. Unless I let his memory, the restrictions he placed on me, continue to dictate what I do—how I behave.

"Nope. Not happening." And I take another slug from the bottle to prove my point then grin. "I answer to no one but me."

The emotions flowing through my veins along with the bubbles of champagne, are freeing.

For years I was forced to toe the line. My whole life, even before my parents died, was what my grandfather dictated—demanded. As much as I loved my father, he had no spine when it came to his own father.

Our lives were ruled by a man who cared for nobody but himself. His own flesh and blood no more than property he ruled over with an iron fist.

Until college.

Until I met three women who changed my life in ways I never could have dreamed of. The memories of those years rush in and I let them.

That was when Natalie Redding finally broke free of her suffocating existence and lived, became the woman I am today.

The COO of a billion-dollar global sportswear brand, owner and GM of a professional hockey team.

With a grin I bring the bottle to my lips again. The cold liquid fills my mouth, popping on my tongue, then sliding down my throat with ease. I'm more of a red wine drinker, but this isn't so bad.

Maybe my dislike of champagne has more to do with my past than taste. With a shrug, I walk toward the bedroom. I need a shower before I crawl into bed and catch a few hours of sleep.

Chase remains motionless as I make my way through the

bedroom; the sight of him sprawled out on the bed makes me stop and smile. I hope he isn't hungover in the morning. I don't even know if he's ever been this drunk before.

It's not a year since he's been legally allowed to drink, and I know everyone sneaks beers or whatever before that, but I'm not sure if he did.

His sole focus was hockey. Until he was forced to take on the responsibility of his sisters. I frown.

Things could have been so different for the Hawkins siblings. If I hadn't—

I shake my head.

No. They would have found their feet. Chase would have gotten back on the path of his lifelong dream.

But he wouldn't be passed out on that bed after a night of celebrating his game winning goal. And it isn't only the game he won for the Rogues.

He put us in contention for the Cup.

The Cup!

Our first year in the league and we're in the Cup final!

I'm not sure I believe it yet. At the start of the year—hell, when the franchise was announced—no one could have predicted the team would do this well. We were definitely the underestimated, unwanted stepchild of the league.

Not anymore.

The league is on notice. Hell, they've been on notice since preseason last September when we hit the ice and won every game.

Entering the bathroom, I close the door and put the champagne on the counter. Stripping out of my clothes, I step behind the glass wall separating the shower from the rest of the room and turn the water on.

A squeak bursts from my throat when the freezing spray hits me in the face. "Dammit." Moving back, I wait for steam to rise before getting back under the spray. And grab the bottle of bubbles while I'm at it.

There's a convenient shelf to place the bottle on while I wash off. I don't bother washing my hair, I can do that in the morning, but I use the vanilla scented soap the hotel supplies to rinse away the day.

I've got my back to the spray, the warm water rushing over my tired muscles, letting it soothe the tension left over from the final moments of the game as I once again reach for the champagne.

Putting it to my mouth, I tip my head back and wait for the cool liquid to hit my tongue.

Lowering the bottle, I stare at it. "Huh."

Flipping it upside down, I watch one final drop fall to the floor, mixing with the water flowing down the drain.

"Well, damn. I drank it all."

It's only then I notice the slightly woozy sensation taking me over. Well, double damn. I think I've gotten myself in the same position as my star goalie.

With a laugh, I shut off the water and press a hand to the wall when my legs wobble. It isn't until I'm in the cooler air of the bathroom that it really hits me.

"Shit. I think I'm drunk." A giggle escapes me and the sound echoing around me only makes me giggle more.

I don't bother drying off, I just giggle my way into the bedroom and fall into bed.

CHASE

There's a soft, warm body pressed against me. Pressed against my hard dick. And I'm helpless to stop myself from pressing back.

A sexy moan fills my ears, and the scent of vanilla fills my nose, and my dick wants to get closer.

My hips are in agreement because they're jerking forward, thrusting my hard length against the plush swells encasing it.

A shudder rolls through me, pre-come oozing from the throbbing tip of my dick and I slide my arms up, my hands finding plump, weighty flesh.

That moan sounds again and my dick twitches. My hips buck.

I must be dreaming.

I haven't had sex in months. Not since...

The woman in bed with me arches her back, pops that sweet ass against my straining dick and all bets are off.

If this is a dream, I'm taking advantage of it and getting what I want.

And even though my dream girl doesn't smell like Gem I'm going to pretend that's who I'm touching.

Soft and sweet and so responsive, dream Gem is everything I knew she'd be. Moaning and moving and pushing into my hands —my dick—dream Gem is riding the wave of lust with me.

My hips keep thrusting, my hands keep roaming, and when it gets too much, I roll, press her beneath me as I work my legs between hers.

Hands on her hips, I tilt them until my dick slips between hot slick folds.

Dream Gem's moan fills my ears, and a growl rumbles in my chest. We're moving together now, rocking back and forth, my dick getting harder, her pussy getting wetter.

I'm not inside her. Not yet. I'm pumping between her legs, dragging my shaft through her swollen, slippery flesh until we're both soaked and breathing hard.

It's a simple lift and punch, and I'm balls deep inside her.

Surrounded by heat. Clenched tight within her pulsing pussy. Her silky muscles holding me still.

But only for a second, because the throbbing need in my dick can't be ignored, not now I'm finally where I've dreamed of being.

Pulling back, I shunt forward, hard, and impale her again. And again.

The moans and groans are echoing around me, threatening to pull me from this incredible dream, and I clamp my eyes shut tighter. Thrust my hips faster. Harder.

And when the pleasure finally breaks me, hits the peak of my resistance, when the blaze of lust is too hot, too sharp, I shove a hand beneath her and pinch her clit.

It's like a short wick on a stick of dynamite.

Boom!

Pleasure explodes through my balls and up my dick.

Explodes inside the hot pussy clamping me tighter than a vise.

Our rhythm is manic.

Stuttered and desperate.

Raking in the last of the sensations as satisfaction starts to numb my limbs.

Breathing hard, gasping for air that's filled with sex and vanilla, I manage to mutter, "I love you, Gem," before the blackness of blissed out sleep takes me under.

NAT

"I slept with my husband."

Even referring to Chase as my husband doesn't make what we did feel any better.

I thought I was dreaming. Thought I was having another of the vivid dreams I've been plagued with since my libido decided Chase Hawkins was worth jumping.

What he thinks is anyone's guess because we haven't talked about it.

And the only reason I know it wasn't a dream, and we really did have sex is because I woke in bed beside him, the sticky evidence of our union between my legs, spread all over my thighs.

I can say with one hundred percent certainty I have never flown out of bed faster.

The shock of waking with come dripping from my pussy only outdone by the man lying beside me. Sound asleep.

Staring down at Chase, I'd debated what to do. Wake him? Get out of the room and pretend it never happened?

The latter seemed the best option.

At least until he wakes up and remembers.

Or doesn't.

Other than being in bed naked, there's no signs he's had sex.

Men are lucky like that. No come-soaked panties to deal with all day after the deed.

I've shut myself in the main bathroom on the other side of the suite from where Chase still sleeps.

It's been twenty minutes since I leaped out of bed and scrambled for clothes.

Twenty minutes of going over and over what happened. And I still can't get my head around it.

I slept with a twenty-one-year-old!

I'm his wife, yes, but having sex isn't part of our deal.

Then again, neither is falling in love and as much as I want to deny it, I can't. I love Chase Hawkins just as much as I love his sisters.

Only I don't want to jump them.

I never, *never*, had this problem the last time I married a man for convenience.

But then Johnathon Whitman never had my heart squeezing with concern or joy or lust. He was a man five years my senior, the son of one of my grandfather's *friends* who I knew would be an acceptable choice and give me access to money that was mine.

Money that would set me free.

Marrying Johnathon broke the first chains on my inheritance, unlocked the resources I needed to break free of my grandfather's rule.

I'd never regret doing it. Even now, with Johnathon continuing to plague my life, I'd do it again.

But marrying Chase? Yeah, not about freedom.

And if I'm honest—and I need to be after last night—marrying Chase was a selfish act. Yes, I wanted to help him with his sister. Help the girls. Help keep their fractured family together.

But mostly I wanted the connection having the girls in my life would give me. The family I always wanted and didn't believe I'd get.

"Fuck!" Head tipped back, I stare at the ceiling and mutter, "What have I done?"

I choke back a laugh.

I fucked my husband, that's what I've done.

A growl of frustration rattles my vocal cords, but I hold it in. I'd give anything to do what Blake does to celebrate and scream as loud as I can at the sky.

Except this isn't something to celebrate—be proud of.

I took advantage of a sleeping—probably still drunk—man.

Even if I was asleep too.

And slightly drunk.

That fucking bottle of champagne!

Fucking hotel!

"Fuck!" The curse grinds through my clenched teeth and my eyes focus on the water stain on the ceiling.

Sound in the other room grabs my attention and my eyes, my gaze snapping to the door.

With a muttered, "shit," I dive for the shower and twist the knob. Water rushes out, drowning out any noise from beyond the closed door and I jump beneath the cold spray, grit my teeth, and suck a harsh breath through my nose. "Fuck that's freezing!"

The first bang on the door gets ignored. But when the second and third are harder and louder, I know I can't pretend not to hear.

"What?" I yell.

"The girls." The door swings open and a naked Chase barges in. "The girls. I can't find them. They're not here. Something's happened to them."

He's frantic, his gaze bouncing around the room searching for his sisters. I don't even think he realizes I'm in the shower.

When his relentless search of the bathroom comes up empty, he grabs his head and fists his hair. "They're gone. They're all gone!"

The agony in his words has me moving before I think. I'm in

front of him, my hands cradling his face, dripping water onto his feet. "They're okay. Chase. They're fine."

"They're not here!"

"No. The twins are with Whitney, they stayed with Fenton and Dana Barnes. And Deanne Harper has Candace. She's had her since after the game."

His head shakes in my hands, but I fight the movement.

"They. Are. Fine."

"Fuck!" The curse is rough and raw, lined with the jagged edges of his distress and relief.

"I promise you, Chase, your sisters are fine."

His head lowers, his forehead bumping on mine. "I thought…"

I can only imagine what he thought. He would have woken in a daze after drinking last night, not to mention the rigors of a tough game; the adrenaline climb and plunge from yesterday, along with the alcohol he consumed would have his brain in a muddle.

And then to find his sisters not where he expected…

"They're fine. Probably having the time of their lives. And you know Deanne dotes on Candace. Spoils her rotten whenever she gets the chance." My words are meant to reassure him and when he nods, I let out the breath I didn't realize was lodged in my chest.

"They're okay." His eyes close, his forehead still resting on mine, as he blows out a puff of air. "They're okay."

We're quiet for a few seconds. Both coming down from the panic of the last few minutes.

"Um, Gem?"

"Yes."

"You're naked."

My eyes bounce between his. His lids are still lowered. He hasn't opened them since he accepted my words as truth. "I was in the shower."

"I'm also naked."

I roll my lips inward. Fight to keep my gaze from lowering.

"I had a dream…"

Oh shit.

His eyes open, pin me under his stare. "It was the best dream of my life."

Pulling my head away from his, I open my mouth to speak, but I can't say anything. Because the words on my tongue are agreement. I want to tell him it was the best sex I've ever had even if I wasn't fully awake for it.

"Don't say anything." His fingers cover my mouth. "I want to live in the dream a little longer and I'm pretty sure you're going to say it was a mistake to have that dream."

When I go to speak, he presses harder against my lips and shakes his head.

"No. We're going to leave the dream in that bed. Let it rest there until we have time to talk about it. For now, we'll do what everyone says you do here. What happens in Vegas, stays in Vegas."

Why do I want to argue? It's the best thing to do. Forget it happened. There's too much at stake—

"Switch that brain off for a second." His command has me jerking back a little more. "Nope. Don't go away."

His hands over mine still on his face hold me in place.

"We will not think about last night and what it means until after the season is over. We'll put it aside to look at later. When we're not staring at the Cup." His grin is blinding. "We're playing for the Cup!"

He wraps his arms around me and lifts, spins. Exactly like he did with his sisters at the end of last night's game. I want to laugh, shout with joy but Chase has forgotten something that I'm incapable of forgetting.

We're both naked.

And right now, we're plastered together—skin to skin—from chest to thigh.

My body clenches and weeps and breathing becomes a struggle. And it has nothing to do with the strong arms banded around my chest.

"Chase."

"We're playing for the Cup!" He spins a final time then starts walking.

"What are you doing?"

"Putting you back where I found you."

I don't understand until I feel the water on my back. "Oh."

"Yeah. So..." He smiles at me with such hope in his eyes I know I'm not going to be able to deny what he says next. "We're still in Vegas, and everyone knows what happens in Vegas stays in Vegas."

"It's a bullshit statement and everyone knows that too."

"Maybe." He moves us both completely under the shower. "But I need to clean you up after I defiled you in your sleep."

He slowly lowers me to my feet, every inch of him rubbing over every inch of me, and I know I should object. Tell him to get out or get out myself. Except the way he's looking at me. Like I'm the only thing in the world he wants. I can't move. Can't deprive either of us of this moment.

Because he's right.

We need to shove what happened last night—what happens now—aside and get on with playing for the Cup.

"What happens in Vegas, stays in Vegas." My words are a whisper. Barely audible over the water pounding the floor beneath our feet. But he hears them.

"For now. What happens in Vegas, stays in Vegas, *for now*." He waits for my nod of acceptance before asking, "So when do the girls come back?"

"This afternoon. After lunch."

The grin he gives me is all mischievous cocky man, and I know, whatever is running through his head right now is going to mark me. He's already marked me. And I'm not referring to last night.

Chase Hawkins has had me behaving in ways I never have

before. Had me wishing for things I thought had passed me by. I thought him allowing me to adopt the girls was the best part of our partnership.

But maybe we haven't reached the best part yet.

Maybe, maybe, the best part is just around the corner.

"You know what my favorite thing about you is?" he asks.

I shake my head, water flicking around us. "No."

"You're a strong leader, determined, focused, but it's this, you taking a step back and letting me lead that's my favorite thing about you."

I don't know what to say, what to think or feel. And then he goes and blows my mind further. Except this time, he takes my heart too.

"Because you, Natalie Redding, don't let many people in. Your inner circle is tight, and for whatever reason, you've let me inside it. I will never make you regret that choice. I will cherish your trust for the rest of my life."

"I..."

"I'll guard it with my life."

"Chase."

"Because you deserve to have that. A person who will do anything to protect you and this soft heart you keep hidden from all but a few."

He places his hand on my chest, over my heart, and in that moment, he owns it. Owns me.

"Now." He grins. "Let's get to making more things to talk about after we win the Cup."

CHASE

My wife is a gem. She's my Gem. And right now, with the prospect of winning the damn Cup closer than it's ever been, I want to show her my appreciation.

I want to kiss the ever-loving hell out of her too.

But I can't.

We agreed.

What happened in Vegas, stayed in Vegas.

And it has. For two weeks, one day.

For fifteen days I've trained and trained and trained and she's taken care of every other aspect of my life. The girls, the house, everything. She's even filled my car with gas. All I've had to think about is me. Hockey.

I get that it's for her benefit too. I mean, she stands to make the history books. Entering the NHL with a brand new franchise and getting to the Cup final the first year in already has her in the history books.

I'm proud of her. Of what she and Oakley and Blake and Cami have done.

I'm proud of the team too. We've pulled together in a way no one expected. The whole league paid for their lack of confidence.

Five games into the last series of the season and we're up.

Three to one. And if we win tonight? On home ice? The Cup is ours.

Boston has put us through the wringer to get here. They might not have won as many games as us, but they haven't let us walk away with the wins either.

We've fought with everything we have to get those games to go our way. And tonight, we stand to win double if we can keep ahead of Boston.

The game and the Cup.

The coaches have been doing their best to keep us grounded. To keep us from, as Oakley says, counting our goals before they're scored.

Win or lose, we can hold our heads up high. We came into the league determined to prove we belong, and we didn't just show them. We slapped them in the face with it.

The locker room is buzzing even though no one is really talking. It's hushed words and pre-game rituals. Equipment prep and lucky sock wearing. It's Zen music and hard rock and complete silence.

Each of us has a different routine to get our heads in the game. Ways we either repeat over and over every game or try and push aside when we feel they aren't working.

I've never really had a ritual. I prep my gear, lay it out on the floor in front of me, then put each piece on. I guess that's a kind of ritual.

"All right, guys!" Coach Alcott shouts to get our attention. "The GM wants to have a quick word."

My gaze darts up. I hadn't expected to see Gem before the game. She usually waits until after to speak to the team. When she steps into the room she's dressed in a pair of dark blue slacks and a Rogues jersey. I'd love to see my name on the back of it—my number.

But that's a pipe dream for later. I'll slot it alongside our Vegas encounter.

"Let me start with this. Thank you." Her gaze moves around

the room, making eye contact with each man before moving to the next. "If it wasn't for all of you, we wouldn't be here. I can stand here and pretend it's because I brought all of you to Baton Rouge, but we all know that's just the vehicle that got you to the ice. It's what you all did when you got on the ice that matters most."

Her gaze moves around continuously, and the expression on her face is one of genuine affection, appreciation.

"You go out there tonight and hold your heads high because you deserve to. You made this happen. For yourselves, each other, the Rogues' org, and the fans. You, not this puppet master with her strings. And when we're done, when the last puck has been sent over the goal line, no matter what the score reads, you come back to this room with those heads just as high."

Her watch beeps and she lifts her arm, but her eyes are still on the room, not the device on her wrist.

"That's my cue. And yours. Time to show the world this season is not a fluke. Get out there and give a lesson in game winning hockey!"

The room erupts in hooting and hollering and clapping and stomping feet. And with a smile on her face and a wave of her hand, Gem leaves us to finish our game prep.

I can see her words have resonated with all of us. She's right. It doesn't matter who got us here, it's what we did when we arrived that made us the team we are.

Concentrating on getting dressed, I play a game in my head, roll through the moves I'll need to make, possible places the puck can come at me, ways to stop it. Always stopping it.

"Okay, this is it!" Coach Alcott calls out. "Last minute. Get your shit together, boys, we're about to make history."

He turns to Coach Watts, and they open the door wide, hold it that way ready for us to head out. I see some of the guys do their last second rituals. Mikel Vinter kisses his stick, Cutter Jepson crosses his chest and says a prayer, and Gannon Byrd removes the necklace from around his neck, presses the ring it holds against his lips then his chest before placing it in his locker.

Me? I put on my helmet and lower the mask. I won't take it off until the end of the game. It's the final act that puts my head into game mode.

As I walk down the tunnel, I can hear the crowd, feel the vibrations of the cheers and stamping feet. This is it.

Getting to play in the NHL was the dream.

Playing for the Cup? The ultimate fantasy.

Waiting in line, I close my eyes and whisper, "This one's for you, Mom and Dad."

Everything is a blur after that. Warm up, player announcements, the first puck drop. It's as though I enter a trance, like some Tibetan monk; I'm here but not.

We dominate in the first period. Enter the locker room with a score of two zip. When we hit the ice after the break, we seem to get better. Maybe it's the fact we know the Cup can be ours tonight. Or maybe it's that we're just playing better.

Four to nothing entering the third period seems ridiculous for a Cup final but that's what we are. The crowd is going wild but we're keeping our heads, not letting any of the hype affect our game.

We've played fantastic all season. From the first game to the last one. But tonight? We're on a different level.

Boston is scrambling. They can't seem to control the puck or keep it. I've barely seen any action. Unlike my counterpart who's been working non-stop to keep us at bay.

It's not until the crowd starts screaming numbers that I look at the clock.

Eight seconds.

Seven.

Six.

Five.

Four.

I stand upright.

Two.

One.

I can't even hear the horn, the noise in the arena too deafening. My gaze scans the ice, the seats, the bench, before turning to find the team racing across the ice toward me.

There are words, lots of words, but the ringing in my ears makes it impossible to decipher them. When Bex grabs my mask, shakes my head, I concentrate on his lips. Try to read them. And the second I do it sinks in.

I just played a shut-out game in a Cup final.

A game that wins us the Cup.

I yank my head from Bex's hold and search for the only person I want to see right now.

It's pandemonium on the ice. In the stands. Chaos of the best kind.

"They're keeping everyone near the bench," Gannon yells in my ear with a tip of his head toward it.

When I look, I can't find Gem or the girls in the crowd. What I do see is carpet. They're laying carpet over the ice in sections and shuffling people onto them.

Officials in suits, kids in jerseys, held in place by moms, wait for their dads to come over.

And there they are. The twins are jumping up and down, their mouths working so I know they're screaming. I still don't see Gem. Or Candace. Worried, I push through the melee and head for Cass and Stell.

Reaching them, I wrap them up in an arm each and pull them against me. I ignore their congratulations and ask, "Where's Gem? Candace?"

"Well," Cass says with a smirk. "Candace decided the last minute of the game was a good time to fill her diaper."

"You're joking."

"Nope."

I turn to check with Stell who shakes her head, but she's grinning. "It seems her big brother making history isn't as important as pooping her pants." She laughs then.

"She'll never live it down," Cass adds.

"Gem missed the end of the game?"

"No. I certainly did not." The woman I'm looking for moves next to me. "I handed that girl off to Deanne."

"Smart." I grin. "We did it."

Nodding, she says, "Yes, you did. Now go join your team so you can get your hands on the Cup."

"But." My gaze drills into hers.

"Later. We'll be right here. Waiting."

I know she means the girls. But I take it a different way. I take it as a promise from her that she'll be waiting for me once the presentation of the Cup is over.

"Don't you have to go up and get the Cup, too?" Cass asks.

"I do. But then I'll come right back here and wait with our girls." Her eyes never leave mine as she speaks, and my heart beats double-time in my chest.

"Promise?"

She nods. "Promise."

"Okay." A hand claps down on my shoulder.

"Come on. We've got a Cup to lift," Bex says with a tug on my jersey.

Holy fudge sticks.

It's real. Not a dream.

We won the Cup!

The Rogues won the Cup!

NAT

"I'm pregnant."

The last time I stood in a bathroom saying words out loud in a vain attempt to make myself feel better didn't work either.

Not sure why I thought it would this time.

With another glance at the stick proclaiming me 'pregnant', I sigh.

I knew what the answer would be. After the night—and morning—in Vegas, I came home and checked my calendar. I'm not on birth control, never have been. I've spent my entire sexual life with one mantra and one only.

If it's not on, it's not on.

The one and only time I don't follow that, I get knocked up.

With my husband's baby.

At least I won't be a single mother.

"Crap." I dump the stick into the trash can to rest beside the other three.

Four tests can't be wrong, right?

Not that I need to see the results. I knew I stood a good chance of getting pregnant from my night and morning with Chase the second I looked at my calendar.

Add in sore boobs, upset stomach...

Yeah, time to admit it and talk to the man of the hour.

We've been so busy since winning the Cup that Chase and I have barely had five minutes together. And not all at the same time.

Things should settle down now. And by settle, I mean not so many media requests. Or celebration parties. Or parades.

The last is scheduled for tomorrow.

The Rogues will be driven through the streets of Baton Rouge before being deposited at Rogue Arena where a huge carnival party is to take place for fans and players.

I'm tempted to leave it and tell Chase after the parade.

Tempted. So so tempted.

But he's already questioning my nausea. Worried I'm sick and not taking care of myself.

No. There's no putting it off now I've got irrefutable proof, not just suspicion.

The twins are at school; they slotted right back in after the last game of the season. Candace is in Rogue Arena's daycare with her second favorite mother figure, Deanne Harper.

Since I brought Deanne down for the playoffs, she's stayed. Melody mentioned her dad was no longer in the picture, but I haven't pushed Deanne on the subject.

She'll talk to me if she wants. In the meantime, I've got her helping with the arena daycare and preparation for the one set to open in the new mall.

I think Chase is in the basement working out. He hasn't left the house since he got back from dropping Cassidy and Crystal off this morning. I thought he'd come looking for me when he saw my car in the garage, but I haven't seen him.

We've been like ships passing in the night these last few weeks and if we are near each other for an extended period, there's a million other people around too.

It's why I decided to take the pregnancy test without him.

Then again, maybe I've got a yellow belly again.

I don't know, can't even imagine, how he's going to react to this news.

Honestly, I'm not sure how I feel about adding another member to the household.

Especially when Chase and I haven't hashed out what Vegas meant—means.

Guess I know what it means now. Baby Hawkins arriving in under nine months.

I'm only a few weeks along. Too early to announce the impending arrival, even to the closest to us. The first trimester is always a risk...maybe I should wait to tell Chase—

"Dammit, no. He deserves to know. Just get it over with, Natalie."

Pulling my shoulders back, I hold my head up and leave my bathroom. I can hear things banging around in the kitchen. He must have finished his workout.

When I get to the end of the short hallway that leads to my suite, I stop short.

He's finished his workout all right.

Shirtless, with a pair of Rogue compression shorts spanning his hips, sweat clinging to his skin, he's standing in front of the open fridge, head back, a bottle of water at his mouth.

His Adam's apple bobs with every swallow. And he swallows a lot. The entire bottle to be exact.

I have the urge to lick the sweat from his chest.

And I'm not even sure I like sweaty men.

Although I have to admit, I like Chase.

"Hey."

My gaze snaps from his defined torso to his face. "Ah, hi."

He lifts one eyebrow. "You okay? Still feeling sick?"

"Um, about that."

"What? Did you go see the doctor? Do you have the flu? A couple of the guys mentioned their wives have had it."

"No. Not the flu. And I didn't go to the doctor."

"Oh, okay." His puzzled expression doesn't change, and I know I need to explain myself.

"I found out why I've been feeling sick."

He turns to face me fully. "And?"

"Remember that thing we were leaving in Vegas for later?" God, why am I beating around the bush?

Chase remains perfectly still, as though waiting for the next word to decide how to react.

"I, um, so…" Shit. Just spit it out. "I'm pregnant."

He doesn't move. Not a muscle. I don't think he even breathes.

"Say something. Don't leave me hanging out here."

"Are you happy?"

"What?"

"Do you want a baby?"

"I… Yes. I think so."

"You think? You've never mentioned children. Other than my sisters."

"I love your sisters."

He nods. "I know. But this is not the same. This is a baby. Your baby. My baby." He swallows after forcing the last two words out.

My hopes sink and I didn't even know I had any. "You don't want the baby."

"I didn't say that." He takes a step toward me. "This is not something I ever expected to hear you tell me."

"I can do it on my own. I don't need—" He demolishes the distance between us in three steps and palms my face in both his large hands.

"Did you not hear me say I love you in Vegas?"

A muted memory flits through my head.

"Gem." He waits until he's sure he has my attention. "I get that we got married for convenience, for the girls, and that this baby isn't planned, but I love you. And before you argue about ages and sisters and teams or whatever else is rolling around in that big brain of yours, I want this baby. With you. I want our marriage to be a real one. I've wanted that for months. Vegas was a dream come true for me."

"Not the Cup?" My mouth twitches with a smile.

"Yeah, the Cup too, but if I had to choose, I'd pick you and our baby. Every time. Every day. Always."

"This isn't what you agreed to."

"It's not what you offered either." He smiles. "I like this offer better."

"How could you? You're only—" His thumbs press into my lips.

"Don't say it. I don't care how old I am, how old you are. It's irrelevant to what's in my heart. Gem, you saved me. I was drowning. Sure, I could do what my parents expected of me, what I expected. But you showed me I was capable. More than capable."

"You would have been fine without me."

He eyes me. I can see the argument and brace for it, but he surprises me.

"You're right. We would have been fine. Eventually. But this, the life we have here, is better than fine. It's the best. It's given all of us Hawkinses our greatest wishes."

"I'm glad you and your sisters—"

"I'm talking about all of us. You're a Hawkins too. And now you're making one." He drops a hand from my face and presses it against my flat belly. "There's a part of you and me in here, growing. Do you know how awe-inspiring that is?"

He shakes his head, his eyes sparkling with unshed tears.

"Gem. You came out of nowhere and handed me a dream I thought was dead. Now I've given you yours."

"What?"

"A family. I already gave you a family and this baby is building on it."

Oh. A smile curls my lips. His words are true. For as long as I can remember, I wanted a loving family. People at my side who loved me unconditionally, stood beside me when I made choices instead of telling me what they should be.

I got more than a star goalie for my NHL team when I went to St. Paul. I got three younger sisters. I got a friend turned husband turned lover. And now I have the one thing I wanted and believed would never happen.

A baby.

I thought Candace would be the only child I'd ever raise as my own. And I will raise her like my own. But this baby, the one Chase and I made in a moment of unexpected pleasure, would be the next piece of our patched together family.

"I'm going to change my name. Before next season, I'll be Natalie Hawkins."

The smile my words put on Chase's mouth is blinding. "There you go again. Making all my dreams come true."

"Thank you."

"For what?"

"For loving me. I never expected to have this. With anyone. With you. When we agreed to marry for the girls' protection, I thought the family we made would be it for me. Never dreamed I'd get to experience the love of a good man or have his baby."

"I think I loved you from the minute I let you into our house. I can't describe it or explain it but there was something there, something pulling me toward you, holding me in your orbit."

"Chase."

"It was your circle. The one you keep so few people in. You let me enter that sacred space and I told you once I would never let you regret that choice. I meant it then, I mean it now. Being with you, as co-parent, friend, husband in name only, was enough. But this, being your lover, getting to love you openly and having a baby together..."

He shakes his head again.

"Fuck, Gem. Holding the Cup doesn't compare to what you've given me."

I believe him. He might be young but he's mature beyond his

years. And when he loves, he loves with his whole heart, with everything in him. He gave up on the career he worked his whole life for because of the love he has for his sisters—his parents.

If what he feels for me and this baby is only a fraction of that, we'll be two of the luckiest people in the world.

CHASE

"I'm pregnant."

Gem's words from yesterday run on a loop in my head. And I'd be lying if I said the smile on my face is for all the people lining the streets of Baton Rouge. Or the Cup sitting in the first car of this motorcade.

Nope. The grin stretching my mouth so wide my cheeks hurt is because I'm having a baby with the woman I love.

My smile slips.

I told her I want the baby.

I told her I love her.

And she never said it back.

"Well, fudge sticks."

Gannon laughs next to me. "No kids to worry about here."

"If I don't do it all the time, including in my head, I slip. And the last thing I need is for Candace's first word to be fuck." I grimace. "Fudge! Fudge! Fudge! Fudge!"

Gannon's laughter rings out drawing the attention of Coach Alcott and Russell Young, who are in the back of this truck with us. There are four of us in each truck bed. We're on the final stretch of road leading to the Arena where the Rogues' org has put together the party of all parties.

It's like the fan barbecue from earlier in the season except the parking lot is filled with carnival rides. Temporary fencing has been erected and there's security at every entry point because the org isn't taking any chance something might go wrong or get out of hand.

The ring of a phone has all of us reaching for our pockets. It's Gannon who comes up with the call.

Frowning, he looks up and says, "It's a New York number."

"Shelby?" Coach Alcott moves over to our side of the truck.

"No. Her number is programed in."

"Answer it," I say.

"Nah." He shoves the phone back in his pocket. "If it's important, they'll call back."

The truck pulls to a stop outside the entrance players will use to enter the arena and we all jump out as Gannon's phone goes off again.

Glancing over I say, "Looks like it is important."

"Yeah. Okay." Bringing the phone to his ear, he says, "Hello," as we make our way between the two security guards at the open door to the Rogue Arena. "Yeah, this is Gannon Byrd."

I can't hear the other side of the conversation but when Gannon stops and says in a shaky voice, "Say that again," I stop and wait.

His gaze is on mine, the look in his eyes one I recognize. Whatever is being said in his ear is not good. The worst kind of not good.

"Where?" he chokes out. "I can be there in a few hours but if you need anything before that, permission, whatever, call me. I'll have my phone on."

I glance at Coach who is studying Gannon intently.

When he hangs up, I take a step toward. "What's going—"

"My wife." He swallows. "My wife. She's in the hospital. She's been assaulted."

"Wife! What fucking wife?" Coach grabs the front of

Gannon's shirt and lifts him onto his toes. "Since when do you have a wife?"

I don't understand the anger Coach is directing at Gannon but I'm not about to let them come to blows in the hallway. Not when Gannon has just received the worst news.

We're surrounded by more players now, the trucks behind us arriving at the arena. I grab Coach, and Russell steps between him and Gannon.

"When the fuck did you get married, asshole?!"

"I..." Gannon shakes his head. "I have to go. I need to get to her."

"The fuck you do. What about Shelby? Huh? What about my sister, you two-timing prick? Does she know you got married?"

I glance over at Gannon, and I know before he says anything the next words out of his mouth are not going to be what Coach expects to hear.

"She does. She was there. We got married the day I signed the paperwork for the trade."

Coach goes still. Not a twitch. Then he bursts to life and spins out of my hold, his fist flying and connecting with the wall beside us. "Fuck!"

"Walker!" Oakley is pushing her way through the crowd, Gem right behind her.

I block Gem's path. "You need to get them to New York."

"What?"

"Gannon got a call. His wife, who I think is Coach's sister, is in the hospital, she's been assaulted."

Gem's eyes shift to Oakley who's already on the phone. "Okay. Let's get everyone else moving into the party."

"I'll do that." Russell steps forward.

"Trevor is at the family room, go get him, tell him Gannon, Oakley, and Walker need to go to New York. Family emergency. Tell him I'll be there as soon as we get their travel sorted."

"Okay." Russell turns to the rest of the players. "Come on. Let's go make sure the fans aren't disappointed."

It takes a few minutes for the hallway to clear and when it does, I do the only thing I can. I offer to help.

"What can I do? What should I do?"

"Can you call Blake and Cami?"

"I messaged Blake. She's on her way. Said she'd get Cami," Bran says behind me.

"Okay, Pa has the jet ready to go. We just need to get to the airport."

Gem frowns. "There's no way that will happen quickly. Even if I ask the BRPD to give you a lights and sirens escort."

"I can get a chopper on the roof."

Everyone turns to look at Ray Denim, the Rogues head of security. I haven't had much to do with the man, but I know from Bex he's a retired SEAL who has connections all over the country.

"To fly them to New York?" Gem asks.

"No. It'll get them to the airport."

"Right. Okay, do that."

"Already on its way."

"Huh." Gem eyes him with a small smile on her face. "Ready for anything."

"Always."

"Can we go? However we're doing it, I need to go." Gannon's voice is strained. Tight with the emotions I can see flashing in his eyes.

"Oakley, you and Walker go with Gannon. Don't worry about anything except getting on the helicopter then the jet. I'll organize bags or whatever for the three of you and send them on to New York later. Gannon. Call that number back, give them mine. I'll be a secondary point of contact until you get to Shelby."

I can tell he doesn't want to do it, but Coach puts a hand on his shoulder, squeezes in support.

"It's a good plan. We might not have connection on the plane, and you don't want to miss anything."

I can't decide if Coach is happy deferring to his best friend or not. I know they haven't reconnected the way Coach expected.

And maybe a secret marriage to the man's sister is the reason for Gannon holding back since he arrived in Baton Rouge.

"Chase. Go find the girls, see if Micky is with them." Gem turns to Oakley and Coach. "We'll take care of Micky for you until we know what's happening. It'll be easier to keep your absence from upsetting him if he's busy."

"Pa's on the phone with someone from the hospital." Blake rushes down the corridor toward us. "But I got hold of my brothers, they're still in New York, and are heading over to where Shelby is now."

"How the hell does anyone know where she is?" Gannon yells.

"Because as of ten minutes ago the breaking news across every media outlet in the country is the senseless bashing of Cup winning hockey player Gannon Byrd's wife, Shelby."

Cami's words have stunned silence cloaking the hallway.

It's Gem who cuts through it. "Get them out of here! Ray, take a couple of your men and go with them. Cami, get me your father. Blake, where's Mason and your dad? I need them to help me stop this event turning into a media circus."

I stand back and watch as my wife, the mother of my unborn child, does her thing and has people disappearing to do her bidding. She's one of the smartest women I've ever met and if she never says the words 'I love you' I won't care. I don't need her words to know how she feels.

Because words are only air. It's the things she does, the way she takes care of the people she loves, that is the real proof.

EPILOGUE - NAT
FORTY-EIGHT HOURS LATER...

As much as I want to be in New York supporting Oakley and Walker—Gannon—I know it's best if we keep the media targets going in and out of the hospital to a minimum.

Not that any of them have left the building since they entered it two days ago.

We all moved into Pa's house when it became obvious the media wanted to get information from any member of the Rogues' org.

I sent a directive through the whole org that until further notice we are on a media blackout. Including anyone who says all they want to talk about is the team winning the Cup.

Everyone knows that line is bullshit.

Because it isn't just that Shelby Byrd was assaulted. She was beaten into a coma by a man who Gannon believed was his biggest fan. I don't have all the details. Ray has been keeping me abreast of developments in the investigation, but the man has gone underground.

Even Amos can't find him.

But it's only been a few days. They'll get him. I refuse to believe anything else.

"Gem?" Chase stops next to the chair I'm sitting in while I

watch the kids on the outdoor playground Pa has set up on the grounds of his estate.

"Hmm…"

"When was the last time you had a drink?" He crouches beside me. "What about sunscreen? You've been out here awhile."

"I don't remember."

"You need to take care of yourself as much as you do everyone else." Gripping my hand, he tugs as he straightens to his full height. "Come on. Cami and Bex are going to stay out here with the kids."

I glance over to see my best friend and her husband sitting in chairs at the table with the umbrella. Pa has a number of different seating options out here, covered and not. When I first followed the kids outside, there were clouds covering the sky.

Now there isn't one in sight.

"Blake is making you something to eat too."

"I'm not hungry."

"You still need to eat, Gem, especially now."

We haven't told anyone about the baby. Or that we're married. We're even sleeping in separate rooms so as not to cause a scene. Although I can't imagine anyone will be surprised when we tell them.

It's hard to hide what's going on between us now that everyone is under one roof. And I'm pretty sure Pa has worked out the baby part. He handed me a packet of crackers from Oakley's stash last night before I went to bed.

For my 'upset' stomach in the morning.

"We should tell everyone. As soon as Oakley calls today with an update on Shelby, we should tell them about the baby. Give everyone some good news."

"We can," Chase hedges. "Or we can wait a few more days until they bring Shelby out of her induced coma."

Yesterday's update was good. Shelby is getting better every day. The swelling on her brain reducing every hour, but they're keeping her medicated. I can't even imagine how Walker feels.

Gannon. Oakley mentioned Gannon blaming himself for not forcing Shelby to move when he was first traded.

None of us were aware she was moving here this summer.

"Okay, let's see what Oakley says, then go from there." Chase guides me inside to the kitchen. Lowering his voice, he says, "Although I think Pa and Blake have worked things out."

"Pa has." When he looks at me, one eyebrow cocked, I explain, "He gave me some crackers to take to bed last night so they would be on my bedside table this morning."

"Ah, right. Is the nausea getting better or worse?"

"Can't tell. My stomach is churning with worry over everything so it could be that or the baby."

"I knew it!"

Blake's voice has me jolting back against Chase. "What the hell, woman! Scare me to death, why don't you."

Laughing, Blake wraps her arms around me, brings her mouth to my ear. "I suspected. After the finals in Vegas."

"What? Why?"

"Because you two were different. And yes, I know your relationship has been evolving all along but those weeks after, during the Cup final series, there was something...I just got a hunch I guess."

Pulling out of Blake's arms I glance around to make sure no one else can overhear us talking. "We were just discussing telling everyone."

"Some good news in the face of this horrible situation."

"Yes, but I don't want to until they bring Shelby out of her coma, and we know how she'll do."

"Oakley messaged us about an hour ago. Didn't you read it?"

"No. I left my phone in here on charge."

"Well, they took Shelby off the sedation meds this morning. Or they're weaning her off them as of this morning."

"I still think I should wait un—"

"Yeah, might be best because if you read the text, you would know that Shelby was ten weeks pregnant when she was assaulted. She lost the baby."

"Oh fuck!"

Chase's growl makes me jump but it's Blake's words that has me pressing a hand to my belly and my eyes filling with tears. "Did Gannon…"

"I don't know any more than that." Blake shakes her head, her own gaze filled with tears. "I can't even comprehend what this will do to the two of them."

"Nothing good and everything bad," Chase murmurs.

"We need to bring them home. Here. So they're surrounded by family. Can we do that? Bring Shelby here?"

"Not yet. Pa said he's looking into things. He's talking to Oakley and Walker more than the rest of us, but I think Gannon is keeping a lot from them at the moment. Oakley only knows about the baby because she overheard a couple of nurses talking."

"Oh, and she told us?" I can't imagine how hard it is for Oakley and Walker to keep that to themselves. "Did they question Gannon?"

"I don't know."

"Sorry. Of course." Blake would tell me if she had any other information on Shelby's condition. "I don't like not being able to help."

"Keeping Micky occupied is helping. Not talking to the press is helping."

I glance at Chase. "It doesn't feel like enough."

"Would Oakley ask for more help if they needed it?" Blake and I nod. "Then you're doing enough."

"Natalie."

I turn to find Pa standing in the archway leading to the hall at the back of the foyer. My stomach drops at his expression. "Yes."

"Ray Denim and Amos Powell are here. I took them into my office so you can have privacy."

"I…" I reach for Chase's hand. "I'll be right there."

With a nod, Pa disappears, I assume to inform our unexpected guests I won't be long.

"I can come with you but maybe take Blake." Chase's words have me looking at him. Before I question him, he explains, "She's part owner. I think she should be there for whatever the Rogues head of security and on retainer PI have to say."

"You're right." I take a deep breath and turn to Blake. "Let's get this over with."

"Can you let Bran know I'm in a meeting and he needs to listen for Drew?" she asks, although it's not really a request.

"Sure. Do you want me to get Cami?"

My gaze connects with Blake's, and I can see she's just as torn about that as I am. "No. Let us find out what's happened for them to come here, then we can let her know if we need to."

"Okay." Before he moves away, he bends and drops a kiss on my forehead. "I'm here if you need," he whispers before pulling away and walking back outside.

"As much as I want to dive into whatever that was, we have other things to deal with." Blake grips my hand. "We've got this, Nat."

"I know. I just wish we didn't have to."

"Come on. Let's get it over with."

By silent mutual agreement we let go and walk side by side in the direction of Pa's office.

When we step inside, it's to find both men standing, their faces giving nothing away.

"Hello, gentlemen." I don't bother with more pleasantries than that. "What happened?"

"I got a call from the BRPD," Ray says. "The alarm on Gannon's apartment went off in the early hours of this morning. When the police arrived, the front door was kicked in and most of his possessions were trashed and scattered on the floor in every room."

My gaze moves to Amos. "And you're here because?"

"I followed Banks' trail down here." He looks at Ray. "I was on the phone to Ray when he got the call from the police."

"Okay. Do they have him?"

"No."

The quiet after that one word has the hairs rising on the back of my neck. "Out with it."

"Banks left a message for Gannon on the bedroom wall."

"What kind of message?" Blake asks. "A threat?"

"Yes."

"And?" I can't hold in my anger, my voice sharp.

"I think you need to go media blackout on Shelby Byrd's condition. And move her to a secure medical facility."

Ray's words have me taking a step back. "What?"

"The threat wasn't against Gannon. It was against Shelby."

"I don't understand."

"Banks isn't Gannon's fan. He's been stalking Shelby since she finished college," Amos explains. "I can't work out if she came across his path because of his proximity to Gannon or if he already knew her."

"Have you told the police?"

"Yes. The NYPD and BRPD have everything I've gathered. But I'm telling you now, I'm also passing the information on to the FBI."

"The FBI? What the hell for?" Blake demands. "Surely this doesn't—"

"I think he's responsible for a number of missing women."

Amos's words stop my heart. And I don't even try to hide my need to hold onto Blake while I ask my next question. "Missing?"

"Presumed dead."

"The assault on Shelby Byrd was interrupted," Ray adds. "I believe he planned to kill her."

"Fucking hell." Blake's fingers squeeze mine.

"All right. Give me a second. I need to think."

I shove aside any panic and focus on what we need to do to protect Shelby. We need Pa to work out a way to get her here. I can have the medical rooms at the arena fitted to take care of her.

"I need my phone." I turn to leave only to be pulled up short when Blake tugs on our joined hands. "What?"

"You can't bring them here. Her. You can't bring Shelby here."

"Why not?" I glare at Blake. "We can lock her down in the arena, we have medical staff on the payroll, medical facilities we can use."

"Banks is here."

"We don't know that for sure. He could already be on his way back to New York."

"I don't think so." My gaze bounces over to Ray.

"You don't?"

He shakes his head. "No."

"And you?" I ask our PI who has never steered us wrong before.

"I think he's sticking close to here. I think what set him off was Shelby packing up their apartment to move here."

"So, where then? We need to move her somewhere safe. Need to stop this guy from getting to her again."

"Miami."

I eye Ray and wonder where the hell—"Oh! Can you arrange that?"

"Yes."

"Do it. Keep me in the loop."

"No."

"What?"

"I won't keep you in the loop. You will know when we leave the hospital in New York and where we're going but there will be no contact with anyone once she's released into my care. That includes with her brother."

"You'll take Gannon, though, right? You can't leave him behind."

"Yes. Gannon and Shelby will stay together."

I glance at Blake, get a nod, and return my eyes to Ray. "Okay. Make it happen. I'll get Oakley and Walker on video call."

"Use my phone." Ray holds out a phone that looks like any other, but I know it can't be. He wouldn't be insisting on me using it if it was.

Taking it, I turn to Blake. "Get Cami. And Pa. We can fill the men in later, but we'll need Pa in on this call."

"I'll ask Mr. James to come in. I can talk with the men while you all get things rolling," Amos offers. "I haven't seen Micky in a while and I'm sure Sara would like an update on how he's doing."

"Thanks."

When Amos leaves the room, Blake sighs and heads for one of the chairs in front of Pa's desk. Flopping into she says, "I don't give a shit what you say or think, Nat, I'm asking Amos to hunt this guy down."

"I don't think you have to ask that," Ray answers.

"No?"

"No. He saw inside this guy's trophy room."

"I'm sorry?" "Trophy room?" Blake and I speak at once.

"Yeah." He scrubs a hand over his face. "He hinted at it but I'm not sure either of you really took notice. Amos thinks Anton Banks is a serial killer."

"A…" I shake my head. I have to. This can't be real.

At the thought of Shelby Alcott, now Byrd, in the hands of— bile rises in my throat and I race for the trash can at the side of Pa's desk.

"Ray, get everyone in here, including Amos. Ask Whitney, Cassidy, and Crystal to organize the little ones in the theater room to watch a movie." Blake's instructions are spoken above my head which is still over the trash can.

Pushing up, I draw in a deep breath. "I'm okay."

"You are not. Sit your ass in the chair, Nat. I'll grab you some water."

Doing as I'm told, I lean back and close my eyes only to pop them back open again when my brain fills with horrible images. "How is this even happening to someone I know?"

"No idea." Blake presses a cold glass of water into my hand. "Stay here. I'll be back in a second."

When my eyes focus on the room, I see I'm alone. Ray has obviously gone to do as Blake ordered. Blake is also gone to do whatever else she deems necessary.

How have we gone for the highest of highs to the lowest of lows in only a few days?

Forty-eight hours ago we were looking forward to a day with fans after winning the Cup in our first year competing in the NHL.

Now we're faced with the possibility of a serial killer targeting one of our own.

Epilogue - Chase

Six weeks later...

I've watched my wife work her ass off on many occasions. But I've never seen her as tired as this.

It might be the baby she's growing draining her, but I don't think so.

I think the situation with Gannon and Shelby Byrd is having a bigger impact on her energy.

And as of two-fifteen this morning, the threat to Gannon and Shelby is over.

Anton Banks was caught, by a routine traffic stop of all things, on his way to search for the one who got away. Shelby.

I don't know the details, but I do know the FBI had set a trap for him, and while they didn't catch him where they expected, they still caught him.

And my wife took the news in a way I've never seen.

She burst into tears.

I'm sure it's the pregnancy hormones.

I've never known her to show such deep emotion outside of her circle of close friends and the look of horror on Ray Denim's face confirmed my thoughts.

She's resting now. Sleeping soundly. Thankfully. I'm not sure she's slept more than a few hours at a time since Gannon got the call Shelby had been assaulted.

Luckily, I've cut back on my training now the season is over, and I've picked up the slack in our lives that Gem normally deals with. Plus, Cass and Stell are on summer break, so having them around all day has helped.

"Chase?" Speaking of the twins.

Slipping from the room I now share with Gem, I close the door behind me and turn to find my sisters at the top of the stairs. "Hey."

"Is she sleeping?" Stell asks, the worry for Gem she hasn't hidden still stamped on her face.

"Yeah. I think she'll be out for a few hours." I walk toward them. "Need something?"

"Um, yeah," Cass looks over her shoulder before her wide eyes meet mine. "They're all here," she whispers.

"Who's all here?"

"Everyone."

The closer I get to the twins, the more audible the murmur of voices from downstairs. "Everyone? I need you to be a bit more specific."

"Oakley and Blake and Cami," Stell says, her voice low.

"And Walker and Beck and Bran," Cass adds.

"What? No kids?" I'm joking but when the girls both shake their heads, the smile on my face drops. "Okay. Let's see what they want."

Leading the way downstairs, I see Deanne Harper hovering near the front door. "Deanne?"

"Oh, hi, Chase." Her smile is unsure and only adds to my concern.

"Is something wrong?"

"No. She's here to collect the girls. Take them to Pa's for the night. He's declared it grandparent night." Cami walks toward me. "Mom and Dad are going too. And Blake's parents are arriving in the city in about an hour, so they'll join once they drop their bags at home."

My gaze moves behind her. "And you're all here because…"

"We figured it would be good to get together."

"Gem's sleeping."

"Let her. Go get the girls ready to go with Deanne and then meet us in the kitchen. We've got food and drink. Nat can join us when she wakes up."

"She'd want me to wake her up."

"Then do that. But not yet." Cami indicates the stairs behind me. "Go help Deanne pack the girls up for a night with their grandparents and cousins."

Turning, I find the foyer empty, and I don't fight the smile tugging at my lips. "Guess the girls are ready for a night away from us."

"I'm sure it's more they're ready for a night of being spoiled." Cami laughs, her hand rubbing her round belly. "Shame I can't let this one join in yet."

"Soon." My smile grows. "Soon there will be another three for the grandparents to spoil.

"And Aunt Deanne. Don't forget me." Deanne is coming down the stairs, Candace on her hip, the twins behind her.

"You two okay to—"

"Yep."

"Yes!"

Neither of my sisters even stops on their way to the door. "Okay, see you tomorrow I guess."

"Don't worry, Chase. They still love you. They just love their grandparents more."

Cami's words have me looking back at her. "Grandparents… we've never had any. Both sets died when I was a baby."

"Well, they have them now." She slips her arm through mine. "Come on. Let's get something to eat. Little Bit is hungry."

"Ah, give me a minute. I just want to check on Gem."

"You'll find us taking over your kitchen," she says with a grin.

I don't hang around to watch her go back to the others. Taking the stairs two at a time I race back to our room.

It's funny. We haven't told anyone directly—except the twins—that we're together. Although everyone knows Gem is pregnant with my baby. I expected some questions, a few narrowed eyes, but there's been none of that.

Then again, everyone has been preoccupied with the Gannon and Shelby situation.

And now that's been resolved, or the threat neutralized at least, I guess we can all get back to normal lives. Whatever they are.

Nothing about my life has been normal in over a year. But maybe that's how life is supposed to be. Always changing, always growing.

I like to think my parents would be proud of me, proud of the girls, or at least happy for us and where we are now.

If they were here, if they hadn't died, we wouldn't have the life we have, we wouldn't be adding another member to the family in a few months.

As much as I wish my parents were still here, there are so many things that wouldn't be the same if they were.

For one—I push open our bedroom door—I wouldn't have a wife and a baby on the way. I frown when the empty bed comes into view.

A wife who isn't where I left her.

"Gem?"

"Bathroom," she calls out.

"You okay?" I race across the room only to skid to a halt when I find her brushing her hair. "Ah…"

"I heard voices downstairs, checked the security feed until I worked out who was here." She turns a sheepish smile my way. "I'm still in protection mode. Had my finger poised to hit the second 1 on 911."

I smile, but it's not a happy one, it's more a grimace. I hate that we've all been scared the last few weeks. "I can understand that."

"Once I figured out the girls were safe, we were safe, I jumped out of bed because they have to be planning something if they're all here."

"Like what? Buying another franchise?" I laugh. But the sound fades when Gem doesn't join in.

"You shouldn't joke about that kind of thing."

"Oh."

"Yep. The plan was always, build a successful NHL team then look to start or purchase a PWHL team."

"The women's national league?"

"Yes."

"You want to own a team in both leagues?"

"Sure." Gem shrugs as she grabs a band and slips it over her hand to stretch it. "Why not?"

"I..." I snap my mouth shut.

"Don't worry, I don't think that's why they're here. Besides." her gaze connects with mine in the mirror. "I plan to resign as GM in a few months."

"You what? You can't. What would you—"

"I'm handing it over to Mason Watts."

I shake my head. I couldn't have heard her right. "Mason?"

"Yes. We talked, well joked about it really, just after we won the Cup." She twists her hair up into a tail and feeds it through the band on her hand. "I think he's the perfect choice to carry the torch from here."

"What will you do?"

"Have a baby. Spend time with my husband." Turning to face me, she leans back on the counter. "I realized something today."

"Yeah?"

"Yes. I've never told you I love you."

My heart bangs against my ribcage. "You've shown me."

"I hope so." She pushes off the counter and comes toward me. "But I need to say it. I'm not used to saying it. Not sure I've said those three words to anyone more than a handful of times in my life."

"I don't need them." And I don't. I feel her love every day; even when we're in panic mode over possible danger, Gem shows me she loves me. "Feeling your love, seeing it in the things you do for me and the girls is more than enough."

"Maybe. But you deserve to hear the words from my lips, and I want to say them. To you."

Wrapping my arms around her, I keep my gaze on hers. "I always think there's no way I can love you more and then you do something, and I fall a little deeper. I'm so deep I don't see myself ever finding my way out."

"Are you mad about that?" She smiles up at me.

"No. The question is, are you mad about it? Because there's not enough money in the world to buy my signature on divorce papers."

"Good. Because I don't ever want your signature on divorce papers."

"Only Rogues' contract papers." I grin.

"Oh, I definitely want it on those."

"I love you, Natalie Hawkins."

"I love you, Chase Hawkins."

We grin stupidly at each other until someone—I think Oakley yells up the stairs.

"You two better not be having sex up there!"

"Oh lord." Gem drops her forehead to my chest.

"Ignore her! She's just jealous because pregnancy makes her horny and she didn't get her morning quickie before Micky got us out of bed for breakfast!"

Gem taps her head on my breastbone twice before I slip a hand around her ponytail and pull her back. "I don't think I'll be able to look Coach in the eyes after hearing that."

My comment produces the exact reaction I was after, a burst of laughter that I kiss right off her lips.

When I let us up for air, I stare at the woman in my arms and thank whatever forces were involved to bring her into my life.

"We should get down there and see why we've been invaded."

She smiles. "We should. I need to let them know I'm resigning as GM four weeks before baby Hawkins is born."

"Do you think they'll be upset?"

"No. The team will be in good hands with Mason at the helm. I plan to bring him on as Assistant GM in the next few weeks. By the time the season starts, he'll be well settled into the role so the change in leadership should be a smooth one."

"Is resigning really what you want, or do you think you have to?" Before she can answer, I add, "Because I don't care if you work after the baby is born. We managed with Candace, we can manage with this one."

Nodding, she says, "We did, we can, but I want to spend more time with all the girls. More time with you. I'll still work, just not in positions that take up a lot of my time."

"Wait, you're pulling back from Rogue sportswear too?"

"Yes. I'm handing over both my jobs and taking on the work Eli has been doing with Limitless. I want him free to retire fully. He's incapable of semi-retiring and he should enjoy the hard work he's put in to get where he is."

"He called me yesterday. He's planning to come down next week, wants to talk about offering Kent Quinn the CEO job."

"Are you okay with that?"

"Yes. I want to play hockey for as long as I can and if either of the twins shows an interest in Limitless, they can take over or whatever. I kind of like the idea of retiring from playing and doing nothing except raising our kids."

"Kids?"

"I want more than one."

Gem laughs. "We have more than one."

"Yeah, I guess we do."

"So, one and done?"

It's my turn to laugh. "Hell no. I'll have as many as you'll let me put in you."

"Oh my god!" Blake yells from the bedroom doorway. "They are making more babies up here!"

Gem arches one eyebrow and asks, "Are you sure you want to tie yourself to this lot?"

"Are you staying with them?" When she nods, I say, "Then I'm definitely sure because I don't want to be anywhere except by your side."

"Then let's go downstairs and tell everyone the wedding they're expecting already happened."

Discover the beginning of Gannon and Shelby's story in, Hot Hookup, the FREE Hot as Puck prequel.

For what's coming next, latest releases, sales and more, join
Rhian's Royal Readers
http://www.rhiancahill.com/contact/newsletter/

If you enjoyed this book, please consider leaving a review. It only takes a few minutes and you'll be helping other readers find stories they'll enjoy, as well as supporting authors you love.

Acknowledgments

I cannot believe how lucky I am to get to write the stories that live in my head. The fact I get to share them with readers is mind boggling and a youthful dream I was never sure would happen.

For all you fanatical hockey fans, this is a work of fiction, I made it up, it's not meant to be 'correct', any errors you see in the game or season or coaching or whatever are mine. Also, feel free to email me with those you spot. I've loved learning about this game while writing the Hot as Puck series. I'm happy to continue learning.

For everyone else, thank you so so much for taking the time to read Hot Puck. I cannot express how thrilled I am you spent your precious time reading my work.

I hope you enjoyed Chase and Nat/Gem's journey as much as I enjoyed (most of the time!) writing it.

xoxo

Rhian

About Rhian Cahill

Rhian Cahill is the alter ego of a former stay-at-home mother of four. With motherly duties rapidly dwindling, Rhian is able to make use of the fertile imagination she used to keep herself sane for all those years of slavery. Years spent living overseas and visiting tropical climates have helped inspire some steamy stories.

Multi-published in erotic romance, paranormal romance, and contemporary romance, Rhian, with the help of Mr. Muse, spends her days and nights writing.

When not glued to the keyboard you'll find her, book or knitting in hand, avoiding any and all housework as much as possible.

For more on Rhian

Website
http://www.rhiancahill.com/
Newsletter signup
http://www.rhiancahill.com/contact/newsletter/
FaceBook
https://www.facebook.com/RhianCahillAuthor
Instagram
http://instagram.com/rhiancahill/
BookBub
https://www.bookbub.com/authors/rhian-cahill
Goodreads
https://www.goodreads.com/rhian_cahill

OTHER TITLES BY RHIAN CAHILL

CONTEMPORARY ROMANCE

Hot as Puck

Hot Stuff

Hot Shot

Hot Damn

Hot Puck

Hot Hook

Hot Date

Love Beach

Summer With a Fake Date

Merry With a Scrooge

Spring Break With a Baby Daddy

Evergreen Lake

Jingle Balls

Winter Lake Series

Love Me Like You Do

Love The Way You Are

When You Love Someone

Let Me Love You

Wild Rush Of Love

Party Games Series

Truth Or Dare

Spin The Bottle

Pass The Parcel (novella)

Are You Game? Series

7 Minutes In Heaven

Catch'n'Kiss

Red Light, Green Light

Hearts Are Wild Series

No More Talking (novella)

Dare You To (novella)

Mad Love

Boys Of Summer

Bondi Beach Boys

Sand, Surf And Sunnie

Only You Series

All Of You

Passport To Passion Collection

One Night In Bangkok

Singapore Fling

Holiday Romances

Christmas Wishes

New Year's Kisses

Valentine's Dates

Secret Santa

Frosty's Snowmen Series

A Touch Of Frost

A Kiss From Kringle

A Taste For Kandy

Hot and Bothered

Doing Logan

Shut Up And Kiss Me

PARANORMAL ROMANCE

Coyote Hunger Series

Coyote Home

Coyote Wild

Coyote Whispers

Coyote Law (novella)

Coyote Lies

For a full list of available books visit

http://www.rhiancahill.com/books/

For what's coming next, latest releases, sales and more, join

Rhian's Royal Readers

http://www.rhiancahill.com/contact/newsletter/

9 781925 375718